ENERGY X

NISFAN NAWAZ

WORLD

New World Order Publications

Edition ISBNs:
978-0-9856377-0-5 (Paperback)
978-0-9856377-1-2 (Hardcover)
978-0-9856377-2-9 (E-book)

First Edition 2015

This edition was prepared for printing by
The Editorial Department
7650 E. Broadway, #308
Tucson, Arizona 85710
www.editorialdepartment.com

Cover design by Tara Mayberry
Book design by Morgana Gallaway

For Denise: Thank you for questioning everything I do. If it weren't for you, I'd be in a lot more trouble than I am in already.

To Omar and Safiyyah: What treasures you are and what a delight it's been to watch you both grow into inspiring and thoughtful young leaders.

For my relatives, friends, anyone making a stand for justice and equality, the courageous, the visionaries for a better world, the humans and nonhumans of Planet Earth: stay busy doing all the amazing things you do . . .

CONTENTS

ENERGY X

CHAPTER 1
BLUE RIDGE PARKWAY

ALEX WATSON EASED UP ON THE GAS AND MENTALLY willed his father's Jeep Grand Cherokee not to stall out and leave him stranded. With nearly three hundred thousand miles on its engine, the Jeep was temperamental at best and exceptionally moody today, which he supposed was only natural as this was the day he'd chosen to navigate a particularly challenging stretch of off-road trail that branched off North Carolina's Blue Ridge Parkway. The trail itself seemed like something out of an extreme sports documentary on ESPN. The torrential rain that loosened the earth and beat on the windows didn't help. He could barely see the trail ahead.

Alex's best friend, James Campbell, sat in the passenger seat, his dark skin paling as the Jeep's tires fought for traction on the steep slope.

"Can you see anything?" James said, yelling to be heard over the rain thrashing the Jeep.

"Absolutely," Alex told him with a disconcerted grin. "I see wipers."

"Anything else?"

"A candy-ass passenger?"

James mumbled something Alex didn't catch. He was too busy concentrating on what was left of the trail and wondering how a storm of this intensity hadn't made the weekend forecast.

Everything had been fine until this morning. They'd had two days of perfect weather for hiking, mountain biking, and camping—the kind of idyllic conditions that drew tourists to the more easily accessed areas of the Blue Ridge Mountains in droves and compelled the boys deeper into the wilderness each year. But now they were miles away from pavement and the trail they'd started out on was all but unrecognizable.

"Maybe we should stop and wait it out?" James said.

"Are you kidding? The minute these wheels stop turning, we'll slide down the mountain."

"Aren't we already doing that anyway?"

Alex gazed through the foggy windshield at what little he could see of the sky: moving slashes of gray trailing close behind the overworked wipers. He hit the brakes and waited for his vision to return as thunder pealed overhead, endless and deafening. After the thunder finally stopped, a tremor ran through the vehicle, as if some giant hand had shaken it briefly by the tires.

"What the heck was that?"

Alex's hands were white on the wheel. "No idea."

There was a sudden, sharp crack, and the truck started to move—sideways. Everything else moved with it: trees, boulders, everything. The whole mountainside was moving.

"*Landslide!*" Alex shouted. Adrenaline surged through him;

there was nothing to do but hold on, ride it out, and hope for the best.

The Jeep tilted sideways as it slid. It would have tipped over completely had it not been engulfed on both sides by mud, halfway up the doors.

Alex looked at James, who was rolling down the passenger-side window, then at the next stretch of road coming into view below them. Just beyond it was a sheer drop-off. The good news was that the road below looked to be holding steady. The bad news was that when the portion of the mountainside that was sliding with them reached that point, it just kept going. Like a waterfall over a cliff. And they were headed right for it.

But the slide lost momentum quickly, and he began to think they'd stop before the truck reached the edge. He and James watched the precipice approach, until it disappeared from view—and the vehicle stopped.

James stuck his head out the window and looked down. "All I see is the bottom. I don't know what's holding us up."

"Let's not wait to find out." Alex tried to open his door, but couldn't; the truck was locked in place by settled earth reaching almost to the window. Sudden movement caught his eye: a giant boulder careening down the mountainside. "We got a problem," he said.

James turned just in time to see the massive rock slam into them, shoving the driver's door in by nearly a foot. Flying glass shards pelted the interior. The windshield and back window cracked—and the truck lurched halfway over the cliff.

Alex considered their options. James's window was certain death, and his was now blocked by the boulder. The windshield would have to be kicked out, rocking the already precariously balanced truck. That left the flat back widow—small, but big enough. "Out the back!" he yelled.

They crawled hurriedly into the back—but their mountain bikes and gear made it impossible to reach the back window.

"How are we supposed to get out?"

Fortunately, Alex's father had converted the Grand Cherokee years ago to a hardtop convertible. "See those T-handles in the corners?" Alex said. "Pull and twist, and we can shove the roof right off." A moment later, the roof was unlocked, and the two of them muscled the convertible top up and over the side.

A fierce wind battered them, driving the rain through their clothes. The Jeep's hardtop sailed into the empty space beyond the cliff. Several seconds later, they heard it hit bottom.

The truck shifted beneath him. "Stay on the driver's side," Alex said, fearing any extra weight on the cliffside might tip the whole truck.

Alex worked the clamps holding the bikes in place.

"What are you doing? We need to get off this thing."

"What, you wanna walk home?"

"I just wanna *get* home. *Alive!*"

"Then you jump out first, as carefully as you can. I'll pass you the bikes!"

James clambered over the side, found the ground solid enough to stand on, and took the first bike. As Alex unclamped the second and turned, the truck started moving again. He threw the bike and managed to get one foot on the bed rail as the truck began to roll, and he pushed off just before it slipped over the brink. A bike pedal jabbed him in the gut when he landed on top of it. The two of them watched the boulder follow the truck off the cliff, and they waited to be swept over the side after it, but nothing else moved.

Raindrops pelted them like tiny bullets, and the air carried the distinctive musty odor of the North Carolina outdoors, a product of the area's heavy clay soil. After a moment, when the paralytic fear had mostly worn off, Alex ventured close to the edge and peered over. The truck was upside-down on the trail at the base of the seventy-foot cliff, the boulder on top of it.

Alex was the first to speak. "My dad is gonna be so pissed."

"He'll just be happy you weren't in it," James said.

The ground shifted beneath them, and they scrambled back toward the bikes. Alex looked to James. "Let's go before our luck runs out!"

"I hear that!"

They grabbed their bikes and slogged through the muddy earth, which sucked at their feet as if unwilling to let them go. They were completely spent by the time they reached a tree-lined outcropping up the mountain a ways where the ground was more stable. They rested for a moment and decided to circle around to the bike path on the far side of the mountain rather than continue on the switchback and risk the landslide coming down on top of them.

They both had rain gear stowed in panniers on the bikes, but neither saw much point in donning it when they were already soaked to the bone. They'd zipped their cell phones into baggies just before the storm hit, but there was no reception up here anyway, so calling for help was out of the question. Besides, Alex wanted to ease into the bad news about his father's truck, and a mountain rescue wasn't part of that plan.

Off-trail, the terrain was rough and uneven, forcing them to carry the bikes until they reached a gravel bike path. Alex half expected to find the whole thing washed down the mountainside, but it looked pretty good, considering. Things should be okay, as long as they reached the bottom before dark.

They rode down slowly, feet skimming the ground half the time to help keep the wheels from sliding. Getting off the mountain would normally have taken them an hour; instead it took five. Alex had never been so glad to see blacktop. They'd have to circle back around to the parkway, which connected with the 694 that ran back to Asheville. All told, it was another nine miles or so to the University of North Carolina at Asheville. Still, compared to what they'd just been through, it'd be a breeze.

As it turned out, the torrential downpour kept the roads mostly empty, and they made good time while the rain cleaned the mud off them and the bikes. About an hour after setting out, they rolled onto the UNC Asheville campus after dark. The dorm building was a sight for sore eyes.

They stopped beside the bike racks and dismounted. After all that riding, Alex found he could barely move his legs. He looked over and saw James was in the same condition. Squatting was impossible, so Alex bent at the waist to reach the bike lock and secure his ride to the rack.

They hobbled toward the dorm like two old men who'd forgotten how to walk. Alex's legs felt like burning marshmallows, spongy and painful.

"Remind me never to go camping with you again," James told him.

"Don't ever go camping with me again."

"I'm hungry."

After agreeing to meet at the dining hall, they parted ways in the dorm lobby, each headed for a hot shower. Alex briefly considered visiting the nearest kiosk where there always seemed to be an ad for "Thai massage" posted, but thought better of it.

CHAPTER 2
FOOD FOR THOUGHT

AN HOUR LATER, ALEX AND JAMES SAT FACING EACH other across a table in the Lifestyle Dining Hall, as far as they could get from the cafeteria line, the source of the big room's ever-present, clattering din. A mountain of food sat on the table before them. James inhaled the mixed aromas, then plunged into a chicken pot pie after loosing the steam inside. "Hot food never tasted so good." He shifted the cabbage and cauliflower away from the pie, as though they were interfering in some way.

"You talk to your dad yet?"

"Yeah."

"And?"

Alex swallowed a forkful of carrots and roast beef before answering. "He's glad we're okay. Not happy about the truck. Mom's a bit shaken, and he didn't even give her all the details. He said something about salvaging the truck, but the thing's totaled. Someone's going to take a look at it when the rain lets up." Alex shook his head and stabbed another forkful of food.

"It's not just us, you know."

"What isn't?"

"I checked the weather," James said. "The whole East Coast is swamped. It's already a record summer for rainfall, and this latest storm just blows us off the charts."

Alex shoveled down another forkful of food and shook his head in disgust.

"Must be a coincidence, right?" he mumbled after a moment. "I mean there's no way pumping billions of pounds of smog into our atmosphere every year could have any effect on—"

"Let's not go there, okay?" James said. "You're preaching to the choir on this thing."

Alex knew his friend was right. They were both still sore over what happened at a lecture they'd attended last week sponsored by a well-heeled UNC alum who made millions lobbying for the oil industry. What was promoted as "a constructive dialogue on today's energy challenges and tomorrow's energy future" ended up being a diatribe on the "myth" of global warming and an attack on a progressive North Carolina senator whose support of a new solar-incentive program got him branded as an environmental extremist.

"Okay, then tell me something," Alex said. "Don't they teach environmental responsibility in business classes?"

"Only as a marketing tactic, I'm afraid. And they wouldn't even be doing that if it wasn't for people like you."

Alex grinned, happy for the opportunity to riff on one of his favorite topics. "That's just it, James. You, me, lots of our friends . . . we all want all this nonsense to stop. There's a whole new generation of people who get it and will soon be in positions of influence. It'll be a whole new world if we can stop government subsidies to nonrenewables, open things up for real competition."

James shook his head. "Not in this lifetime, not against an old guard that's this entrenched. No sense in wasting your life trying for something that'll probably never happen."

Alex straightened up. "Why so cynical, man? You want a better world too."

"Sure, but I want a paycheck for doing it. Going green has to help the bottom line if it's ever going to gain real traction. We can't all be born to society." James froze suddenly, obviously wishing he could take the words back.

Alex just stared at his food.

"Oh man. I'm sorry. That didn't come out right."

"Forget it." Alex knew the words hadn't been ill intended. But it was a sore subject, not so much for him as for his parents, and it made him feel bad for them. They'd made a lot of sacrifices to keep up appearances.

"I wouldn't be here if it wasn't for your father," James said. "You know I haven't forgotten that." Years ago, Alex had persuaded his father to pull a few reluctant strings to get James into UNC Asheville on a scholarship. James continued, "You can take the boy outta the hood, not so easy to get the hood outta the boy."

"Forget it," Alex insisted. "Really. Between you and me, there's not all that much money. Stock crash wiped out the family reserves. Most of what's left is reputation. I'm up to my ears in student loans, just like everybody else."

"No wonder your dad's upset about the Jeep, then."

Alex nodded. "Hey, I was thinking about a home-cooked meal later this week with the folks. You want to join us?"

"Can't. Got an interview with G-Tek. Lots of prep work to do. "

"The green energy guys? That's great. But aren't they in New York?"

"Video interview."

Alex smiled. "See? You do want to make a difference."

"And get paid for it, like I said. These guys are well funded, very connected. Rumor is some big government money's coming their way."

Alex was about to answer when his attention drifted to the TV mounted on the wall behind James, who turned to follow his gaze. It was a CNN report, with silent subtitles running over a map, war footage, and photos of two men.

"In the southern African nation of Zimbabwe, President Botu sent troops to confiscate land atop recently discovered oil reserves . . . Local citizens were reportedly shot for resisting, and civil unrest became an armed revolt led by Patrice Mahna, son of former Zimbabwe president Philippe Mahna, who was exiled after a military coup twenty years ago . . ."

"You believe this crap?" James said.

"Same crap, different country. Maybe you and your new job can do something about that, huh?"

"Gotta get the job first." They finished their food like two starving men and washed it down with orange juice and milk. "Man, I'm beat."

Alex signaled his agreement by pretending to nod off at the table. They hit the tray return and stepped outside. The rest of the week would be taken up with studying and finals.

"Hey if I don't see you, good luck with the interview," Alex said.

"Good luck with your checkride!"

CHAPTER 3
THE WATSONS

THE WATSON HOUSE SAT ATOP A HILL AT THE END OF A quiet cul-de-sac in one of Asheville's most desirable neighborhoods.

The next night found Alex in the detached two-car garage, flying an airplane. Or, more accurately, a flight-simulation program consisting of software, a MacBook Pro, a fairly realistic flight-stick assembly, and a big-screen TV.

Nighttime flight was challenging, the landmarks on the screen difficult to make out. Alex steadied the Cessna 172 on approach, aiming for the ribbon of darkness between the strip-lights bordering the runway. He paced the descent, carefully monitoring airspeed and altitude. The simulator threw in an unexpected crosswind for good measure, but Alex's stick and rudder skills were solid and he actually enjoyed the challenge.

He shuffled in the salvaged pilot's seat and added just enough rudder to compensate for the mild crosswind. He leaned forward and scanned the instrument panel on the MacBook screen for any irregularities while watching the TV display to monitor his progress. The plane continued its gradual descent, and he started to relax, confident of a textbook landing, so much so that his mind began to wander to his surroundings. His half of the garage could use a good cleaning. Unlike his father's "workshop" half with its tools neatly hung on pegboards, the "Alex" section was littered with geek-science-lab equipment, a collection of interesting rocks he'd found or bought over the years, and a smattering of airplane parts. Dangling above it all was a model World War II Hawker Sea Fury, the fastest prop plane ever built and Alex's personal favorite.

He was just turning back to the landing screen when the garage's pedestrian door opened and his sister, Samantha, poked her head inside and stared at him through oversized-but-stylish glasses. Though only three years older than Alex, Sam had a certain worldliness about her that he feared he'd never possess. Blonde and bookish, she nevertheless radiated idealism and self-assurance. Alex often thought that if they'd lived in Nazi Europe, Sam would be the French resistance.

"Crash yet?" she asked.

Alex snapped his attention back to the simulation screen, one hand whacking the MacBook and sending the Cessna into a dive. The engine whined as the Ground Proximity Warning System droned, *"Terrain, terrain, pull up, pull up, pull up!"* He tried to save the plane, but was already too close to the ground. Tarmac filled the windshield, followed by orange flames.

Sam smiled from the doorway. "Dinner's ready," she said sweetly. "I've been sent to fetch you."

"You couldn't have texted?"

"Dad says no more texts or calls to people we can walk to in sixty seconds. He thinks it makes us lazy and isolationist."

Alex whipped out his cell and speed-dialed. "Hey Dad, just wanted to let you know we're coming up for dinner. Sam thought we should call ahead."

Samantha shot him a dirty look and headed up to the house. Alex shut down the simulation, spun the prop on the hanging Sea Fury, and followed. The sky still trailed scarlet from the setting sun, creating an impressionistic mural of rosy pinks on the house's west wall.

REACHING THE TOP OF THE WALK, ALEX FOLLOWED the unmistakable smell of alfredo chicken tortellini to the kitchen, where he found Sam with their parents, David and Mary. His mother turned her emerald eyes on Alex, features lighting up as they always did when he came home to visit, even for a weekend. Her still-blonde hair was tied up in a bun behind her head, because the old house's air conditioning just didn't cut it in the kitchen when the oven was on.

His father nodded from behind the counter, where he fussed with a homemade salad dressing. He looked tired, which he seemed more often than not lately, largely because of financial worries, Alex guessed. He was now a disillusioned middle-classer who'd expected more from a world that hadn't delivered and likely never would. His salt-and-pepper hair suited him, but now tended more toward the former than the latter. The shadows under his eyes were new, no doubt put there by lack of sleep. Alex wondered about his health, but knew there was no point in asking; he was always "just fine."

"Anything I can do to help?" he asked instead. His father shook his head.

"You just sit down and enjoy, young man," his mother told him. "That's why I cooked your favorite and the mister over there did his Iron Chef routine with the salad." She looked meaningfully to Samantha—who carried the food to the table, knowing better than to debate her parents' "traditional" views when it came to domestic roles in the kitchen. Alex watched with amusement. Moments later, everyone was seated, breaking bread and digging in.

"It's too bad James couldn't make it," his mother said. "I do enjoy his company. But it's very nice to have just family here."

Alex nodded. "He's doing a job interview, but says hi."

"Speaking of jobs," his father said, his British accent still intact after decades in America, "how goes the search?" Having experienced firsthand the havoc a stock market bubble or economic downturn could wreak on the unprepared, he was determined to see the same fate didn't befall his son.

"I'm still considering my options," Alex said, trying to keep things neutral. He didn't want to rush into the wrong thing simply because it offered a quick paycheck. "I'll keep tutoring until I decide." He realized that tutoring other students was a stopgap, but he also had very little interest in work that didn't appeal to his scientific curiosity.

Ultimately, he wanted to do something he really loved, even if that meant not having an official or titled job. The problem was, he wasn't quite sure yet what that something would be. Creative, meaningful, valued—but those were qualities and not the thing itself. He couldn't picture himself behind an office desk, answering to some corporate boss, unless maybe *he* was the boss, and the work wasn't just about money. The whole thing seemed a bit like searching for an endangered species: he knew it was out there somewhere, and he was on the watch for it—but just when he might catch his first glimpse was anyone's guess.

"There must be a lot of open doors for someone with your grades in physics and math," his mother said, interrupting his thoughts.

"Well, yeah, but they're mostly government labs. It's not like it used to be. I just read about a physics PhD who killed himself because the only job he could find was working in a call center."

"My God, that's awful," his mom said.

"Brave new world. I do have a couple of offers from government labs."

"Good," his father said. "You need something steady. Solid."

Alex didn't bother pointing out that, like everything else these days, government was standing on shifting sands, and today's jobs might be gone tomorrow. Instead he said, "I want to do something I believe in. Something that makes a difference. Like Sam." The last words tumbled out of Alex's mouth before he could stop them. He shot an apologetic look Sam's way. She kicked him under the table.

"Oh?" their father said.

"I was going to mention that." Samantha said.

"You took the job with Fairchild Communications?" their mother asked.

"No, actually. I'm going with OTW."

"OT-what?" their father said.

"Occupy the World."

"What do they pay?"

"Room, board, airfare, and enough to get by."

Mom froze, knife and fork paused in midair, food sitting in her mouth waiting to be chewed on. "Airfare?"

"They're in London," Sam told them.

An awkward silence descended, broken only by silverware on china, muffled chewing, and the chirp of a lone cricket just outside the window. Eventually, Mom said, "That's so far."

Dad joined in at once. "*Enough to get by?* Don't get caught in that trap. You need security . . . Occupy . . . Are those the people camping out in parks, taking over buildings? In my day, we wrote our representatives when we wanted something done."

"It's not like that anymore, Dad. Our representatives aren't *our* representatives, and they really don't care what we want. That's why the world needs—"

Mom tried to play peacemaker. "Let's not talk politics at the table, shall we?"

"Anyway," Sam said, "OTW is pretty established. It's a worldwide movement with a ton of public support, and more coming all the time."

"They do important work," Alex said. "And they could use a good PR person."

"Maybe they don't have a good PR person because they can't afford one," Dad noted.

"They do have someone good," Alex assured them. But that only dug the hole deeper, as their parents' inquiring gazes demanded an explanation.

"He's in jail," Samantha told them. Predictably, that comment provoked a heated discussion that kept the whole family up late. Mom and Dad had visions of their daughter being arrested at a demonstration and languishing in some foreign prison for decades on end, and that image proved hard to dispel. But in the end—reluctantly—they conceded that Sam's career path was ultimately up to her.

CHAPTER 4
OPPORTUNITY KNOCKS

ALEX WOKE LATE THE NEXT MORNING, DESPITE SET-ting the alarm. He must have turned it off and gone back to sleep again. That, or Sam had come in and switched it off as payback for his slipup at dinner. He threw his clothes on, snagged a banana for breakfast, and sped to the campus.

He hurried through the college science building entrance and down the hall to the classroom. He peered through the door's narrow window. Professor Fitzhugh despised tardiness yet never remembered to take roll until just before dismissing the students. Of which there had to be a hundred, so he could hardly have noticed one empty seat near the back.

Alex waited until he turned to the whiteboard, eased the door open and slipped inside, then eased the door shut behind him. It all went very well, until the latch *clacked* like a gunshot in the silence. All heads turned to the door, except Professor Fitzhugh's. "Good of you to join us, Mr. Watson," he said without turning.

Alex froze like a deer in headlights, chest still heaving from the mad dash to class. With that and getting busted for being late, he felt like an asthmatic at twenty thousand feet.

Professor Fitzhugh turned around and looked to Alex, summoning his best disapproving frown. The dry-erase marker in his hand was still paused on the board, and his frizzy white hair stuck out at all angles, as if drawn by a globe of static electricity around his head. But for the pencil-thin bald strip running down the middle of his scalp and the Coke-bottle bronze-framed lenses perched on his forehead, he looked like some sort of demented Einstein.

After an excruciating moment, it occurred to Alex that the professor was expecting him to say something. He tried, "Sorry."

The professor nodded, finished writing, and stepped aside. On the board were the words "FINAL EXAM TODAY." Below that: two equations. The tests were handed out as Alex took a seat. He copied the equations from the board on the back of the test.

For the next two hours, Alex and everyone else sat scribbling with heads down while Professor Fitzhugh wandered aimlessly about, glancing at the occasional test and clucking to himself. He returned to his desk and hovered there when students began handing in their papers. He riffled through them and looked at the answers, sometimes smirking, sometimes scowling.

Glancing up from his test, Alex realized he was the only one left. He was usually among the first to finish. In fact, he'd sailed through most of the test fairly quickly—but the two equations from the board had him sweating. He thought he'd solved the first one, but the second was impossible. When Professor

Fitzhugh cleared his throat and tapped his watch, Alex admitted defeat, handed in the test, and headed for the door.

"Just a minute!" the professor called after him.

Alex turned in the doorway.

"LET ME GET THIS STRAIGHT," JAMES SAID AS THEY jogged the university's Bulldog Boundary Trail. "He writes this never-been-solved equation on the board, then you come in late, think it's part of the test, and freaking solve it?"

"There were two equations," Alex said. "I only solved one. Now he wants to coauthor a paper with me. Can we slow it down a bit?" He was struggling to keep up with his friend's pace. James was the runner, a six-foot-four lean machine that seemed to float above the trail. Alex just tagged along every now and then to keep in shape.

The course meandered more than two miles along the campus perimeter, through urban and natural terrain, affording views of woodlands, wildflowers, and the occasional botanical garden. Now and again, a curious squirrel would watch them pass.

James slowed to a more reasonable pace. "I'm telling you, that brain of yours needs to get out of the lab and do something useful."

"Working on it." Despite what was for him a strenuous workout, Alex always felt better after their runs: tired in body, perhaps, but refreshed in mind and spirit. He tried to hold that thought as they approached the trail's hilly Glenn Creek stretch, where the less athletically inclined studied under majestic oaks and hickories on either side of the path.

"Is Sam home now? I forget," James said.

"Yeah, but not for long. She took a job doing PR for OTW in England."

"Sweet. How'd that go over?"

"It didn't, but they can't really stop her."

"She have a British passport?"

"And U.S., just like me. Born to a British dad."

"Tell her I'm happy for her."

"Will do."

"Then tell her to get it out of her system and find something that pays real money."

"Think I'll skip that part."

"Good advice," James told him.

"Yeah, yeah. How'd the interview with G-Tek go?"

"Great. Job starts next week, but I leave tomorrow. The usual summer-job thing: late nights, early mornings. I try to impress them by working like a dog. If I succeed they hire me full-time after I graduate."

"Seems like everyone's getting out of this town but me." Though to be fair, this was James's last year of college, and Alex still had one more to go.

"You've got another year to figure things out," James said, as if reading his mind. "You late bloomers are the ones to watch out for. Any offers?"

"A few lab-geek jobs, but . . . it's got to feel right, you know? Where are they putting you up in New York?"

"Ritzy hotel the first week, till I find a place. Money doesn't seem to be an issue for them. Or maybe they want me to get a taste of the good life first so I'll work harder. I don't know. I did some apartment research last night. I might be able to swing Upper Manhattan, by the Columbia campus. Be kinda like I never left home, but New York's right there. Ethnic cuisines, people from all over the world. Some cool running and biking routes on the West Side Hudson . . ."

"Sounds like you're already moved in."

James pointed to his own head. "In here." His gaze went to the sky above them. "Weren't you supposed to fly today?"

"Final solo checkride to get my pilot's license," Alex said.

James gestured at the sky. "Guess that's off."

Alex looked up. The blue sky they'd started under was swiftly turning gray as he felt the first light patter of raindrops on his face and hair. From the look of the clouds rolling in, they were in for another storm. They made their way back to the dorms before it got too bad.

"So, I guess this is it till August?" Alex said.

"Nah. I'll be back to visit my dad. He likes the company. Probably see you in a few weeks." He turned to go, then swung back, looking puzzled. "How do you afford flying lessons, anyway?"

"I don't. It's a trade for tutoring my flight instructor's son with his high school classes."

CHAPTER 5
LONDON

THAT NIGHT, THE WATSON FAMILY RODE IN SILENCE for five hours, traveling to Raleigh-Durham Airport, where Sam's flight would depart for JFK and then London. Alex sat in the back with Sam, exchanging glances while both parents kept their eyes on the road—or what little they could see of it through the downpour. The Audi Q9 Hybrid was virtually silent, making the rain seem all that much louder.

Alex caught their mother's somber face in the rearview mirror; she looked like she was holding back tears. He turned to Samantha and tried to smile. He could tell she was nervous, at least for the moment. Knowing her, the first week on the job would dispel any residual anxiety and have her looking at the bright side of everything.

Sam tipped her head toward the front, indicating that Alex should say something.

"Getting you ready for British weather," he said to break the silence.

"I don't mind the rain," Samantha answered.

"Good. I hear it's like this all the time over there."

"Not quite."

Apparently their little conversation starter worked, because Mom spoke next. "Nigel is set to pick you up at Heathrow?" she asked.

"He'll be there right on time," Sam told her. "No worries."

"I'm a mother; it's my job to worry."

"What's your first order of business?" asked their father, ever the practical one.

"I'll be working on planning and logistics for a demonstration in Canary Wharf."

"Demonstrating . . ."

"It's a protest against new UK laws favoring banksters over ordinary citizens. Like it's not bad enough already. They're just following in Wall Street's footsteps and setting a precedent for other European governments to do the same."

"Sounds dangerous," their mother said. "I mean, you're putting yourself in the middle of a political quagmire."

"Mom, we talked about this. It's what I want to do. Besides, I won't be alone. I have Nigel and the other OTW board members, and we have professional security people who double as bodyguards."

"It must be dangerous if you need bodyguards."

"Mom. It's just a precaution. Anyway, they're still working out the details."

"You mean for the rally?" Dad asked.

"Yeah. There's this new law in the UK that requires a demonstration permit, and the permit's not cheap."

"You need to pay the government to protest the government?" their father said, voice rising. "That's ridiculous!"

Alex and Sam shared a smile. Alex said, "Welcome to the fight, Dad."

"And that's not even the half of it," Sam told them. "Now they want you to post a bond in case the protestors damage something. The bigger the protest, the higher the bond; for a big demonstration, it can be hundreds of thousands of dollars."

"Maybe you can get a loan from the banksters," Alex joked.

"Right," Sam said. "Then march down Canary Wharf and tell them we don't like their kind. There's a plan. Right now we're just trying to stop the bond thing from passing."

Their mother turned around in her seat, eyes brimming with concern. "Just be careful, Sam."

"You taught me to be tough, remember? Plus I've had a brother to practice being tough on."

"She'll be fine," Alex said, trying to sound reassuring.

Dad pulled into a parking spot, and Alex hauled Sam's bags from the trunk, loading them onto a cart. The family took an elevator, then followed the signs to the airline's departure terminal and ticketing counter. Sam paid additional fees for the extra luggage; this wasn't a vacation, and she needed to take practically everything she owned. If she'd had a French Resistance beret, Alex was sure she would have packed that as well.

Once finished with the check-in process, they walked to the security line. Tears ran down Mom's cheeks. Dad wiped away a few of his own and smiled. "Proud of you, princess," he said and hugged Sam tight, holding her as long as she would let him. Samantha sniffled.

Then it was Mom's turn. "Love you very much, honey!" she said in a quivering voice, embracing her daughter. "You need to take care of yourself and call every day."

"I will, Mom."

Finally, Alex gave her a bear hug. "You're going to love it. Skype me when you get there."

Lightning flashed bright outside, lighting up the terminal windows. Rumbling thunder shook the building just after. "I hope this nasty storm clears before you take off," Mom said.

"I'm sure it will."

"Have a good flight," Alex told her.

Samantha nodded, blew their parents a kiss, and entered the security line.

CHAPTER 6
P-H-O-E-N-I-X

SAM ARRIVED IN FINE SHAPE, AND A WEEK LATER THEIR parents seemed to have adjusted, somewhat. Alex frequently holed up in the garage at night, tinkering. Tonight he had the big door open so he could watch the rain, Queen's "Bicycle Race" cranked up on the iPod speaker. The model Sea Fury swayed in the cool breeze above him as he worked on a drone-like robotic helicopter he'd built from scratch. Begun as a weekend hobby, the project had slowly and with much effort morphed into something that might actually work. He was thinking of using it for his senior-year thesis.

The cylindrical frame measured about eighteen inches in length, and was constructed of lightweight sheets of aluminum, welded together and secured with short flathead screws. Lift and steering were achieved via main and tail rotors—or would be, once it made its first test flight. Alex designed the prop system to fly the robot much like a helicopter, allowing the main rotor blade to tilt in different directions for forward thrust and steering.

At the front, a dome-shaped glass capsule housed cameras and GPS. His inner geek could never be satisfied with a single camera, so he'd installed two: one with day and infrared night vision, the other a thermal-imaging camera. He'd thrown in a motion detector and a siren for good measure.

Artificial intelligence software controlled electronics and hardware, which mounted securely against the frame inside the hull. Alex's creation would be smart, something employing heuristic programming to learn and make calculated decisions. Enclosing everything was the airtight exterior casing, sealed to protect the craft's delicate innards from the elements. Theoretically, it was all-weather capable.

From the outside, the device looked like the offspring of an airship mated with a helicopter, so it wasn't likely to win any awards for aesthetics. But Alex hadn't set out to create something pretty—not with the first generation, anyway. Rather, the initial idea was to build a sort of robotic watchdog that would patrol the exterior of the Watson residence and intelligently alert the family of any unexpected guests or unusual occurrences.

Alex completed his finishing touch: Flying Tigers-style shark's teeth on the nose, and the letters P-H-O-E-N-I-X spelled out on both sides. They'd never had a dog or cat around the house because of his father's potentially life-threatening allergies. Now this would be their guard dog.

Alex pressed the decals into place, set the copter aside, and rechecked the custom cell-phone app he'd written to issue commands and receive alerts. Everything looked good. Despite the weather, and perhaps to make up for his recent simulation crash, he decided on a test flight. He was concerned about the lightning, but reasoned that a strike was extraordinarily unlikely. He was about to start the copter when the phone rang in his hand. It was Sam.

"Hey Sam, how's it going?"

"Couldn't be better. Just got done roughing it."

Alex knew Sam's idea of roughing it was bringing a cooler full of food and drink on a road trip. "I'm going to die of boredom here," he said, "with you and James away."

"Great, so now you'll be forced to make new friends instead of playing nerdmaster with that junk in the garage."

Alex's gaze took in the stripped-down electronics all around him. "What junk? You would have called da Vinci a hoarder." Thunder pealed overhead.

Sam abandoned the subject. "I hear rumbling. Don't tell me it's still raining there."

"Ever since you left. My checkride keeps getting put off. You?"

"Sunny so far. Eighties, even. Go figure."

"How was the Outward Bound thing?" OTW had signed up Sam and her coworkers for an Outward Bound leadership and team-building course, presumably thinking it would be a bonding experience.

"Very cool. It was in Dartmoor. You know, home to *Hound of the Baskervilles*."

Alex remembered Dartmoor well; the family had vacationed there last summer. "And this is your workday," he said.

"That starts tomorrow. I think Nigel wanted me to have some fun before doing battle with corporate titans. We learned how to tie knots, and did a search-and-rescue response to a simulated distress call. Then we hiked twelve hours on the moors and camped inside an old run-down house, literally in the middle of nowhere. It was creepy, like something you'd see in a scary movie. That took up the whole weekend. I'm exhausted, but it was really fun. Oh, and we rappelled off the top of an old bridge, a hundred and twenty feet to the bottom. Climbed inside a rock fissure. Scaled a sheer cliff. And we almost lost Sunil in a bog."

Alex was glad to hear things were going well after the tense departure. Sam tended to gush when she was excited, so he just let her talk. "Who's Sunil and what's a bog?" he asked.

"You'd like him. He's an engineer techie guy, big-time into geek stuff like you."

"What happened to him?"

"He stepped into quicksand. Well, sort of. Here they call it a bog. We pulled him out. Scary for him, but funny for us. Nigel says that Sunil usually gets himself into some sort of quagmire, this time literally. He's fine now."

"How about this Nigel guy, what's he like?" Alex asked.

"He's a really good guy. Strong sense of community. There's no official OTW leader, but he pretty much runs the whole thing behind the scenes. He's all about making a difference, not glomming the credit. His dad was a senior editor for *National Geographic*, so his family's well traveled and connected in odd places. He has a master's in political science, sees right through the bullshit headlines. He also talks with some international VIPs he thinks might be willing to help change things, where other activists just write them off as one-percenters."

"Are you falling for this guy?"

"Don't be silly. You asked about him, so I'm telling you. Hold on a sec."

Alex heard muffled conversation in the background. After a moment, Sam came back. "Okay, need to run now. That was Nigel. We're off to the OTW headquarters near St. Ives to get cleaned up and fed. Then it's work, work, work."

"Good talking to you, thanks for the call. I'll tell Mom and Dad you said hi."

"*Ciao*, little bro."

Ciao? He'd never head her say that before; she must have picked it up from one of her new friends. Alex looked outside again, and thought better of testing his hard-worked copter in a thunderstorm.

CHAPTER 7
CHECKRIDE

THE RAINS LET UP THAT NIGHT, AND ALEX MANAGED TO schedule his flight for the following afternoon. The checkride was—assuming they passed—every student's final flight before "earning their wings" for the legal right to fly solo. Dark skies loomed over wet runways when Alex arrived at Asheville Airport in his Volkswagen. Skittering clouds offered fleeting passage to occasional bursts of sunshine, which seemed only to accentuate the general gloom. Not exactly ideal flying conditions, but Alex wasn't choosy. He just hoped the semi-clear weather would hold long enough to complete his flight test.

He took a deep breath as he stepped from the terminal, inhaling crisp, fresh air with a hint of jet fuel. There was a surprising amount of activity, with private planes queuing up for takeoff. He made his way to the light-aircraft section, where he found Hank Grissom fussing over his Cessna 172. Hank was an excellent flight instructor, though he looked more like a professional wrestler who could bend a crowbar with his bare hands. He greeted Alex with his usual bone-crushing handshake and rib-rattling slap on the back. "There he is! Good job with the ground test. You passed; results came in today. Ready for the hard part?"

"Been ready forever, feels like," Alex told him. He felt like a coiled spring wound tight enough to shatter.

"Don't get cocky on me now," Hank teased, then glanced at the sky. "We might even see some sun today. Look over there." Hank pointed to an opening in the clouds: a lonely but angelic ray of light pierced a cumulonimbus at an angle, casting a glow on the far end of the runway. "Is that a sign from the heavens, or what?"

"I'll take it."

"Then let's get this party started. You know the drill."

They hopped inside. Alex stepped through preflight and startup, then carefully taxied the plane and performed the run-up checks, completing the departure checklist and preparing for takeoff. So far, so good, he thought; no incidents and all systems go. He felt a twinge of nervous excitement as the tower cleared them for takeoff.

Alex let out the throttle, and the Cessna barreled down the airstrip, lifted off, and quickly gained altitude. It wasn't long before they broke through the clouds into sunlight and leveled off.

"Let's start with the cross-country," Hank instructed.

Alex ran down his checklists while Hank tapped notes into his iPad. As far as Alex could tell, he made no mistakes in the first hour. He even began to relax a bit and enjoy the sights. The clouds had thinned out northeast of the city, giving them a mostly clear view of the Blue Ridge Mountains that had so recently swallowed his father's cherished Jeep.

"I want to thank you again for tutoring Billy," Hank told him. "He never would have passed science without you."

Alex smiled. "And I wouldn't be up here without you."

"When you get your wings, I'm all out of flight lessons to trade. I don't want to lose you next year. If you want some airtime, maybe we can trade for that. Till you can afford that Hawker, anyway."

"Like that's going to happen. Sounds good, though. I may take you up on that. How am I doing, if you can say?"

Hank scanned his checklist. "Great so far. Nothing to call out."

Alex tried to keep from grinning and felt sure he failed miserably. He banked the Cessna to follow the spine of the mountains, heading northeast.

"Hell of a storm," Hank said, indicating the slopes below. "I've never seen so many landslides."

Alex gazed down at the brown, treeless slashes in the sloping forest cover. "James and I were almost buried alive last week," Alex told him. "Off-roading the Parkway in the rain. Dad's Jeep wasn't so lucky."

"Bet you caught hell for that."

"Yeah. He's still waiting to salvage the truck. I think he's holding off until he sees how bad it is."

"How bad is it?" Hank asked.

"Fell off a cliff," Alex told him. "Looks like it's already been in the crusher."

"Ouch."

Soaring directly over the mountains' backbone, Alex looked down on one side of the range, Hank the other. A bluish light caught Alex's eye. The color was completely unnatural. A sudden glitch in the instruments drew his attention; everything flickered, then returned to normal.

"Whoa!" Hank said. "I just had this serviced!"

Alex looked back out the window, but the light was gone. "Did you see that?" he asked.

"My instruments tweaking out?"

"No. A blue glow. Down there. Really strange."

Hank shook his head. "Nothin' on my side."

"We must have flown past. Can I swing around?"

"Any other time, sure. Not on a checkride." Hank zigzagged his thick fingers across the iPad screen, making notes on his student's performance.

Alex whipped out his iPhone and marked their GPS position. If he knew the direction and estimated the distance to the glow he'd seen, he thought he might be able to track it down later. Once done, he put the phone away and concentrated on flying, careful to stick to the flight plan as Hank reviewed his list of remaining check items.

"Just a few more steps and we'll be ready to head back and test your landing skills," Hank told him.

Alex kept his focus, and the rest of the flight went smoothly. He circled back to the airport, steadied the plane on final approach, and took her down gently. A few feet off the ground, he powered back, leveled off, and touched down with a slight bounce. The tires screeched, wind swishing past as they slowed. He taxied back to the light-aircraft tie-down section, coming to a stop at the plane's assigned parking spot.

Alex let out a deep breath, hoping he'd passed. At least he wouldn't have to wait for the results this time, as he had with the written test. He turned to Hank, who was still busy with his iPad. Hank's usually animated face was expressionless. "Let's step outside," he said cryptically.

The two of them deplaned from opposite sides and came around to meet by the prop. Hank consulted his iPad again, frowned, and scratched his head. Alex fought the urge to rip the device from his hands and look at it himself.

"I don't know what to tell you, kid," Hank said at last. "But according to this . . ." He suddenly grabbed Alex under the armpits and hoisted him into the air. "You're a pilot!"

The two of them yelled like their favorite team had just won the Super Bowl. Then Hank returned him to earth and reached back inside the plane. He opened a leather folder from his flight bag, pulled out an official-looking paper bearing an image of a Cessna, signed it, and held it out. "Here's your temporary certificate, good for four months. Your permanent PP certificate will come in the mail, may take a few months."

Alex beamed and reached for the paper. Hank snapped a selfie of the two of them at that instant, the plane beside them. "That'll be in your email today. Congratulations." They shook hands, Hank employing his customary bone-crushing grip, causing Alex to wonder whether he'd have to learn to fly one-handed. "I don't know how to thank you."

"No need; your tutoring is worth a whole lot more, is how I see it. That's how you know a great deal: everyone thinks they got the best of it." He slapped Alex on the arm, no doubt bruising it. "Fly safe, pal. Let me know if you want to swap for air time."

"Will do, sir!" Alex threw him a half salute and floated off the taxiway like he was walking on air. He reached the parking lot, slid behind the wheel of his cherished 1963 VW bug, took a deep breath, and slapped both hands on the dash while stomping the floor with his feet. A distant part of him realized that he must look like an insane misplaced drummer, but he didn't care: he was a pilot!

He stopped when his hands began to sting. Remembering the blue glow, he set his temporary certificate carefully on the seat beside him and hauled out his iPhone. He brought up the GPS program, recalled the coordinates he'd entered, and clipped the phone to the dash mount. The program overlaid the coordinates with a map and plotted a route to the spot.

Alex consulted the screen, put the old car in gear, and headed out. The coordinates marked the spot where the plane had been, rather than the precise location of the mysterious blue glow. He'd use the GPS program to get him into the area, and guesstimate from there. If the glow was constant, he should be able to find the source with a few hours' work.

Already high from the flight, he felt as if he were setting out on a new adventure, like something out of the old pulp novel reprints he'd read as a kid.

CHAPTER 8
CURIOSITY ALMOST KILLED THE CAT

HE LEFT THE AIRPORT AND DROVE TOWARD THE MOUN-
tains northeast of Asheville, retracing his steps along Route 694
until it connected with Blue Ridge Parkway. From there it was
easy, at least until the parkway ended. There was no way the Bug
would take him where his father's four-wheel drive had, so he
parked in a turnout when the going got rough.

He retrieved the daypack he kept in the trunk and set out on
foot. He passed several landslides along the way, their liquid
motion now frozen. The soil seemed solid enough but—having
witnessed firsthand the damage a landslide could do—he gave
these places a wide berth anyway. It took several hours to reach
what he estimated to be the general vicinity of the glow's origin,
but once there, he found no trace of it.

Using an old-school compass for guidance, he began a search
pattern, walking in ever-widening circles. If he was right about
the location, or even in the ballpark, he should come across
the source of the glow, assuming it was still glowing and hadn't
been a reflection. He'd never seen a color like that. He wanted

to call it neon, but that wasn't quite right. More like the really weird-but-cool-looking blue sometimes used in sci-fi movies to depict the glow of spaceship engines.

After a few hours of circling with no success, he began to wonder if his location guesstimate had been off. Frustrated and out of breath, he closed his eyes, picturing the glow again as he'd seen it from the air. This had to be the right area. He'd just have to keep widening his circles until he found it—whatever "it" turned out to be. Just so long as it was still here and not buried by another landslide.

He made his way upslope to a nearby boulder, then leaned back against it and hauled out his iPhone to check the GPS again. The phone flickered suddenly and the screen turned bright white, then died. It was then that he noticed the bluish tinge on his left shirt sleeve.

He pulled his arm in close to his body and watched the tinge disappear. When he extended his arm again, it returned. He pushed away from the boulder and peered around it. There, a recent rockslide had revealed an underground chamber, like a mini-cave with no exit. On the bottom of the chamber, six feet down, was a fist-sized lump of rock glowing with an extraordinary blue light that shone out around some sort of black encrustation.

Alex could hardly believe his eyes. The light was beautiful, but almost painful in its intensity. The rock itself looked natural—rough and pockmarked—but the glow was astonishing. It was all he could do to tear his gaze away long enough to find a stick in the rockslide debris.

He dropped to hands and knees and used the stick to poke

at the rock, then drew the stick up and felt the tip. It was no warmer or colder than his surroundings; despite its radiance, the rock wasn't hot. And it was too bright to be biolumines-cence—so what made it glow like that?

Without warning, the edge of the hole crumbled away beneath him and he dropped into the pit beside the rock. He jerked away from it at first, then tapped it with a fingertip. When no sudden calamity befell him, he touched it again, and finally grew bold enough to pick it up. It was lighter than he expected, the black encrustation rough atop the smoother underlying rock that glowed through the cracks. He had to squint to look at it closely.

More rock fell from the rim of the pit. Alex looked around and saw that the chamber itself was larger than the hole above him, undercutting the surface soil on all sides. The eight-foot boulder he'd leaned against was supported by nothing more than a few inches of earth and rock—which began to crumble as he watched.

The boulder shifted above him, blotting out the sky as the ground gave way. Alex tossed the rock upward and jumped for the pit rim opposite the boulder. He managed to pull himself out as the boulder thudded into the hole behind him, so close it ripped his shoe off. He sat up and tried his iPhone again; it was completely dead. He frowned at the glowing prize beside him.

Noticing for the first time that it was getting toward evening, he gathered up the mystery rock and navigated back toward the car. If he hadn't kept a compass in his pack, he'd have been com-pletely lost.

The hike back was uneventful, and he found the car toward

dusk. He slipped behind the wheel, set the rock down on the passenger seat, and turned the key in the ignition. The familiar sound of the two-stroke Wankel engine signaled the start of his trip back.

CHAPTER 9
PET ROCK BLOO

DARKNESS DESCENDED BEFORE HE REACHED HOME, streetlights blinking on. Soon after, Alex noticed a strange, rhythmic flickering effect. It was hard to see while bathed in the glow of the rock beside him, so he draped a jacket over the rock to get a better fix on it. After a mile or so, he realized the street-lights were flickering as he drove past—and only as he drove past.

He pulled up in front of the house and hit the remote to open the garage, where he planned to examine the rock more closely. Nothing happened. He hit the remote again. The door remained shut. He scooped up the jacket with the rock, strode over, and opened the big door by hand. The moment he did this, the garage lights, sound system, and TV switched on by themselves. More bizarre still, his father's power tools suddenly came to life in their wall brackets: drills, power saws, weed whacker. Bizarre because they weren't plugged in; he could see their cords hanging loose beside them.

Mouth hanging open, Alex stared at the pandemonium. The spell was broken a moment later when the lights blew out, the stereo died, and TV and tools erupted in showers of sparks before falling silent. Alex opened up the jacket and stared down at the glowing rock swaddled there like a baby. "Bad rock," he told it. At least he hadn't left the MacBook in the garage.

Alex left the rock on his workbench and drove to the local dollar store, noticing on the way that his headlights had stopped working. He returned home with a bag full of cheap penlights and a stack of Post-its. Sitting in his car, pen in one hand and notepad in the other, he brainstormed a list. Then it was time to experiment.

He stepped from the car with one of the lights and walked toward the garage. He'd only gone a few steps when the light turned itself on and flared up; then the bulb exploded. He continued into the garage and dumped the dead light on the workbench. He dug around in a drawer, looking for an old lead apron he'd picked up at a yard sale. He found it and draped it over the rock, then walked back to the car and repeated the experiment with a fresh light. The result was the same.

He dropped the dead light beside its mate, pulled out the list he'd made—titled "Possible Shielding Materials"—and crossed off "lead." An hour later, he'd worked through the entire list and nearly all of the penlights.

Exasperated, he threw the list down on the table. A stray breeze from outside blew the paper sideways. It landed beside Alex's favorite find—well, maybe second favorite, now: a soccer-ball-sized geode, neatly sliced in half to reveal the thousands of purple amethyst crystals growing inside. The crystals hugged the geode's stone skin, leaving a ball-shaped space at the rock's center. Now each half was shaped like a big crystal-lined bowl with maybe just enough space, he realized, to house his new favorite find.

Alex picked up one of the geode halves and used it to cover the new rock. He then marched back to the car for another penlight, reminding himself of Thomas Edison's numerous failures on the way to discovering the proper way to make a light bulb work.

Alex grabbed the second-to-last light and returned to the garage. This time, the light stayed off. Once inside the garage, it occurred to him to wonder whether the light had ever worked in the first place. It was, after all, a one-dollar light. He flicked the switch—and the light came on. A massive grin split his face. He'd discovered something. He had no idea what it meant, but it felt good anyway.

The dome-shaped geode half only covered the rock from the top, down to the surface of the workbench. Alex lowered the penlight beside the bench, to see what would happen. He didn't wait long; the moment the light dropped below the level of the geode, the penlight flared and blew out.

He retrieved his list of shielding materials, added "crystal," and drew a circle around it. Alex uncovered the glowing rock and stared down at it. "I think I'll call you Bloo," he said.

AFTER CATCHING A FEW HOURS' SLEEP, ALEX DRESSED inconspicuously in dark jeans, black tee, and a gray baseball cap, then set out for the college. He arrived at four a.m. As he'd hoped, the campus was deserted. He slipped a gym bag over his shoulder and made his way to the science building. He thought he'd have to be creative about getting inside, but the door by the garbage bins had been propped open, as if by invitation.

The floor inside was freshly polished, the machine still sitting in the hall, so he made a mental note to keep an eye out for the janitor. He navigated to the maintenance room and found the door unlocked. Which was good, because his lock-picking skills—and the picks he'd improvised in the garage after watching an online video—left much to be desired. He listened at the door before opening it, but heard nothing.

Once inside, he checked the key cabinet for the master spare and slipped it from its hook. He turned to leave and reached for the doorknob when it turned on its own. There was no time to hide, and no place to go. With no other choice, he stepped behind the opening door, holding his breath as the janitor passed within inches. For the first time, he noticed that the man was built like a linebacker; there was no way Alex would escape if the janitor got his hands on him.

He eased around the door and into the hall as quickly as he could, then sprinted madly away on the balls of his feet, wishing his shoes would stop squeaking on the newly polished floors. Glancing over his shoulder, he saw no sign that he'd been heard.

He rounded the nearest corner and gave his heart a moment to recover before moving on. Five minutes later, he used the master key to let himself into the physics lab. He set down the gym bag and rooted around inside, peeling back a layer of bunched clothes to reveal the geode duct-taped shut around the rock he now called Bloo. Nothing electrical had blown out on the way there, so he assumed his makeshift crystal shield was working.

He set a small voice recorder on a counter and switched it on. "This is a chronicle of the adventures of Alex Watson and his pet rock Bloo," he began, "which glows blue, by the way. Testing fundamental properties. Don't know who'll listen to this, but it seemed important to have a record in case this blows up or something and I turn into a mutant lizard."

He took a deep breath and got started. He loosened the tape on one side and eased the geode open a tiny crack, just long enough to quickly insert a thin magnet to touch the rock. Feeling no pull on the magnet, he withdrew it and closed the geode.

"Nonmagnetic," he announced.

He held up a metal detector and repeated the action with the detector's probe. "No reaction from metal detector." Then a radiation detector. "Not radioactive. Not alpha-beta-gamma, anyway."

Fortunately, the lab still kept the old-school instruments alongside the newfangled electronic ones, which would likely have overloaded and blown out before giving him a reading.

Alex looked around and found a gauss meter. The instant he cracked the geode open, the reading jumped right off the end of the dial. "Whoa! Significant energy output. Gauss meter's off the chart. Which explains the propensity to start electrical systems at a distance. And overload them."

He glared at the rock. "Just how much energy do you put out?"

He tried a power-energy meter. It also maxed out. "Holy shhh—I mean . . ." He cleared his throat. "Trying to be professional here. Energy output at least ten thousand kilowatts. I'm not going to be able to measure the full output with these instruments."

He found a blade and cut several small slices from the rock. To his surprise, it was no more difficult than slicing through a pineapple: not exactly easy, but not impossible, either. He ran the slices through chemical tests, which told him nothing. Finally, he vaporized a tiny slice in an ancient gas chromatograph. The results baffled him. "Interesting . . . . Sample does not appear to be made of any known element." He gazed at the geode. "I might just have to call you *Energy X* . . ."

Having taken the analysis as far as he could with the instruments available in the physics lab, he packed up, checked the hall, and made his way back to the janitor's room. He returned the key, retraced his steps to the parking lot, and drove home.

AFTER A FEW HOURS CATCHING UP ON MISSED SLEEP, Alex woke and went to the phone store to replace his iPhone. Then he stopped by Enter the Earth, a rock-hound shop that carried a variety of exotic and common crystals, rocks, minerals, and fossils. Cluttered with brightly colored gemstones and other specimens, the place was a delight to the eyes.

The store clerk carefully placed a collection of quartz crystals on the counter. Alex counted the wad of cash in his hand and set down the right amount. The crystals were almost as big as the bills. He drove home in a hurry.

Back in the garage, he sliced the quartz with a wet saw, then glued the quartz slices together, forming a small crystal box with overlapping seams and a sliding lid. Using a drill bit so thin he needed a magnifying loupe to guide it, he drilled a tiny hole in one side, which he covered with a thin crystal sheet. When he was finished, he stepped back, grinned, and admired his handiwork. If all went well, the thinner crystal slice covering the hole would act as a resistor, allowing a useful amount of energy to escape the box—but not enough to wreak havoc with everything in the area.

"Okay, let's try you out." He opened the geode for an instant, sliced off another small piece of Energy X—no bigger than the tip of a ballpoint pen—dropped it in the new case, and slid the lid shut over it. He looked to the ceiling; the new light bulbs he'd installed were still on, so the crystal case was a success. A handheld gauss meter confirmed no power readings, except near the hole with the resistor. At that spot, the needle registered a very small output. He assumed a thinner resistor would yield a higher reading, but he wanted to play it safe for now.

Alex inserted the crystal box into a stripped-out MacBook Pro battery casing—taking care to line up the resistor with the battery contacts—and snapped the casing into his laptop. He turned the MacBook over, opened the lid, and touched his finger to the start button. He closed his eyes, whispered "Please don't blow up," and pressed the button.

He squinted at the screen. The familiar whirring sound and the Mac startup melody told him he hadn't just nuked his laptop. He felt his pulse race as the laptop continued its normal startup sequence, finally displaying his custom wallpaper: a red Hawker Sea Fury sitting in a meadow of St. John's wort under blue skies. He looked at the geode and its hidden cargo. "Good rock," he told it. His next project would be building a larger case for Bloo, so he could look at it without blowing up everything in the room, followed by a half-dozen smaller cases and a variety of resistors for future applications.

First, though, he wanted to talk to Sam. He tried Skyping her, but got her video mail. "Hi," the recording greeted him. "You've reached Samantha Watson with Occupy the World public relations. Leave a message, thanks!"

Alex checked his watch. "I forgot you guys are five hours ahead," he said. "Guess you're asleep. Call me when you get this."

He had to burn off some of the excitement he felt; even if he couldn't reveal the secret just yet—not over the phone, anyway—he had to talk to someone. He placed a video call to James.

"Hey, Mr. Wizard," James answered. "How's it going?"

"Spectacular. How's the new job?"

"Busy."

"You coming back anytime soon?"

"Yeah, I'm gonna come down and visit my dad this weekend. Why?"

"Been working on something new," Alex told him, trying very hard to contain himself. "I think you'll like it."

"What is it?"

"A surprise. Text me your flight and arrival info for Friday; I'll pick you up at the airport and fill you in. This is gonna blow you away."

"Come on. You can't say that and not tell me what it is."

"Sorry, pal; can't share on a corporate phone."

James sighed through the line. "Fine, but why the secrecy?"

"You'll see."

FRIDAY NIGHT, ALEX WOVE HIS WAY THROUGH THE crowded terminal at Asheville Airport, trying not to get lost among hordes of commuters and business travelers. There were weary-looking men with loosened ties and unbuttoned collars, wailing babies comforted by parents, lovers welcoming their soul mates back home.

He went in as far as security would allow and checked the boards; James's flight had already landed. A short while later, he saw James walking briskly toward him, smiling and waving. They shook hands on meeting.

"Hey, man. Thanks for picking me up," James said.

Still the same old James, Alex thought, despite rubbing shoulders with big-city movers and shakers. "Good to see you, pal. I'm parked in short-term."

He led the way through the long airport hallways while the two of them caught up and exchanged news.

"Thanks for the ride," James told him when they arrived at the car.

Alex nodded.

"What's with the Cheshire Cat grin? Last time I saw one of those, you solved an impossible equation."

"Got something to show you."

"Ohhh, right, the big surprise."

"Little, actually. But also big."

"Okay. So let's see it, dude."

"Not near the airport." Alex drove them to a local mall and parked in the middle of a huge, crowded lot. He took the MacBook from his backpack behind the passenger seat and set it upside down on the dashboard. "Hold on a sec." He'd made a few modifications to the battery compartment, which made things easier to see. Now removing the cover revealed the

Energy X fragment in its clear crystal case. Its eerie blue glow suffused the car's interior.

James held a hand up to shield his eyes. "Whoa, I think you may have violated the warranty agreement there." He squinted for a better look. "*What is that?*"

"*That* will keep this MacBook running continuously. No power cord, no recharge, nothing."

"That's your big surprise? Some glowing blue rock that's gonna solve your laptop's energy troubles? What's the gag?"

"It's real."

"Right." James checked his watch. "My father's expecting me. I mean, you made this sound important, and you show me a laptop? I don't get it."

"Indulge me." Alex slid the lid off the crystal box and gestured at the parking lot around them. "Look out there." The cars around them suddenly started up, headlights flicking on in the darkness like a wave of light, expanding outward from the old Volkswagen. There were hundreds of cars.

Alex slid the cover back into place. James watched as the cars around them fell quiet and dark.

"Now do you get it?" Alex asked him.

It was a moment before James could arrange his suddenly jumbled thoughts. "Holy crap!" he said at last.

"Yes."

"I mean, *holy crap!*"

"Clearly."

"This is incredible!"

"That's my big surprise. Also little. And this is just a small piece of the rock I found."

"How big is that power source? The one in the laptop, I mean."

"Ten grams. Smaller pieces don't work. I don't know why yet."

"How much energy are we talking here?"

"I can't measure it with anything they have at the college, and I can't waltz into someone else's lab with a glowing blue rock and not explain it. So . . ."

"You have no idea."

"Of course I have an idea. Well, sort of. I tried to measure the output of the ten-gram piece with an energy meter, but it's off the charts. The whole chunk maxed out the meter at ten thousand kilowatts, so I thought the small piece would be measurable, but it wasn't. It maxed the meter just like the big one."

"Is ten thousand kilowatts a lot?"

"Enough to maybe run three hundred homes in your average neighborhood, with a good bit left over. If this scales, and I don't see why it wouldn't—if anything, there might be some kind of multiplier effect—then based on the minimum output-to-weight ratio of the smaller piece, the whole rock could theoretically run the whole country."

"*What*? For how long?"

"Maybe forever."

James leaned back, shook his head quickly, and closed his eyes. After a moment, he opened them again. "I just can't wrap my head around that. What if it runs down? How do you recharge something like that?"

Alex laughed. "You don't. But as far as I can tell, you'll never have to. The rock this came from is already ancient. There's a black crust on the bigger piece, like what you find on meteorites. It carbon-dates to over a million years. So my guess is this thing isn't running down anytime soon. I tried to measure the energy depletion rate, but couldn't find one. Probably because the output's off the scale."

"Dude, do you know how much money this is worth?"

"Hopefully enough to pay for my last iPhone and the stuff in the garage. All of which it fried when I brought it home."

James looked at him in disbelief.

"Kidding. This could change the world . . ." Alex's expression turned troubled. "If I can figure out how to replicate it."

"Why would you have to do that?"

Alex sighed. "Yeah, well, here's the thing. This rock? I don't think it's from here."

"What do you mean by *here*?"

"Earth. I put a sample through a gas chromatograph."

"The gizmo that tells you what something's made of."

"Right. The partial encrustation is classic meteorite shell, superheated and slagged on entry into the atmosphere. But the rest of it—the rock itself? It doesn't show up. At all. It's a completely unknown element. I'm calling it Energy X."

James nodded. "I like it. EX for short."

"Nice."

"But I have a better name. Why not call it Kryptonite? Because that's what it's going to be for Big Energy. "

Alex thought about that. "And would you shed a bitter tear?" he asked.

"I would throw a party, man. So, your one rock is all there is?"

"Probably, yeah."

"It's still worth a fortune. You should meet with the guys at G-Tek. They're even more connected than I thought. They could get this off the ground fast."

"I don't know. Can any corporation really be good?"

"Clean energy's what they're all about. This could rock the world, no pun intended. Actually, scratch that: pun definitely intended. Even if it only powers one country, think of all the money we won't have to spend on fossil."

"You're right about that. And all the fossil we won't burn."

"Zero carbon emissions," James added. "This could buy years, maybe decades to develop alternative energy sources for the rest of the world. You gotta meet, man. I can set it up. I guarantee you, they'll go nuts over this."

"Okay. Don't tell them too much, though. And don't promise anything. And don't tell them I found it. Or where it came from, or—"

"I get it! I get it! You're paranoid."

"Cautious."

"This is radical. Totally revolutionary."

Alex heard the sound of approaching footsteps and replaced the battery compartment cover, killing the blue glow. A man and woman got into the next car, eyed them suspiciously, and drove off.

"Maybe not the best place to have this conversation," James noted.

"Agreed."

"Now can we go? My dad's expecting me for a southern home-cooked dinner. You're welcome to join us."

"Thanks, but it's been a long day. Changing the world, you know."

"Hard to argue with that."

CHAPTER 10
IF I HAD A MILLION DOLLARS

THE NEXT MORNING, ALEX WOKE TO A VIDEO CALL from Sam. They caught up quickly. He could hear the sound of people working in the background as they spoke, and saw the occasional torso pass behind her. After a few minutes, she reached out and stopped one of the torsos. "Hold on a sec. Nigel, say hi to my brother."

Nigel leaned down and gazed into Sam's webcam. Alex guessed him to be mid-to-late twenties. Like Sam, he looked bright and idealistic. Unlike Sam, he had long brown hair and sported fashionable stubble. "Hello, brother!" he said, in a proper English accent.

"Hi there," Alex replied.

Nigel waved and moved on.

"That's Nigel," Sam said.

"I gathered."

"Sorry I didn't get back to you sooner. We're in crisis mode here."

"Why, what happened?"

"Remember I told you about that huge march OTW has planned to protest the new bankster laws?"

"Yeah."

"The city caved and passed the updated permit bill." Somewhere in Samantha's background, Alex heard a motorcycle start and then race off.

"Sounds heavy-duty."

"So the revised law means that in addition to the demonstration permit fees, you also have to post a bond to pay for any damage that *might* be done by demonstrators."

"Right, I remember."

"The bond requirement alone will cost us one hundred thousand pounds."

"Where'd they come up with that figure?"

"Estimated size of the protest. OTW's last protest was huge, so . . . But we don't have that kind of money. We're doing a fund drive, but there's not much hope."

"Wow. Anything I can do?"

"Not unless you know someone ready to part with a hundred grand. But thanks. Don't let me bring you down."

"No, hey, my day seems much better after talking to you."

She frowned at him. "What are you up to?"

"Got my pilot's license."

Sam's face lit up. "That's fabulous! Congratulations!"

"I'm also working on a new power source."

"You mean like a battery?"

"Something like that. I'll fill you in next time you visit."

X

AFTER HANGING UP WITH SAM, ALEX DID SOME QUICK research on G-Tek. From what he could tell, they were poised to make waves. There were rumors of government R&D grants in the works, and alternative energy was the company's primary focus. A typical entry on the company read:

Cited by Incubator Magazine *as one of America's fastest-grow-ing companies, G-Tek (short for Green Technologies, and formerly Green Investment Partners) is a global renewable energy research and development company based in New York. Their research port-folio includes geothermal, solar, wind power, and energy-efficiency products. Additionally, project management and financial services are rendered through their operational wing.*

They seemed legitimate. He looked up the *Incubator Magazine* article, which turned out to be impressive. A group of venture-capital companies and a handful of angel investors had seeded G-Tek with $120 million. Based on projects slated for comple-tion over the next few years, they were projecting profitable annual revenues of close to $500 million within five years. The company was helmed by an experienced CEO and an equally qualified chief operating officer.

Alex sat back and popped the geode open for a quick peek at the rock, then closed it before his MacBook exploded. His eyes were drawn to the model dangling from the ceiling. On a whim, not really expecting to find anything, he ran a search on "Hawker Sea Fury for sale." There were three: two overseas and one in Georgia. He winced at the prices; the one in Georgia was $600,000. Not many had been built to begin with, and few had survived the war and all the years since. That rarity demanded a high premium.

His mother poked her head in the side door. "Lunch soon, young man. What are you so busy with lately?"

Alex smiled. "Changing the world," he told her.

"I wish you luck."

"What do you and dad owe on the mortgage?" he asked.

"About $200,000, I think. Why?"

"Just curious."

"Well if you're curious about lunch, come up to the house."

A moment after she left, Alex's ringtone sounded: the original sixties *Star Trek* theme. "Hey, buddy," James told him, sounding jubilant. "Got you a meeting with the CEO and the chief attorney in New York. They'll spring for the plane ticket."

"Cool! When?"

"Monday, after hours. Bring your best game; these guys are heavy hitters."

"You got it. Thanks!"

CHAPTER 11
G-TEK INC.

MONDAY NIGHT, JAMES SCANNED THE ARRIVALS TERMI-
nal at JFK, but saw no sign of Alex. He was about to call when his
phone rang. It was Alex. "Dude, where are you?" James asked.

"Delayed at Asheville, some kind of mechanical issue. They
fixed it but we sat at the gate for an hour."

"Been waiting in arrivals for a while."

"You could have checked the boards."

James looked up; sure enough, Alex's flight was listed as
delayed. "Oops," he said.

"Would have called you, but they had us shut our phones off.
We're deplaning now. I should be there shortly."

"Okay, see you soon."

Alex appeared soon after. "Good to see you, man!" James said.
They shook hands and navigated through the mob, heading for
the exit. "What's with the plane?"

"I don't know. I wish they'd update their fleet. It's not exactly
calming when they say they have mechanical issues but won't
tell you what they are."

"As long as they get you here. Got the laptop?" James asked anxiously.

Alex stopped, slapping a hand to his forehead. "I *knew* I forgot something."

James stared at him, aghast.

Alex grinned. "Relax." He patted his carry-on. "Right here. Why so nervous?"

"Ah, you know. I'm still the new guy, and I sold you pretty hard."

"I'll try not to disappoint," Alex told him.

"Any trouble at security?"

"Not a bit. The thing is undetectable unless you're scanning for power output, and the crystal shielding takes care of that. How did they react to your pitch?"

"They took a bit of convincing, especially when I said it had to be the top guy. I played on paranoia; if it really is huge, they can't afford to have some lower-level guy cut his own deal and bolt. Still, not sure how serious the CEO is about it."

"He'll get serious in a hurry."

"I heard that. And by the way, you are dressed to kill. Perfect nerd-entrepreneur wear."

Alex nodded. He'd actually spent some time online looking at photos of Silicon Valley wunderkinds and their choice of clothing, which is how he'd decided on American Eagle dark-blue jeans and black T-shirt. The shirt featured a large bald eagle's head front and center, on a backdrop of mountains lit by a full moon breaking through misty nighttime clouds. "I look terrible in suits anyway," he said to James.

They left the building and stepped to the curb. The sun was just setting in the west, glinting gold off arriving aircraft. A sleek black limo pulled up before them: spotless, clean, and so shiny Alex could see his reflection in the metal. Because of the curve of the door, his image was distorted. It reminded him of the funhouse-mirror room in the amusement park he and James had frequented as boys. They would laugh until they cried—sometimes until they couldn't breathe—and that had made them laugh even more.

Alex looked around to see who the limo was for. It didn't come to him until the black-suited chauffeur stepped out and started toward them. "Is this for us?" Alex said.

"This is for us." James told him.

"Sweet."

"Get used to it. You might be leaving here a rich man."

"Let's not get ahead of ourselves," Alex told him.

The chauffeur opened the door for them, and they slipped inside. Despite seats facing in four directions, Alex took one facing forward; for as long as he could remember, any other position in a moving vehicle triggered motion sickness.

James sat across from him, facing backward. The chauffeur closed the door and resumed his place behind the wheel. "Welcome to New York, sir," he said. "I hope you have a very pleasant stay here."

"Thanks." Alex replied.

The chauffeur closed the divider to give them some privacy, and they got underway.

Alex scoped the limo's interior. There seemed to be room for ten more.

"Ready to change the world?"

"Ready as I'll ever be."

The chauffeur navigated the city's notorious traffic expertly as cabs vied aggressively for gaps in lanes that hardly seemed fit for even a bicycle; local pedestrians jaywalked across multiple lanes; and lost or gawking tourists did their best to become roadkill.

So this was Manhattan, Alex thought. For reasons unknown, the Watson family travels had never included New York. The city was everything he'd expected it to be: busy, loud, lively.

Eventually, they glided to a stop. Alex had to remind himself not to open the door because someone else would do it for him, and the chauffeur did an instant later.

Exiting the limo, they stepped to the curb before a gleaming skyscraper. Alex craned his neck, gazing skyward. "You work here?"

"Just another rat in the maze. For now."

"This all theirs?"

"The top two floors."

Alex tipped the chauffeur, who thanked him and quietly disappeared.

Alex opened up his carry-on and pulled out a blazer. It was more wrinkled than he expected. He slipped it on anyway. James eyed the wrinkles.

"It doesn't matter," Alex told him. "EX matters."

MOMENTS LATER, ALEX AND JAMES WAITED QUIETLY IN a well-appointed reception area. Alex finished some calculations on his iPhone, then leaned back and placed his hands on the big chair's armrests, caressing the aged leather. The whole room conveyed an undeniable upscale exclusivity—but subtly and tastefully done. The only item that appeared a little out of place was a large photo on the wall behind the reception desk. It depicted an older man shaking hands with the president of the United States.

After a few moments, the heavy mahogany doors beyond the reception desk swung open with a light squeak. A well-groomed and cultured-looking man stood in the doorway. Alex judged him to be in his mid-to-late fifties, and even standing still, he had a certain intensity about him. He stepped forward, clasped James's hand, and greeted him like an old friend. "James, good to see you."

He turned to Alex. "And you must be Alex. Jack Miller. Great to meet you."

Alex thought he sounded Texan. "Same here." Alex shook hands and glanced at the photo on the wall; the man in the photo with the president was Jack.

"The current administration's very interested in innovative forms of alternative energy," Jack said. "We just haven't found the right breakout technology. James tells me you mean to change that."

"I hope to," Alex told him.

Jack guided them through the doors into a corner office with floor-to-ceiling windows. Aside from the top floor of a darkened skyscraper across the street, the room offered a panoramic view of the city and, in the distance, Central Park. The room was richly decorated. An antique desk with a modern chair rested on Berber carpet, along with an antique conference table. There was an en suite gym next door—also with floor-to-ceiling windows—a private restroom with a shower and, beyond that, what looked like a bedroom.

"Comes in handy for marathon projects," Jack explained, noticing Alex's gaze. "This is Pete Bowman, our lead counsel."

Alex's head snapped around; he'd been so taken with the view and the size of the place, he hadn't even realized someone else was in the room. He'd have to get a grip on that; he wasn't here to sightsee.

Pete Bowman stood and offered a hand. He was in his early forties and, like Jack, wore a tailored suit that fit him like a glove. He had a doesn't-miss-a-trick look about him, and gimlet eyes behind designer lenses. His cologne smelled expensive. "Pleasure to meet you, Alex."

Alex nodded.

"We usually don't accept meetings like this," Jack began as everyone took a seat at the table. "Both Pete and I have extremely busy schedules. But James convinced us we'd see something extraordinary, and that piqued our interest." Jack spoke like an untouchable celebrity, brimming with confidence.

"I think you'll find this worth your time," Alex told them. He set his MacBook on the table, removed the battery compartment cover, and lifted out the crystal box containing Energy X. The tiny rock's brilliant blue glow suffused the room. The sun had set outside, and the office lighting was dim; Alex couldn't have asked for better conditions to show off EX.

"It's very pretty," Jack said. "What does it do? What is it?"

"It sits there and looks pretty," Alex said. "Oh, and it also puts out enough energy to power the entire city. Indefinitely."

Jack and Pete exchanged glances. Alex knew exactly what they were thinking because in their shoes, he'd have been thinking the same thing: "Is this guy nuts?" He'd brought a few instruments and videos along to help substantiate his claim, but he knew no corporate exec in his right mind would accept it without repeating the measurements with their own or third-party instruments.

But fortune seemed to have smiled on him because now he saw a shortcut to force an immediate decision. He gestured out the window to the darkened skyscraper across the street. "What's with that?" he asked.

Jack and Pete seemed baffled by the odd segue. "Just renovated. Opens next week," Pete told him.

Alex stood and walked the few steps to the window, taking the case with him. Once there, he slid the crystal case's lid aside and pressed the box top-first against the window.

The skyscraper across the street lit up. Top floor first, then all the rest, moving down. Jack and Pete rose to their feet and watched in astonishment. When Alex closed the box, the skyscraper fell dark.

"What do you think it costs to power that building for a year?" Alex inquired. "Ten million? This," he said, holding up the tiny glowing cube, "can power the whole city for eternity. And I have more. Green energy is here, gentlemen. But it's blue." He couldn't help but smile at this last line; it had taken him an hour to think it up.

Jack searched for his voice. Alex thought he made it sound remarkably steady, considering. "At this point, I can't say I'm convinced it's more than a parlor trick," Jack said. "How does $50,000 sound? All rights."

Alex laughed.

"Did I say something funny?"

Alex shook his head. "James told me you were sharp."

"In a good way," James added quickly.

"Your watch cost more than that." Alex said.

"All right. We can make you vice president of R&D, starting salary $200,000 a year. Pending confirmation of your claims. Bottom line, even if what you say is true, it could take weeks, even months to verify."

"Let's get real," Alex said.

"What do you want?" Jack asked, suddenly serious.

Alex gazed out over the city. "I want the whole world to have this. I want it to be affordable. And I want to put the fossil fuel and nuclear power industries out of business. They can buy into this if that will lower their resistance, but they can never control it. Then maybe we can get this planet back to what it should be."

Jack and Pete exchanged nervous glances.

Alex turned from the window. "With your resources, I think we can make that happen."

"How much do you want?" Jack asked.

"Right now . . . one million, nine hundred ninety thousand, thirty-seven dollars and twenty-two cents. A lease, not a sale."

"Two million then, is what you're asking."

"One million, nine hundred ninety thousand, thirty-seven dollars and twenty-two cents. I'll even throw in the laptop."

Jack caught Pete's eye and held it for a moment, then looked to Alex. He puffed up his chest, clearly about to play hardball.

"Don't even pretend to think about it," Alex told him.

Jack deflated. "It would have to be exclusive."

"Of course. Do all the research you like. See if you can duplicate it. But you can't exploit without my approval. I won't sell or lease to anyone else for six months. If you want to move forward then, we'll talk. If not, I'll take my rock back and go play somewhere else."

Jack stepped up to shake hands. "I'll have Pete draft an agreement for you to look at."

Alex fitted the crystal box back in the battery case and secured it back in the laptop. He'd already replaced the hard drive, so there was no personal or business information to worry about. "If you want me to leave this, I'd like a contract today and the payment in my account before I leave the building."

Jack laughed without humor.

"I say something funny?"

"You're not so dull yourself," Jack said. "Give us about thirty minutes to paper the deal and set up the transfer."

"We'll need your bank account details," Pete added.

Alex slapped a Post-it down on the table, the info already written there.

Jack and Pete rose. Pete took the note. "Enjoy the view," Jack said. He and Pete departed, leaving Alex and James alone.

"Holy shit," James whispered.

Alex wrote on a Post-it and held it up: "Bugged?"

James shrugged, as if to say "No idea." They restricted themselves to small talk until Jack and Pete returned thirty minutes later, bearing contracts.

"We had to call in some favors to get the money in your account on short notice this late in the day," Jack said, "but the transfer is ready to go through the moment you sign." He and Pete placed three thick contracts on the table. Jack held out a Montblanc pen. "I'll even throw in the pen," he said.

Alex smiled. "I'll have to read before I sign, of course." Jack looked disappointed. "Also, I'd like to video the signing and the power source." He used his iPhone to shoot a brief video and explain the basics, even holding a power-energy meter beside the rock to demonstrate a minimum power output. Then he propped the phone on a shelf with a view of the table and got down to business.

The reading and contract-tweaking took another three hours, during which Pete apologized for half a dozen "errors" he said must have resulted from the quick modification of an existing contract to fit their unique situation. He was convincing—so much so that, had all of the "errors" not favored the company, Alex might even have believed him. He supposed such legal maneuvering was to be expected. What mattered was the final agreement.

Pete made the changes on a laptop as they hammered things out and, once everything was settled and Alex went over the new draft—in triplicate—he signed and pressed his thumb beside the signature line. Pete switched windows on his laptop, put the payment through, and showed Alex the confirmation. Alex's phone beeped a moment later with a text from his bank, informing him of the deposit.

"You're a rich man, Alex," Jack told him.

"This is just the beginning," Alex said, "of a new world." He shook hands with Jack and Pete. Alex couldn't help but glance longingly at his trusted MacBook.

"Not to worry," Jack told him. "You can afford a few new Macs now. Pleasure doing business with you, Alex." Jack turned to James, "And you, we'll be hiring full time. You were right to bring this to us."

"Oh and, uh," Alex said to Jack. "Tell your guys not to handle that outside of a crystal shield. I used quartz."

"Is it dangerous?" Pete asked.

"Not that I know of, except to electronics. The real challenge is filtering the output so it doesn't overload whatever it's powering. That and the shielding, so it doesn't blow out everything in the area."

"We'll keep that in mind," Jack told him.

Alex and James headed out through the reception. Glancing back over his shoulder, he saw Jack and Pete exchange grave looks, but he wasn't sure why.

Alex and James floated down the hall, walking on air. "I wasn't sure you could do bank transfers at night." Alex said.

"That's all you have to say?"

Alex grinned. "Yeah."

"Man of few words."

They spilled onto the street, giddy with victory. They did a little dance as the stone-faced limo driver waited patiently.

"And what was with that whole 'and twenty-two cents' thing?" James asked.

"There are some things I want to do right now. That's how much it costs."

"Like what?"

"Like paying you a 10 percent commission for brokering the deal, or introducing us, or whatever. Point being, it wouldn't have happened without you."

James stared at Alex, speechless, then welled up and hugged him.

"Hey! Hey! Save that for the girlfriend."

James released him from the man-hug. "I don't know what to say, man. Thank you!"

Alex nodded. "Hey, we've been good friends since kindergarten. Now we'll be wealthy friends. Same diff."

"Who were you in there? I've never seen you like that."

Alex thought about that. "Someone who's not afraid anymore."

"Of what?"

"I don't know . . . of what other people might say or think or do. I can be me . . . yeah, that's it, I think. For once in my life, I'm the guy holding all the cards."

"Did you see the look on their faces when you lit up that building?"

"Shock and awe. But they didn't look too happy as we left. What was that about?"

"Didn't catch that. Maybe they're afraid the thing runs down next week and they're out two mil."

"One million—" Alex started to correct.

"Yeah, yeah."

James checked his watch. "It's past my bedtime. Hey, I'll see you on my next trip back."

"Will do." They shook hands beside the limo. At that moment, every light in the building they'd just stepped from lit up and went nova. An instant later, the whole thing went completely dark.

"Oops," James said. "It's not like you didn't warn them."

"I think it's time for me to make a graceful exit," Alex told him, and he slipped into the car.

"Safe flight," James said.

The chauffeur closed the door and took the wheel. Alex waved through the window as the car pulled away, bound for JFK.

CHAPTER 12
A TOP PRIORITY

THE MOMENT THE ELEVATOR DOORS CLOSED BEHIND Alex and James, Jack said, "We need to get our hands on the rest of this before someone else does. Or, worse, this kid goes solo." He could hear the edge of panic in his own voice, but was unable to prevent it.

"How?" Pete asked.

"I don't know yet, but I'll come up with something."

"Okay."

He removed the EX power pack from the MacBook and held it up, eyeing it suspiciously. "And find out if we can patent this."

"We should brief O'Donnell and Whitley," Pete suggested.

"How much did we contribute to their campaigns?"

"Not sure; couple of million between them."

Jack considered their situation. It was rare—unheard of, really—for something to catch him completely off guard. But he was nothing if not quick on his feet. "I wonder if we can't play the national security card on this with Homeland or Defense."

"That could work."

"If this gets into the wrong hands . . . *damn!*"

After sending a few emails to arrange calls the following day, Jack stormed into the research lab, hoping to find Dennis, who often worked crazy hours so he could access the company's distant supercomputer when no one else was using it. The kid was some kind of ubergeek they'd hired straight out of high school. He also looked like a squirrel with giant, black-framed glasses. Jack found him doing something perplexing, at least to the average observer.

"Sir?" Dennis jumped up and stood at attention, as if the two of them were in the army.

"I don't care what you're doing, or who it pisses off," Jack told him, holding up the glowing crystal box. "From now on, this is your priority. What is it, where it might have come from, how does it work, can it be patented, how do we make more of it? Got it?"

Dennis nodded like a bobblehead, already fascinated. "What is it?"

"Some kind of power source. Get started right away. You'll have a staff of twenty tomorrow, and we'll move you to the big lab." He handed the box to the kid and turned away. Remembering Alex's warning, he turned back in the doorway. "Oh, and don't—"

But he was already too late; Dennis stood there with the box in one hand and its lid in the other. The ceiling lights suddenly became blinding, and all of the electronics in the room turned themselves on. Seconds later, the light bulbs exploded and everything else blew out in showers of sparks, leaving dark silence behind.

Jack and Dennis stared at one another's blue faces.

CHAPTER 13
OCCUPY THE WORLD

ALEX STEPPED UP TO THE AIRLINE TICKET COUNTER.

"Next please. Destination, sir?" the attendant greeted him.

"Asheville, North Carolina," Alex said, handing her his ID. "Can I change my destination?"

"Where do you want to go?"

"Atlanta, Georgia."

She worked the keyboard with lightning-fast fingers. "You're in luck. There's a flight leaving in an hour. There is an additional charge."

"That works." Alex presented his credit card. Not having to ask the price was a new experience for him. It felt strange.

"Do you have any luggage?"

"Just this carry-on. Short trip."

"You're all set then. Here's your boarding pass."

Alex cleared security and walked to the lounge area, where he found a seat by a TV. No sooner had he slouched down in the chair than an anchorman said, "And coming up next, we have an exclusive interview with the chair of Occupy the World, Nigel Schaefer."

Alex snapped upright and waited impatiently for the commercials to end. "As promised," the anchorman continued, "we bring you Jennifer Brooks's interview with OTW chair Nigel Schaefer, recorded earlier today."

The image on the television switched to a view of an over-dressed Jennifer Brooks in front of the British parliament buildings. "Polls show the general population increasingly dissatisfied with government policies that favor large multinational corporations while discriminating against the middle class," she began. "Which goes a long way toward explaining why both European and global membership in Occupy the World continue to grow rapidly. Earlier today, I had the pleasure of speaking with OTW chair Nigel Schaefer."

The TV showed footage of Nigel and Jennifer in a studio interview room. "Mr. Schaefer, thank you so much for agreeing to meet with me. I understand you're typically selective with interviews, so we really do appreciate it."

"My pleasure, Jennifer. Anything I can do to help get the word out."

"From the recent membership data and continuing growth curve, it appears you don't need much help on that front. We're all closely following the much-publicized demonstration planned for Canary Wharf."

"Yes, we're hitting the pavement hard, fundraising to meet the new permit and bond requirements—which we will, by the way, be challenging in court. For right now, it's tough, and we still have a big funding gap. So we welcome any and all donations."

"What would you say are the driving factors for the incredibly rapid growth of your membership?"

"I'd say primarily the promise of equality under the law. Also, the simplicity and wide appeal of OTW itself. There are no executives, no CEOs, or any of that. I'm the chair only because someone has to speak for the rest. And while we do have a board of directors to propose and implement new ideas, all two million-plus OTW members, including myself and every member of the board, have equal voting rights."

"That sounds good in theory. How does it work in practice?"

"It prevents the kind of corruption we see in politics because instead of just bribing—pardon me; making financial contributions to—a couple of guys at the top, now, even if they were bribable, you'd have to pay off over a million people. No one can do that, so we remain free of undue influence from special interest groups."

"Can you talk about OTW's mission?"

"Happy to. Our primary goal is to level the playing field and ensure that all people—and not just corporate interests—have a voice in shaping the policies that affect their lives and the planet we live on. In addition to seeking to reform politics-as-usual, that means exposing and fighting injustice and the complete disregard for individual and collective rights engaged in by corporations, governments, and other entities."

"How have you structured your organization?"

"You could call it a blend of the classical cooperative and trade union organizations. A large group of individuals working together to achieve common goals. Strength in numbers, basically."

"OTW has had an interesting history; can you highlight some of the key milestones?"

"Well, the trigger was obviously Occupy Wall Street in the United States. That inspired a small group of British university alumni to ask, *why just Wall Street*? Why not occupy the *entire world*? Because the same things that were going on in America were also happening in other places. America exported the problem, so to speak—so why not export the solution?

"So that was the driving force?"

"Yes, and as you can imagine, the time was ripe. Social media and technology were there as never before, and all of these ingredients came together to create a sort of perfect storm. A peaceful revolution was born as people who were no longer willing to tolerate the status quo finally saw a way to change it without resorting to violence."

"What do you think about the future of OTW?"

"The whole world's social, economic, and political systems are in a death spiral. Anyone who cares to look at the facts can see that we're circling the drain. If we're going to have a future at all, it can't be based on the same model that led us here. OTW offers a way out. Our future, or something like it, is the only possible future."

Alex snapped out his phone and dialed Samantha. It went to voicemail. "I keep forgetting you're five hours ahead," he said. "I'm at JFK. Watching Jennifer Brooks interview Nigel on TV. Just thought I'd call to say he's pretty impressive. Okay, bye for now." He hung up and continued watching.

"How is your membership distributed globally?" Jennifer asked on the TV.

"Primarily in Europe and the States, but we also have hundreds of thousands of members across Africa, Asia, and South America. The movement has no borders."

The interviewer laughed. "Where do I sign up?"

Nigel feigned shock. "You're not a member? You can sign up on the website in less than a minute. Membership is free; all we ask is that you bring your ideas, energy, and dedication to the cause. And if you care to donate, we're happy to accept that too."

They wrapped the interview and Jennifer moved on. "After speaking with Nigel Schaefer, I asked U.S. Senate Transportation and Energy Committee chair Senator Brenda O'Donnell about her views on OTW."

The image on the screen split to show Jennifer on one side in London, and Senator O'Donnell in Washington, D.C. Alex checked the time and glanced toward the gate. A crowd had gathered, but there was no sign of his plane yet, so he continued watching.

"Thank you for being with us today, Senator," said Jennifer.

"Of course, Jennifer. Happy to be here." The senator pushed her silver-gray bangs off her forehead.

"What role do you see OTW playing in U.S. and global politics?" Jennifer asked.

"Large numbers and followings alone do not necessarily frame success," the senator replied. "So far, OTW is simply a platform for voicing opinions and dissatisfaction. They're basically activists. I have not seen any real action to effect substantial change of any nature whatsoever. It's going to take more than demonstrations and sit-ins to achieve the goals spoken of by

Mr. Schaefer. Right now, OTW seems more about propaganda than actual constructive participation in the political process."

"They've certainly been successful at building membership quickly."

"I don't mean to marginalize their success in recruiting new members. But without any tangible results to point to, OTW remains just another noisy movement lacking real substance. I would ask how their actions have benefitted our society. To me, they appear to incite conflict and disruption by contrasting the divide between the privileged and the rest of us. Similar social circumstances have existed since the dawn of civilization. Those who work the hardest gain the greatest rewards."

"Senator, how do you respond to their allegations that a wealthy, privileged elite and a small number of multinational corporations exert an undue influence on the politics of the United States, and indeed the world, through financial campaign contributions and lobbying power?"

"That's nonsense. Legislators introduce legislation for everyone. It's what we do."

"Have you yourself not taken significant contributions from many large corporations?"

O'Donnell scoffed. "Jennifer, you know very well that we all do that, but again, the legislation we write and pass is for the benefit of the broader population."

In other words, Alex thought, politicians do what they do out of altruism, and just happen to be paid by corporations that receive no special treatment for their repeated contributions. Same old, same old. It was hard to tell who was the better recruiter for OTW—Nigel or Senator O'Donnell.

He noticed a sudden commotion and saw that his plane had finally arrived at the gate. Soon people were standing in front of him, making noise and blocking his view of the TV. He decided to spend the remaining wait time online, booking a place to stay in Atlanta.

AFTER THE BUILDING WENT DARK, JACK MILLER MADE A few calls to open up the main lab in New Jersey, arrange extra security, and get Dennis situated there. He could hardly explain what had happened to the building's electrical system—nor, fortunately, could anyone else—so he'd simply claim ignorance if anyone asked.

A few hours later, he grilled Dennis over the phone to see what he'd learned. "Can anyone make more of this?" he asked.

"Maybe if they have their own hadron collider," Dennis told him. "No, scratch that. There's not even a place for this on the periodic table."

"How is that possible?"

"I'll need to do a bit more research to figure that out. My guess right now would be that we're not going to be able to make any more of it or duplicate its power output. And neither is anyone else."

"So the person who brought this to us . . ."

"Has all there is. Maybe all there ever will be."

"Keep digging," Jack instructed.

CHAPTER 14
HAWKER SEA FURY

AT ASHEVILLE AIRPORT, HANK WHISTLED A TUNE WHILE working on his plane. The afternoon sun bore down, making him sweat. Still, the heat was a welcome break from the recent streak of rainy days. A low rumbling noise in the sky caught his attention. The kind of deep, throaty sound modern planes didn't have. It was distant, but approaching quickly. A moment later, a World War II fighter thundered overhead like a bat out of hell, moving faster than any prop plane he'd ever seen. He watched it bank to come in. The outline was unmistakable. "I'll be a sonofabitch . . ." he said.

Alex guided the Hawker Sea Fury onto the tarmac and touched down with a bounce. The large tires squeaked as they kissed the runway. The plane itself was mostly storm gray. There were broad latte-cream stripes front to back on the sides of the fuselage, starting behind the oversized propeller and running all the way to the tail fin and rudder. Red, white, and blue bull's-eyes were painted atop black and white stripes on each wing. A bubble canopy covered the elevated cockpit, which offered excellent visibility. The wings were short, semi-elliptical, and underslung. The aircraft had the appearance of a stylized bullet in flight, even when on the ground. Alex taxied to a stop near Hank and shut the engine down.

"Hawker Sea Fury!" Hank said by way of greeting. "Where the hell did you find that?"

Alex climbed down. "Georgia."

"How the hell did you afford it?"

"A bit of good fortune sort of . . . fell from the sky."

"Sure is a beauty."

"That she is. Even came with a satellite phone." Alex showed it off to Hank. It was one of the latest models, with all the bells and whistles, including a camera to capture and broadcast high-definition video and a screen to display incoming pictures and video.

"That'll come in handy. No more dead zones and poor reception in-flight." Hank frowned. "I'm gonna hafta find another tutor, aren't I?"

"Probably. You wouldn't know where I can buy a Santa hat, would you?" Alex asked.

"In June?"

A SHORT WHILE LATER, ALEX SAT WITH HIS PARENTS AT the dining table, using his brand-new MacBook Pro to connect with Sam via videoconference. Once she was online and everyone had said their hellos, Alex pulled out a Santa hat and put it on.

"I don't understand," his father said.

"Christmas came early," Alex told him. "I bought myself a plane."

"What are you talking about?" Samantha quizzed.

"I'm talking about me owning a plane."

"A plane, my goodness," their mother said. "Isn't that expensive?"

"Yes, but Christmas came early for everyone. I'm paying off the mortgage on the house and our college loans . . . and I thought I might take care of OTW's little permit problem in the bargain."

They all stared at Alex, speechless. He looked to Samantha. "I get that back if they don't trash the city, right?"

"Umm. I think so. I-I don't know what to say, Alex."

"How can you afford this?" Mom asked.

"A simple thank-you will suffice." Alex smiled softly.

"Thank you!" they all said at once.

"You're not into anything . . . illegal, are you?" Dad asked.

"Da-ad!" Samantha scolded.

"Well . . ." their father said.

"No, you'll be happy to hear I'm not into drugs or anything remotely like that. I'll tell you more later, but for now, let's just say one of my hobbies paid off. This thing I'm working on is going to pay the bills for a very long time. And, by the way, eliminate fossil fuels and nuclear, put some bad companies out of business, change the course of history . . . and, with any luck, put an end to global warming. I'd like to say it will cure cancer and bring world peace, but that would be taking it a little too far."

Mom bit her lower lip and fretfully fluttered at Alex. "We can get you help if you're under stress or something."

"Yeah, call for a straitjacket!" Samantha said.

"I'm not crazy."

"We're going to need some kind of explanation," his father said. There was silence around the table. Alex sighed. He reached inside the backpack on the floor and pulled out a black cloth bag. He set the bag on the table, stuck a hand inside, and removed the crystal case he'd built a few hours before. Inside: Bloo. Its eerie light suffused the room. The family gawked at it, captivated.

"What is it?" Dad asked.

"I honestly don't know, but it has an awful lot of energy. Not sure how much."

"Is it dangerous?" Sam asked.

"Not that I know of. But this crystal box is the only thing keeping it from blowing out every electrical system in the area."

"So that's what happened to my tools in the garage," his father said.

"Sorry. It overloads everything in the area. That was the night I brought it home. I'll be replacing the tools, of course."

"Brought it home from where?" Samantha asked.

"I found it in the hills."

"It looks so . . . unnatural," his mother said.

"It's not from around here."

"So how did you make all that money?" Dad asked.

"James got me a meeting with G-Tek. I leased a small chunk of it to them."

"So your plan is to get G-Tek to help you change the world," Sam said.

"They have the reach, I have the rock, so, yeah."

CHAPTER 15
ENVIRONMENTALLY FRIENDLY

THE NEXT MORNING'S SUN WAS BRIGHT. ALEX SLID ON his gray-tinted Oakley shades and taxied the old plane into the hangar designated for light aircraft. The few planes inside were in various stages of disassembly and repair. Hank stood by one of these, head buried under the cowling.

Alex rolled the Sea Fury to an empty corner and climbed out.

"There's a delivery for you over there," Hank said, pointing to a large crate near the Hawker. "I signed for it yesterday."

"Thanks. I got their email notice last night."

"What's in it?"

"New engine."

"Looks like you have more money than you know what to do with."

"Oh, I'm coming up with ideas on how to spend it." They chatted briefly, and Alex set to work on the old warbird. After removing the body panels covering the Hawker's engine, he spent most of the day hauling the old Bristol Centaurus eighteen-cylinder from the plane, occasionally calling on Hank for help. It took another day to install the new mounts and secure them firmly.

Then, when no one else was in the hangar, he lined the engine compartment with crystal shielding and spent the better part of that same day building a replica of a lithium-ion battery pack. But instead of lithium-ion cells, this pack housed a small bit of Energy X, shielded by a protective one-inch crystal box fitted with the appropriate resistor sheets. Wires terminated outside the battery pack as contact points.

He inspected the firewall and mounted his EX battery nearby with a couple of clamps. Moving inside the cockpit, he built another crystal box, this one big enough for a flight bag.

Finally, he pried open the crate and hoisted out a gleaming new engine. The elevated letters *Yuneec* were stamped on the side.

"That electric?" Hank asked.

"Sure is. The new Yuneec Power House."

"Something wrong with the old engine?"

"Not a thing."

"Can you crank that electric job fast enough to get the speed you want?"

Alex smiled. "Got it covered."

"Let me know if you need a hand," Hank said, then scratched his head and returned to his own work.

Alex lowered the electric engine into place.

After triple-checking everything he could think of, Alex held his breath and started up the old plane. The new engine softly hummed to life. Unlike the original power plant, this one caused almost no vibration. There was no jet-fuel odor and no exhaust. He was now the proud new owner of the world's first environmentally friendly, electric-powered World War II aircraft.

He taxied to the runway, got clearance from the tower, and eased the throttle open. The plane streaked down the runway and lifted off. The only sounds were a faint electric hum and the racket of the madly spinning propeller.

Once airborne, he opened her up for a test run. More than half a century after its birth, the Hawker Sea Fury was still the fastest production prop plane ever made. It quickly reached its stated maximum speed of 490 miles an hour—and then, to Alex's surprise, climbed past 500, a speed he'd been unable to reach on the flight from Georgia. Of course, he thought; the new engine was aluminum and over a thousand pounds lighter than the old one.

Grinning like a madman, he set course northeast, toward the Blue Ridge Parkway east of Asheville. He slowed as he approached the spot where he'd first seen Energy X. But there was no blue glow today. He picked up speed and looped back to fly south, passing over Biltmore House to get a bird's-eye view of the historic French château-style home and its exquisitely groomed English gardens.

CHAPTER 16
BURNING THE MIDNIGHT OIL

JACK AND PETE STEPPED FROM THE LIMO IN FRONT OF G-Tek headquarters. It was late, almost midnight. Senator O'Donnell and Senator Phillip Whitley remained inside. "I'll get the wheels spinning with the Transportation and Energy Committee," O'Donnell promised.

"I can pull some strings with Homeland and Defense," Whitley told them. "No guarantees right now, though."

"I understand," Jack said. "Do what you can. We're on the brink of disaster here—all of us."

"Of course," Whitley said.

"If this goes unchecked," O'Donnell opined, "it could result in global economic unrest, turmoil, and—potentially—a meltdown. Rest assured, we'll act in the nation's best interests."

"Glad we're on the same page." Jack said.

Senator O'Donnell nodded. "We are. And thank you for dinner. Daniel is one of my favorites in New York."

"My pleasure, senators," Jack said.

"We'll be in touch," Whitley told him.

Jack and Pete watched the limo drive off, then went inside. The building's owner, deluged by tenant complaints, had managed to repair the entire skyscraper's electrical system in three days, and had promised to replace all tenants' damaged electronics to avoid multiple lawsuits.

Pete slid his card through the reader beside the door, and they went inside. They grabbed an elevator and rode up in silence. The elevator bell dinged as the doors opened on the top floor, and they walked the deserted hall toward the executive suite.

"Not sure how much help we'll actually get from O'Donnell and Whitley," Jack remarked. "They talk a good game, but that's their business."

"We've got their attention," Pete said. "That's something. Why are we here?"

"I left the new phone in the office."

"That's not the kind of thing you can leave lying around," Pete said seriously.

"My wife goes through everything at the house."

They entered the suite. Jack shuffled through the messy stack of papers on his desk, searching for the phone.

WORKING LATE, JAMES TAPPED AWAY ON THE KEYboard in his cubicle on the next-to-top floor. Jack had personally asked him to arrange a meeting with the CEOs and COOs of the top ten U.S. energy corporations. He'd been running ragged all day, trying to reach their administrative assistants and working with their calendars to come up with the earliest possible date and time that suited everyone's schedule. On top of that, he was working on an important deliverable due the next day, a report on comparative sales forecasts for G-Tek's current portfolio of energy offerings against projections for proposed Energy X-based products and services. It didn't make any sense to James because when it came to Energy X, there were just too many variables. But he did the best he could, noting a list of ballpark assumptions to support his calculations.

James rubbed his sleep-deprived eyes, undid his top button, and loosened his tie. He leaned back in his chair, rubbed the stubble on his face, and let out a sigh. He needed a break. He got up, stretched to work out the kinks, and headed upstairs. He didn't have the access code to take the elevator to the top floor, so he took the stairs.

James stepped out into the corridor and made his way to the large window at the end of a short dead-end hall. Even through the thick reinforced window, the view was nothing short of spectacular. Rivers of white and red lights snaked through concrete canyons while immensely tall skyscrapers glittered in the distance. It was hypnotic. He imagined he could smell the aromas of cuisines from around the world. He knew they were out there, beyond the glass.

The sound of the elevator bell snapped him out of it. He wondered who it might be, as the cleaners had already come and gone. Muffled voices moved toward the executive suite. One of them sounded like Jack. This could be the perfect time to update him on the big meeting, while also showing his dedication to the job by the mere fact that he was still here working.

He rounded the corner and came to the reception area. The door to the executive suite was cracked open. Striding toward it, ready to knock, he couldn't help but overhear Jack speaking. "Alex Watson is the end of our world," he heard him say. "There are no other choices—certainly no legal options. I think our course is clear."

Shocked, James hovered by the door. He inched closer, hoping to hear more.

"Pay him off," Pete said.

Pressing his eye to the crack, James saw Jack pull a cell phone from the papers on his desk. "Did you read the psych profile?" Jack asked Pete. "He's one of these save-the-world nuts." He dialed a number on the phone and brought it to his ear. "Besides, what are we going to offer him? This thing is priceless." He pressed the phone to his cheek as someone picked up on the other end. "Yeah. It's me. You're a go. Tonight. Make sure you get the rock . . . hard to miss; it glows blue . . . you have the address in Asheville?"

James couldn't believe it: they were going to steal the rock. Tonight! He had to warn Alex. He turned away from the door and felt something touch his shoulder; he was so close to the door, he'd bumped it when he turned. Worse, it creaked.

INSIDE THE ROOM, JACK AND PETE TURNED JUST IN time to see the door move slightly. Jack scooped a knife-like letter opener from the desktop, stalked to the door, and yanked it open. There was no one in sight. He gestured to Pete, indicating that they should conduct a search, and that Pete should take the floor below. The two of them left the office and split up to begin the hunt.

JAMES RUSHED DOWN THE FIRE STAIRS AND DIALED Alex on his cell. The call went to voicemail. He slipped back onto the next floor, hurried back to his cubicle, and switched off the work light he'd been using. He collected his belongings and shoved his work in a drawer, then raced for the elevator. He was reaching for the call button when the elevator dinged loudly. It could only be Jack or Pete, searching for the eavesdropper.

James turned and sprinted for the nearest corner. He heard the elevator doors slide open as he darted into the next hall. He moved back to the fire stairs, eased the metal door shut behind him, and started down, dialing Alex again.

ALEX GROANED WHEN THE CELL VIBRATED AGAIN ON the nightstand. He snatched it up and checked the caller: James. Reluctantly, he answered. "I know you want to impress the new boss," he said. "But don't you ever sleep?"

"Alex, listen to me. We got problems."

The tone of his friend's voice had him wide-awake in an instant. "What problems?"

"I'm at the office. Jack and Pete are here, talking about you like you're the Antichrist."

"What? That doesn't make sense. This is everything they could dream of."

"All I know is what I heard five minutes ago. They're sending someone to your house to steal the rock. Tonight, right now."

"I'll sue their asses off."

"With the connections these people have, I don't think so. You can't hide from that. They can pick up a phone and call the White House."

Alex was silent for a moment. He paced the room in shorts and T-shirt, feeling a panic he'd never known welling up inside him. "Who are they sending?" he said.

"What does it matter, man? Just get outta there. Think about it later."

"What are you going to do?" Alex asked.

"Go home and lie low. Then come back to work like it never happened. Watch your back, Alex."

"I will. Thanks, buddy."

Alex hung up and reached for his clothes.

CHAPTER 17
PHANTOM

THE FREELANCE AGENT KNOWN TO HIS EMPLOYERS AS "Phantom" appeared to most to be an unassuming man of few words in his early forties. His skills were for hire by those desiring covert execution of sensitive missions involving item procurement or elimination of difficult targets. There was a closely guarded listing of the top professionals in his occupational niche, seen by only a handful of governments and corporations, and it was a point of pride that his own position on that list had never fallen below the top five.

Dwelling largely within a fiercely secretive underground network hidden from the public, Phantom had trained himself to dispose of threats in a highly efficient manner, with zero traceability to the contracting entity. Whether the threats so addressed were real or perceived was not his concern. Contracts were entered into and confirmed via customized and disposable mobile devices. Payments were offshored and electronic.

His given name lost in the midst of assorted aliases, Phantom held multiple passports and chose the "Robert Karson" identity for U.S.-based missions. Over the course of a successful eighteen-year career, he'd completed hundreds of kills. He'd ruthlessly suppressed early feelings of remorse, which with time gave way to indifference.

Poker-faced and calculating, he focused like a laser on the task at hand and was exceptionally skilled with a variety of weapons and concealment techniques. His unarmed combat abilities were on a par with the Navy Seals; he knew this because he'd killed one. He was fluent in English, Russian, German, Arabic, and French.

Phantom's last assignment had wrapped a week ago, and he'd been enjoying the time off at home. He sat back in his deck chair, enjoying the cool breeze and spectacular view from his rear patio. He'd designed the mountaintop home himself, hiring an architect to implement his vision. Construction, complicated by the location, had taken three years. The home itself was simple by modern standards, but built with precision and much care. What the house lacked in elaborate appointments, it more than made up for with spectacular views of Wyoming's Big Horn Mountain Range.

He sipped coffee, his thoughts lingering on the just-completed contract in Uzbekistan. The close call bothered him, and his own post-mission evaluation didn't sit well. He mentally stepped through the sequence of events, as he always did, analyzing and seeking lessons to improve future performance. This one had been a particularly grueling mission, requiring him to navigate through a highly charged political climate in the middle of a small war ignited by rival factions. The job nearly compromised his identity when one of the opposing parties he'd infiltrated came to suspect him of spying. In the end, training and experience had been his saving graces and allowed him to complete the mission intact.

His internal deliberations were suddenly interrupted when one of his satellite phones vibrated with a new message. He opened it, seeing two photos: one of a young man with angular features, the other of what appeared to be a small, glowing blue rock in a glass case. He inspected them closely, then read the specifics of the proposed mission. In his line of business, there was no room for error, and little tolerance for back-and-forth communications. He insisted on concise, detailed mission statements, articulated in an unambiguous manner that presented no possibility of misinterpretation.

He studied the requirements a second time. The payoff was curiously larger than any of his past contracts, and he had to wonder why when the mission seemed simple enough. Time was obviously a factor, but not enough to account for the discrepancy. So it must be the rock; for some reason, it was valuable. Beyond such basics, he preferred not to know the reasons for things. Too much info opened up windows for conflicting interests, and muddied his focus. His job was to execute his assignments as flawlessly as possible, no questions asked, and to collect his payments. The message ended with the statement, "Will send go/no-go confirmation within 48 hours. Holding fee already transferred. If accept, prep and head to Asheville, North Carolina."

This could be the last job, he thought; the pay was enough for him to retire comfortably. Not because he was tired of killing; the only thing he felt these days was indifference, a mental numbness that made him think he should get out of the game. He couldn't quite imagine himself holding a gun in shaky hands and straining to see with aging eyes. The break had to be made at some point, and now would be as good a time as any.

He finished his coffee, texted back "Accept," and got to work. From the weapon room, he selected the Para P18 9mm and an SG 550 tactical snipe rifle. The attractive stainless-steel-framed P18 offered mild recoil and a fully adjustable rear sight, and provided a more-than-adequate capacity of nineteen rounds. The Swiss-made 550 was relatively compact and light, but still very accurate. He packed both in his custom carry case, and gathered the other items he'd need. From what he'd seen in the job proposal, the assignment should be fairly straightforward.

Although, to be sure, one never could tell.

CHAPTER 18
HIT MAN

ALEX HUNG UP WITH JAMES. HIS HEART RACED, BUT HIS body seemed paralyzed, frozen by fear. After a few panicked moments, his brain snapped out of its stupor and began firing on all cylinders. James was right; there was no time to think this through, or even wonder whether his friend may have misunderstood what he'd heard at G-Tek. The safest play was to move, now.

The house was still, his parents asleep. Trying to be quiet, Alex speed-dressed and put the geode in a backpack, along with his passport and the few thousand dollars he'd withdrawn from the bank for the sheer novelty of actually having some serious money on hand for unexpected situations. He remembered the bank teller looking at him like he was some sort of criminal for wanting to withdraw his own money.

He slung the bag over his shoulder, killed the bedroom light, eased the door open, and padded down the hall. The house was dark but for a dim glow from the downstairs hall lamp. Using that for guidance, Alex made his way down the stairs, then raided the kitchen for food and bottled water. When he was finished, he wrote a quick note on a recipe pad and left it on the table, one corner anchored under a bowl of apples.

He scooped his keys from the hall table and left the house without a sound. He even rolled his Volkswagen down the sloping cul-de-sac road before starting it. The night was still and quiet, the residential streets lit only by a gibbous moon.

He turned off Hidden Brook Lane onto McKinney Road, then right onto Pisgah View Road, taking a southward route that would cut under Highway 40 and onto Brevard Road. He worked his iPhone while driving, trying to transfer money out of his account. As he neared the highway, a car with its lights out drove past from the opposite direction. An instant later, he heard the sound of screeching rubber. Heart leaping into his throat, Alex glanced in the mirror and saw the dark car coming out of a wild turn and speeding after him.

He pounded his foot down on the gas and felt the car surge forward. But Volkswagens weren't built for speed, and his pursuer was quickly closing the gap. Alex mashed the pedal to the floor, but the old Bug was giving all she could. Seconds later, he was rammed from behind. He fought for control as the Bug veered off the road. Somehow, he pulled out of it, guiding the car back onto blacktop.

The other car pulled up beside him. The driver was in shadow, but Alex could see in the moonlight that the car was a Subaru Outback. As they came up beside a ravine, the Subaru slammed into the side of Alex's car, trying to run him off the narrow road. Alex kept control—barely.

The Subaru's passenger-side window slid down, and moonlight glinted off something in the driver's hand. Alex stomped the brake as the attacker fired. A sudden chain of thundering gunshots sounded as bullets shattered the Bug's windshield. Shards of glass showered Alex as the Subaru sped past, almost too fast to make the turn ahead.

Already braking, Alex spun the Volkswagen around and raced off in the other direction. He'd passed a freeway on-ramp back there, and thought that might be his best chance. Checking the mirror, he saw the Subaru clip several roadside trees and turn around.

Alex gained the freeway and pushed the Bug hard. He saw the airport sign whip past just before the Subaru caught up and bounced him off the guardrail. Sparks flew as metal screeched against metal.

Alex heard a sudden wail behind him, and saw red and blue lights flashing in the mirrors. He'd never been so glad to see a cop. The police car came on fast and rammed its push bar at an angle into the Subaru's bumper. The Subaru spun past the off-ramp, back end smashing into the rail.

Alex veered down the off-ramp. The last thing he saw was the police car pinning the Subaru against the rail. Counting himself lucky, he killed the headlights and sped into the night. No doubt the police would like to speak with him, but he couldn't risk sitting in a jail cell while G-Tek sent someone else after him. The whole thing was insane. Every time he told himself it couldn't be happening, reality begged to differ.

He tried to steady his breathing and think straight. He had to call someone—but who? There was nothing anyone he knew could do against something like this, not when the company behind it was so powerful. He had to get out of the country, away from their home base. He thought of someone he could call, but not just yet. He realized his phone could be used to track him and threw it out the window.

Moments later, the lights of Asheville Airport came into sight. The gate would be locked at this hour, so he ducked below the dashboard and crashed the fence line. The car slid sideways on the grass as the fence resisted, then it nearly rolled when the fence gave way. He sat up and cut the wheel hard left, straightening out.

Alex pulled up by the Hawker, hooked his backpack, and darted to the plane. He tossed the bag inside, removed the wheel chocks, and climbed on board. The electric engine hummed to life in an instant, and Alex taxied to the runway. He was just about to start his takeoff run when a police car appeared on the access road, lights flashing.

Conditioned to obey the police, Alex found himself slowing the plane. But the cop car smashed through the fence and came straight for him, never slowing. Bright yellow flashes erupted from the driver's-side window. Alex heard the bullets ping off the old plane's bulletproof canopy. He opened the throttle, and the plane accelerated down the runway.

The patrol car changed course, veering to intercept. The crazy bastard was actually going to drive his car into a speeding plane. Alex could see the driver duck down, bracing for the impact. Alex hauled back on the stick and the plane leapt skyward, rear wheel ripping through the light bar on the cop car's roof.

WHEN THE IMPACT DIDN'T COME, PHANTOM SAT UP and skidded the car to a halt. He jumped out, steadied his arms on the open door, and fired at the departing plane. The damned thing had a bulletproof canopy, so he aimed for the fuel tanks. He reloaded with incendiary tracer rounds he'd prepared himself and fired empty. The bright white streaks they left behind told him his aim was true; at least half his rounds hit the tanks. But there was no explosion. He didn't understand that, unless the tanks were armored. He'd brought the rifle with him, in its case on the backseat, but by the time he got it out, the plane would be out of range. He'd never seen a prop plane move so fast.

After searching the Volkswagen, he pulled out a throwaway phone and made the call.

"Line is secure," said the voice on the other end. "Is it done?"

"Still in motion," Phantom told him.

"And the rock?"

"I assume he has the package with him."

"Where is he now?" the voice asked.

"Just left Asheville Airport in some old prop fighter with a bulletproof cockpit. Heading east."

"I'll get back to you," said the voice, and hung up. Phantom despised calls like that; they were embarrassing. Fortunately, they were exceedingly uncommon. He hung up, retrieved his gun case from the backseat, and unscrewed the patrol car's gas cap. He stuffed a cleaning rag from the case down the car's filler neck and lit the end with a lighter. Then he picked up his case and walked toward the trees. He felt the hot wind on his back when the car erupted behind him.

INSIDE G-TEK'S EXECUTIVE SUITE, JACK HUNG UP THE phone. "We need to wake some people up," he told Pete.

SUDDEN LIGHT CAUGHT ALEX'S EYE, AND HE LOOKED back to see something burning on the runway. He kept the Hawker climbing. He tipped the wings to get a look at the damage. It seemed cosmetic, particularly when compared to photos he'd seen of World War II planes that had landed safely despite horrifying damage. That said, if he'd been running a gas engine, his flight would have ended in a ball of fire; there were multiple holes where the fuel would have been. For a moment, absurdly, he felt like a fighter pilot of old, and wondered what kind of action the plane itself had seen, whether it had been shot before.

The old-style dial on the instrument panel told him the plane had reached five hundred miles per hour. He ran a few checks, and everything seemed to be running smoothly. He'd probably have his license revoked, though. Then again, who even knew he'd taken off in the dead of night without clearance? Though he did leave his bullet-riddled car beside what was in all probability a burning cop car. So there was that.

A white line appeared in the dimness ahead: waves breaking on the coastline. He flew over, heading out to sea. Moments later, the sun peeked above the vast Atlantic. He watched it rise, then twisted around in his seat to look at the receding shore, wondering if and when he'd be back. Checking his watch, he pulled out his satellite phone and dialed.

CHAPTER 19
COMING TO VISIT

OCCUPY THE WORLD'S UNOFFICIAL HEADQUARTERS was a two-story, Cotswold-style stone cottage surrounded by mature sycamore trees. A foot-high decorative stone wall ran around the house, about seven feet from the cottage. A Cornish hedge grew beside the wall. The closest neighbor was a flower-strewn meadow; beyond that, a small expanse of woods. The place was private enough to get away from it all, yet not overly far from the nearest town. St. Ives was just a few miles north by unpaved road.

Inside, the living room doubled as a command center, where the OTW directors worked computers and planned the upcoming demonstration. Answering an incoming Skype call on her laptop, Samantha was delighted to find Alex on the line. "Well, hello stranger," she told him.

"Not for long," Alex said. "I'm coming to visit."

"Hey, that's great. When?"

"Now, actually. I'm in the air."

"What?"

"Yeah. You know that little project of mine?"

"Uh-huh. I thought that was with James's company for now."

"About that. They had a little change of heart, and now they're sort of trying to kill me."

"*What!* Are you hurt?"

"No, but not for lack of effort. The plane took some hits, though."

"What do you mean *hits*?"

"Bullets."

"You got shot at?"

"Um. Yeah."

"Wait, the rest of the gang needs to hear this. Can you do video?"

"Okay, I'm switching my video on. Can you see me?"

"Yes. Can you see us?"

"A little fuzzy but, yeah."

OTW's leadership gathered around Samantha's computer, staring into the webcam. "You already know Nigel," Sam said. "Meet Sunil, Patrick, and Hana." Samantha gestured over her shoulder. They waved or nodded to Alex.

"Did I hear that right?" Nigel asked. "Someone's shooting at you?"

"They were. Tried to run me off the road, shot out my windshield, and then shot at the plane."

Confusion reigned at OTW. "I don't understand," Nigel said, speaking for the others. "Why would someone try to kill you?"

Samantha looked to Alex, unwilling to reveal his secret before he was ready. For his part, Alex decided that, given recent events, this was the time to reveal it to the world. "They're after Energy X," he said.

"Energy X?"

"It's a wireless energy source strong enough to power a large country and, as far as I can tell, it'll last forever. Super intense. I'm shielding it with quartz."

"No way," Patrick said.

"Trust me for now; I'll show you when I get there. I thought you guys might be interested in helping put this to use. What do you say?"

"If this is on the level . . ." Nigel began.

"It is," Alex interrupted.

"Then clearly, this could change the world."

"Is that a yes?" Alex asked.

"Changing the world is what we do. Of course it's a yes. What can we do to help?"

"People need to know this exists."

"We should stream live on the Internet," Samantha said.

"I'm on it," Sunil told her. "Give me a minute."

"Alex, can you repeat everything you've said so far, so we can stream it?" Sam asked.

"You bet. The more people watching, the better."

"What kind of plane is that?" Hana said. "All I can see is part of the canopy behind you."

"Hawker Sea Fury, World War II fighter. Real beauty."

"And you're where, stateside? That can't have the range to get here."

Alex grinned. "It does now," he answered. Despite the situation, he found himself admiring Hana's appearance. She seemed Eurasian, with an olive-tan skin tone and hazel-brown hair that was mostly straight but ended in gentle curls. Her eyes seemed both alluring and standoffish. She looked like she could either kiss you or kick your ass. He remembered the question and forced his thoughts back on track. "Observant," he told her.

"My job to be."

"Okay, we're live now!" Sunil announced excitedly. "Archiving as well, so people can download later and catch up." Sam did a brief spoken introduction, then asked Alex to bring viewers up to speed.

CHAPTER 20
COME WITH US

JAMES DARTED AROUND HIS APARTMENT, RANSACKING dresser drawers, pulling shirts and pants off hangers, and dumping it all into a suitcase. If the squeaking door had been noticed—as he felt certain it must have been—then it was only a matter of time before Jack and Pete checked the access log to see who'd carded into the building and onto G-Tek's floors. Aside from themselves, there would be only one name on that log: his own. Hell, even if he hadn't been noticed, there was no way he could keep working for them. And so he'd booked the first flight back to Asheville.

He closed the suitcase, snapped the latches shut, and headed for the door. He was reaching for the knob when someone pounded on the other side. His heart nearly stopped.

"Federal agents!" a deep male voice shouted. "Open the door!"

James felt ice water in his veins. He backed away from the door, thinking he might climb down the fire escape. He never got the chance. The door splintered inward and a SWAT team barged in, guns aimed at James. He raised trembling hands. One of the armored men handcuffed him and patted him down while the others fanned out through the apartment, yelling "Clear!" each time they found an empty room. The man searching him took his phone.

When the SWAT team was done, two men in dark suits walked in. "Agent Holloway, National Security Agency," said the larger of the pair. He snapped a leather wallet open, displaying a badge. The other agent stood behind Holloway, poker-faced and indifferent.

"What the hell, man?" James said angrily. "You got the wrong place."

"You are James Campbell." Holloway said, more statement than question.

James nodded.

"Right place. You're coming with us."

"I want a lawyer. I know my rights."

Holloway took James's phone from the SWAT cop and smirked. "In case you haven't heard," he said to James, "since 9/11, you have no rights."

The agents escorted him out of the apartment, down the stairwell, and into the back of a black SUV with tinted windows. The second agent showed James a black hood. "I'm Agent Carter. I'm going to put this on you."

"What are you, a cop or a terrorist?" James shot back at him.

"Mr. Campbell, standard NSA protocol requires us to maintain the confidentiality of our interrogation sites."

James's vision went dark as the hood came down, and he felt the car get underway. "Where are you taking me?" he demanded.

"A secure location where we can ask a few questions," Carter told him.

"Bullshit. You could have done that in my apartment."

"That's not the way we like to do things, Mr. Campbell."

James tried to map out the route they were taking, but there were too many turns. About twenty minutes later, the car came to a stop, waited a moment, then drove over a bump. James guessed they'd entered a parking structure or garage. Shortly after this, the journey ended.

The two agents shuffled James out of the Suburban, and they walked for another five minutes. He was guided into a seat, and the hood unceremoniously whipped off his head. He squinted in bright fluorescent light, finding himself in a stark and windowless room with the two agents. A steel table sat before him, along with two other chairs.

Holloway closed the heavy metal door, and Carter slapped some photos down on the desk: one of Alex beside the new plane he'd emailed James about, another of Alex's house, a third showing the plane tied down at the airport.

"We know you spoke to him by phone," Carter said. "Where's he going?"

"I don't know. He didn't tell me. What's it to you, anyway? Don't you have real criminals to catch?"

"Mr. Campbell," Holloway said, "you'd be prudent to cooperate. We wouldn't want the situation to escalate now, would we?"

"You're gonna shoot me, disappear me, what? These are Gestapo tactics."

"This is a national security matter. We have the authority to do whatever is necessary."

"Same thing the Nazis said. You're telling me some small-town college kid is a threat to national security?"

"We're not at liberty to discuss that," Holloway told him, sounding annoyed. "Now tell us where he is!"

"I told you. I don't know. We had a brief conversation on the phone."

"We've been monitoring Alex," Carter said. "He's been spending a lot of time at the airport. What do you know about his plans?"

"Sounds like you know more than I do. And since when is hanging at the airport a crime?"

"What does he intend to do with the energy source?" Holloway asked.

"You working for the government or G-Tek here?"

"*We'll* ask the questions," Holloway told him. "You'll answer them."

"He wants the whole world to benefit from it, but I have no idea *how* he's gonna do that, other than by bringing it to G-Tek, which he already did. You know they're trying to steal it from him, right?"

"Where did he get it?"

The fact that they didn't follow up on his last comment told James they, or their bosses, were in league with G-Tek. "He didn't say," he replied.

"Is there more of it?"

"How the hell should I know?"

Holloway seemed about to say something when his cell phone buzzed. He checked the screen, and looked to James. "Seems we found your friend. You're outta here."

The hood descended over his head, and he was led back to the car. Twenty minutes later, the hood and handcuffs came off, and he stepped to the curb outside his apartment. Carter detached some kind of device from James's phone and handed it back.

"Expect to be prosecuted for kidnapping," James said.

"Mr. Campbell," Carter told him. "You were detained for national security reasons, not kidnapped. The courts have no authority over such procedures. Have a safe flight back to Asheville."

Before James could think of a response, the door slammed shut and the SUV sped off. He could feel his legs shaking. He dialed Alex on his cell. It went to voicemail. "Alex, James. You're not gonna believe this . . ." He filled Alex in on recent events, then apologized for getting him into this. "I just wanted to do something good and help a friend, you know? Hope you're okay. Call me when you can."

He hung up, caught the elevator back to his floor, and stepped through the ruined doorway. About to pick up his suitcase, he thought to check the time; he'd never make the flight back home. He closed the wrecked door as best he could, pulled his laptop from the suitcase, and went online to book another flight, reconsidering his destination. Realizing he'd forgotten his daily check-in with his father, he called home on his cell. He'd been so proud when James had landed the job with G-Tek. Now he'd have to tell his father there was no job.

"Hey, son. How are you?" his dad asked.

James sighed. "I'm outta G-Tek," he said.

"You wasn't fired, was you? Is this because you black?"

"No, dad; no one cares about that here. I wasn't fired and I haven't exactly handed in my resignation, but it's over. They're not on the up and up. I can't work for them."

"Well if they's dishonest, then I can't blame you none, son."

"And not to worry you, but in case anything happens? You should know I kinda got picked up by the NSA a little while ago."

"Those spy people? What they want with you? James, is there something you're not telling me? Are you mixed up in something illegal?"

"No, it's not even about me. It's about Alex. But I'm worried what might happen next."

"What you gonna to do? You can always come home."

"Thanks, Dad, but I think I need to disappear for a while. I don't feel safe here in New York and I don't want to cause you any trouble. So we may not see each other for a while."

"How long?"

"No idea. Depends on how long it takes for all this to clear up."

"Don't wanna lose you too."

"Don't worry, Dad, I'll be okay. Not sure where I'll go but I need to get outta New York for starters. I'll call when I can. When I feel a little safer."

"I understand. You be careful. If they ask me, I'll tell them I don't know where you is. That's the truth. I'll miss you."

"Me too. Love you, Dad."

"Love you too, son."

CHAPTER 21
RAPTOR ESCORT

ALEX REPEATED THE STORY THUS FAR, SO THOSE TUNing into the stream could catch up, then tried to think of something to say that would accurately reflect the magnitude of what was going on. "If we're willing," he said, "this could change the course of history. It's not often we're handed an opportunity like that. If we can keep this in the right hands, we can use it to benefit everyone, and not just a few corporations." He could see Sam's eyes welling up at his words, so he guessed he was on the mark or close to it.

Sunil reappeared on the webcam, saying something to Sam. "It's already viral," Sam told Alex. "The BBC is on it, and CNN. How does it feel to be breaking news?"

"I'd rather be spending a quiet evening at home," Alex told her. "I plan to land at Exeter. Big airport, lots of people."

"Witnesses," Hana commented.

"Exactly. I should be there in about seven hours. Did I mention this is the fastest prop plane ever built?" Alex heard a low rumble, swiftly growing louder. He scanned the skies, but there wasn't a storm cloud in sight. The sound grew louder still, rattling the canopy as two massive shapes pulled alongside, their sleek lethality a stark contrast to his aging fighter. Alex recognized the planes as F-22 Raptors.

Pilots in green flight suits stared back at him, their mirrored faceplates unreadable. Alex held up the satphone to send video of the fighters.

"Sam, you getting this?" he asked.

"What the hell are those?" Sam said.

A new voice came over the plane's VHF airband. "Sea Fury, this is Commander Albright of the United States Air Force. You are ordered to descend immediately to ten thousand feet and land at Cherry Point Naval Air Base."

"Alex?" Samantha said.

"I'm here."

"We have orders to escort you to Morehead City," the Raptor pilot continued. "If you do not respond, we are authorized to fire on you."

"Alex. Turn around," Samantha said, trying to sound calm. For a moment, the only sounds were the Sea Fury's electric hum, the drone of its oversized prop and the steady roar of the Raptors' jet engines.

"Sam . . ." Alex said, breaking the silence.

"Turn around!" Samantha ordered.

"If you turn around now, you'll disappear," Hana said into the webcam. "You need to keep going."

Sam looked at Hana, incredulous, then turned to Alex. "Don't play with these people, Alex."

"You have one play to make, and that's to keep going. You know I'm right," Hana said to Alex.

Alex thought for a moment, then said, "Keep us on the air, Sam. No matter what."

Hana nodded grim approval.

"Alex!" Samantha called.

He propped the satellite phone inside the crystal case he'd built to hold his flight bag, making sure its camera had a good view through the canopy. Viewers should be able to see him and one of the Raptors, which flew slightly higher than he was. He removed something from the flight bag and closed the case again. "U.S. Air Force Commander, this is Sea Fury," he said into the plane's radio. "I am in international airspace; you have no authority here."

"Sea Fury, I have orders to bring you back or shoot you down. You have thirty seconds to comply and start your descent."

Alex showed his passport to the satphone's camera, then held it up against the canopy. "You see this, Commander? My name is Alex Watson. I am a British citizen. This is my passport. Why are you threatening an unarmed British national?"

"I don't have that information. I do have my orders. You have fifteen seconds to start your descent."

"You should know that I'm streaming live audio and video right now, being broadcast over OTW.org, CNN, and BBC. Technically, shooting me down could be an act of war."

"Time's up," said the commander. One fighter swung wide to the side. The other dropped behind, preparing to fire. "Sea Fury, this is your final warning."

Alex adjusted the satphone to keep one plane in sight. "Commander," he asked, "are those ejection seats electronically fired?"

"With mechanical backup. Why?"

"Just curious," Alex told him. Then he slid the lid off Bloo's box, reached in, and pulled out Energy X, squinting his eyes against the blue glow. The old Sea Fury and its shielded engine were unaffected by the rock's powerful energy output.

Not so the Raptors. The computerized fighters' electronics failed immediately. Not only couldn't they fire their missiles, which were also computer controlled; without electronics, they couldn't fly at all. Alex watched the pilots punch out in their ejection seats as the hundred-million-dollar aircraft plummeted from the sky beneath them. The one casualty aboard Alex's plane was the VHF airband radio, which for some reason he hadn't thought to shield.

He returned Bloo to its container and placed it back inside his flight bag. He pulled the satphone from the case, using it to shoot video of the Raptor pilots' parachutes and self-inflating rafts.

"Did you guys get all that?" Alex asked.

"What the hell just happened?" Sam said. "Why are they after you?"

Nigel leaned in and spoke to Alex. "Excuse me but . . . did you just take down two fighters?"

"Alex, we're still streaming live." Samantha said.

"Ahm, it must have been some kind of electrical failure. My British-built Hawker's running just fine." Alex looked into the satphone camera and smiled. "And by the way, if any of our British viewers are politicians, you might call the White House and ask them to stop sending military fighters after unarmed British citizens."

"Why would the U.S. do that?" Samantha said.

"I don't know," Alex told her. "Ask G-Tek in New York."

Patrick tapped Samantha on the shoulder and handed her a phone.

"Not now," she said.

"It's the BBC."

Sam took the phone. "Hello, this is Samantha Watson."

"Miss Watson, you're the OTW PR contact?"

"I am."

"I'm Henry Baker, director-general with the BBC. I'm calling from Broadcasting House in London. How are you doing today?"

"I've been better."

"I realize that this might not be the best time for you, but we would like to get the exclusive for your story."

"It's not my story; it's my brother's."

"Yes, we know. We would like to interview him when he gets here."

"That would be entirely up to him, but I can't imagine he'd agree to it. First because he's probably cringing right now at his accidental fame. And second because as his press advisor, I'm not sure I see the advantage of an exclusive from his perspective. We want to reach everyone, everywhere."

"Nonetheless, we do have a global reach. Will you speak with Mr. Watson?"

"Absolutely. I just can't make any promises. Stepping into the limelight was an act of desperation, not a first choice. My brother is a physics nerd at heart."

Henry laughed. "I understand. Please, do what you can. I can also offer extensive BBC coverage of OTW's upcoming Canary Wharf demonstration, with global broadcast."

"I'll bring both subjects up with him when I can."

"Thank you. I'm sure you've plenty of pressing matters to attend to, and we're all hoping the remainder of his journey is safe and uneventful. When you have a decision, please call the Broadcasting House here in London and ask for me. They'll put you right through. And on a side note, I'd be happy to give you both a personal tour of our new state-of-the-art facility."

"That's very kind of you."

"Well, Miss Watson, it's been a pleasure. Do I have a verbal agreement that the BBC will get the exclusive on this?"

"If Alex says yes."

"Excellent. In the meantime, we'll continue to cover the OTW live stream. The viewer statistics are quite impressive."

Sam said her goodbyes and returned her attention to her brother.

ALEX'S FATHER, DAVID, THREW A HAND OUT TO KILL THE alarm and tugged the covers over his head. His wife, Mary, groaned and rolled onto her side. "I'll get the coffee started," she said, pulling down the covers to kiss her husband.

"Thanks, honey. Breakfast is on me."

"That's the way I like it," his wife said, sitting up and pausing for a catlike stretch, arms over her head, back arched. She shuffled to the bedroom closet.

"Do you hear that?" David asked.

"Hear what, honey?"

"That noise, outside."

"You're probably still dreaming." She knew he tended to mix things up while caught in the state between sleep and wakefulness; at such times, he couldn't always quite tell what was real and what wasn't. During their early years together, this had frightened her. She worried that the love of her life might be mentally unstable. But as the years passed, she grew accustomed to it, coming to view it as more a charming idiosyncrasy than anything else.

"Could be," he agreed.

"Okay, coffee time." Mary slipped into a robe and headed downstairs. She prepared the Bialetti macchinetta in the kitchen and topped off the filter with Lavazza. She set it on the stovetop, yawning as she waited for it to percolate.

David appeared at the top of the staircase. He sauntered down the steps, running his fingers through his hair. "Ah, the unmistakable aroma. You make the best cappuccino in town!"

"Oh thanks, dear. You're sweet. Now where's my cooked breakfast?"

"I'm on it." David took the skillet from the cabinet under the kitchen counter and rounded up the ingredients for a Spanish omelette. "Have you seen Alex?" he asked.

"Not yet."

"Alex!" he called back upstairs. "Making breakfast. Want any?" Alex didn't answer.

"Must still be asleep," Mary said. "He's full of surprises lately."

"I'll get him." David trotted back up the stairs and gently knocked on Alex's door. "Hey sleepyhead, you up for breakfast? Alex, are you in there?" Getting no response, he eased the door open and looked inside. The room was empty. He went back downstairs. "He's not in his room," he announced. "Maybe the garage?"

"I'll text him," Mary said. It was then that David noticed the small piece of paper tucked under the apple bowl. He picked it up. "'Went to visit Sam,' it says."

"Just like that, going off to England without even telling us? That's not like him."

The conversation was interrupted when someone knocked at the front door and rang the bell at the same time. David went to answer it. "I'm sure he had his reasons," he said, moving down the hall.

David opened the door, then stepped back from the sudden glare of white lights and flashes as the dozens of reporters standing on the lawn hurled questions at him. He saw news trucks with satellite dishes on the cul-de-sac road just down the hill.

Mary walked over from the kitchen. "What's going on?" she asked, coming up behind David. After the initial shock wore off, the reporters' questions snapped into focus.

"Mr. Watson, why is Homeland Security after your son?" was the first question David really heard.

"What?"

"Is your son a terrorist?" another reporter asked.

"He most certainly is not!" said Mary, insulted by the question.

"Why is the U.S. government chasing him? Why is he on the run?"

"What are you talking about?" David asked.

"Is your son responsible for destroying two Air Force fighters?"

"What's his involvement with the police officer murders?"

"I have no idea what you're talking about," David said, and slammed the door. The bell seemed to ring again before it was closed. The house phone also started ringing. Mary rushed to answer it. "It could be Alex."

"It's those clowns outside," David said. Mary answered, then said, "Please leave us alone. We have no idea what's going on. Please leave us alone." She hung up.

"Best leave it off the hook. He has our cell numbers."

"We have to call him. And Sam."

"In a minute," David told her. He moved to the living room and switched on the TV. If Alex was suddenly in the news, perhaps he could learn something there. When the set came on, the first thing he saw was a split screen showing the inside of a cockpit on one side, Sam and some of her coworkers on the other. Text scrolled across the bottom of the screen: LIVE OTW STREAM – ALEX WATSON TRANSATLANTIC FLIGHT. "Found him," he called to Mary. "He's live on TV!" He flipped channels as Mary rushed over, and they watched a replay of the Air Force Raptors going down as the pilots ejected. He switched back to the live broadcast.

Mary dialed a few numbers on her cell. "His cell and satellite phones go to voicemail. Sam's too."

David turned up the volume on the TV as Alex spoke.

CHAPTER 22
TRANSATLANTIC PURSUIT

JACK AND PETE WATCHED THE BROADCAST FROM G-Tek's executive suite. "The fact that I brought this new energy source to G-Tek, and the next thing I know I'm targeted for assassination and the Air Force wants to shoot me out of the sky—that's not a coincidence, is all I'm saying. There's a photo on the wall at G-Tek's headquarters of their CEO shaking hands with the president. At the time, I thought that was a good thing."

Jack cursed at the screen. "Now the press will stick a microscope up our ass. We'll be pariahs in D.C."

"You know the government won't touch him now," Pete said.

Jack nodded reluctantly. "That doesn't mean we can't. If he's out of the picture and the rock's gone, it's nothing but rumor. Where did he say he was headed?"

"Exeter."

Jack dialed another throwaway cell. "New rendezvous in Exeter, UK. I'll have a plane waiting for John Smith at Charlotte." He hung up.

"John Smith?"

"What does it matter?"

"I checked the market futures," Pete told him. "Our stock is getting hammered. The whole industry could tank on this—and who do you think they'll blame?"

For a moment, Jack felt his mounting fear might get the best of him. But he clamped down on it, and the moment passed. "If we can get that rock in our hands, we're all good. There's still a chance to pull this out."

THE FLORENCA CAFÉ WAS UNUSUALLY BUSY AND seemed understaffed, with servers rushing to fill orders. Phantom sat at a corner table on the upscale restaurant's patio, overlooking downtown Asheville. There were stunning views of the city and its art-deco architecture, but his eyes surveyed closer things, like pedestrian traffic entrances.

Phantom had a secret fetish for the world's finer cuisines, an obsession he kept a closely guarded secret, as anyone who knew this would have an easier time finding him, if it came to that. And so he had his favorite places but always dined alone. Keeping an eye on the foot traffic, he sampled the smoked salmon Benedict. While still savoring the morsel on his tongue, he tore off a piece of the grilled focaccia and dipped it in lemon-caper hollandaise, which happened to be the dressing for the asparagus, so generously portioned that it occupied nearly half his plate. He took a sip of grapefruit juice to clear his palate.

The TV, mounted on an exterior wall, cycled a mix of local and national news. He saw helicopter footage from the night before, showing a shot-up Volkswagen and a burning police car at Asheville Airport. It was a bit more excitement than the locals were used to. And of course the Volkswagen belonged to the now-famous Asheville resident Alex Watson, so the café hummed with chatter as patrons followed both stories on the screen. For Phantom's part, he now understood—from his target Alex's broadcast—why he was being paid a premium. The target could bring one of the world's biggest industries to its knees.

His phone vibrated, interrupting his breakfast. He answered it. "New rendezvous in Exeter, UK. I'll have a plane waiting for John Smith at Charlotte," the client said, and hung up. Because of the news reports, Phantom now had an excellent idea who that client was, which was something that almost never happened, as anonymity was as important to the clients as it was to him. Interesting, he thought, glancing at the TV news report.

"Video of Alex Watson and the two malfunctioning U.S. fighter jets has gone viral," the reporter said. "The White House has no comment on the incident, which was streamed live earlier today."

Phantom slapped a fifty on the table to cover meal and tip for the pretty young brunette with pale skin. "No change," he said. The tip was gracious, but not large enough to draw undue attention.

"Thank you, sir. How was your breakfast?"

"Excellent."

Finishing his juice, he walked a few blocks and called a cab. It arrived in minutes. "Charlotte Airport," he told the driver.

As the cab pulled into traffic, Phantom made another call.

"*Guten Tag*," a female voice answered.

"I'll be arriving in the afternoon," Phantom said in German, "destination to follow. Please make all the usual arrangements."

"What time should I expect you?" asked the woman on the other end.

"Around four local time, via charter jet. I'll call with specifics when I'm in the air."

"*Auf Wiedersehen.*"

Phantom hung up, texted EXETER AIRPORT to the same number, and studied a map of the airport on his phone.

Two hours later, he crossed the tarmac to a shiny new Gulfstream IV. On the side of the white plane, stretching across the five large oval windows, slanting flame-red letters spelled out: HEMMINGTON INTERNATIONAL OIL. The noise of the twin jet engines drowned out the sounds around him. He climbed up the short flight of steps, and was greeted by a smiling attendant in an immaculate, neatly pressed navy-blue uniform with gold trim. Everything about her screamed perfection. "Welcome aboard, sir. May I take your jacket?"

Phantom shook his head.

"All right, well, please take a seat. We'll be leaving right away."

Phantom scanned the luxurious but empty cabin. There were ten camel-colored leather seats, and a deep sofa along the starboard wall. All looked more than comfortable. He sat on the couch, thinking to catch up on missed sleep and be fresh for the hunt. The flight attendant closed the door and prepared the cabin for departure. "How long is the flight?" he asked.

"Normally around six hours. We've been asked to expedite, so we'll be taking the best possible route to get you to your destination quickly. Say five to six hours."

Moments later, the pilot opened up the twin Rolls-Royce engines, and the plane leapt from the runway.

Given what he'd learned over the past few hours, Phantom knew now this would be the most important assignment of his career. He thought about how he might go about reaching the target at a busy airport like Exeter. Not the easiest feat under the best of circumstances, which these were not. England was littered with surveillance cameras, and now he'd have to consider the media in the bargain.

As well, the target had OTW helping him. Which meant he might have a security detail; another obstacle. Gretchen was an asset in his column, though. After she'd made arrangements for his arrival, he'd instruct her to do some tracking. In a pinch, she could even engage, though he preferred to complete his assignments himself. All in all, he felt the mission was complex, but still viable. On the other hand, the target had just taken down two U.S. fighters without firing a shot, and that warranted some serious thought.

He leaned his head back and wished he were going to London, one of his favorite cities. He'd never been to Exeter, which meant dealing with unfamiliar roads and traffic patterns. London would have been better. Perhaps the target would head there, if he left the airport alive. And perhaps Phantom would, if he didn't.

He reminisced about meeting Gretchen Dietrich for the first time many years ago, at the Croydon Place Hotel in London. It wasn't the kind of hotel he was accustomed to, but he liked the location, and they had German waitresses serving a British breakfast. The juxtaposition amused him greatly: German discipline and British organizational skills.

The hotel's restaurant service, though, had been questionable at best. Their signature style bordered on rude, but oddly enough, he considered that one of the peculiar charms of the place. He'd become fond of German culture, and liked the fact that communications were terse and direct. The hotel food was average and uninspired: bangers, baked beans, and scrambled eggs. English simplicity. The lobby smelled of cigarette smoke. In fact, now that he thought about it, he really didn't know why he liked the place, unless because it reminded him of Gretchen.

SIX HOURS LATER, AFTER CLEARING CUSTOMS, Phantom stepped to the Exeter Airport curb as a black BMW pulled into the charter-flight pickup area. Sliding into the passenger seat, he faced Gretchen. Her sharp German features and storm-gray eyes were framed by wavy blonde hair. The last time they'd met, she'd been a redhead. They exchanged smiles, and she pulled into the airport loop. Drizzle spattered the windshield. The road was wet but well built, drinking the rain like a parched sponge and channeling it away.

Phantom found himself watching Gretchen, his only trusted friend. More than a friend: a confidante. She looked good, but then she always did. He took note of her driving gloves, which matched the rest of her outfit.

"Schön, dich zu sehen," she greeted him in German whilst sporting her customary half smile.

"Und sie," he returned, speaking like a native German, a controlled glint in his eyes.

"Less than an hour before he lands," she said, anticipating his next question. "The BMW is yours; it's clean. Your bag's in the back. I couldn't risk entering the pickup area with an arsenal, so I've arranged a selection of weapons for you to look at. The seller is close."

Phantom nodded. "Good." He needed to be back before the target arrived. He handed her his passport for safekeeping; his UK papers would be in the bag she'd brought him.

Twenty minutes later, Gretchen turned into a deserted alleyway and stopped by a roll-up door. Stepping from the car, she pressed a button on an intercom beside the door and spoke the code. The old door clanked upward as she slid back behind the wheel, and a heavyset man beckoned them inside. Gretchen edged the car into a dim, warehouse-like interior. The door rolled shut behind them.

The man showed them to a hidden back room filled with weapons on display. Phantom looked them over. "Show me your best breakdown sniper rifles."

The man scuttled around the display, retrieving two modified Parker-Hales and placing them on the central table. Phantom inspected them, deciding on the M-85. "This looks good. I'll also take the SIG P226 over there, and those Minox binoculars."

"You 'ave sophisticated taste," the man said, fetching the SIG and its holster. Phantom checked clip and chamber, then donned the holstered weapon. Gretchen slapped a wad of British pounds in the seller's hand, and he carefully packed the rifle and binoculars in a case with several boxes of ammo, then put the case in the car's trunk.

Phantom and Gretchen climbed into the BMW and headed back to Exeter Airport.

CHAPTER 23
HEMMINGTON INTERNATIONAL OIL

WHEN A GREAT RUMBLING SPLIT THE SKY AROUND HIM, Alex expected more fighter jets. Looking around, he saw what looked like a Gulfstream III or IV passing almost directly above him. It banked as he watched, adjusting its course southward. With the sudden glint of sun off metal, he couldn't quite make out the red lettering on its side. Now that he thought about it, after the debacle with the Raptors, the next thing the U.S. sent after him—if it sent anything at all—would likely be a missile. He'd never hear it coming.

"We did some research on G-Tek," Samantha told him over the video link. "Well, one of us did. Sunil is our resident hacker."

"I prefer the term data-retrieval specialist," Sunil corrected. Someone had plugged in a wide-angle camera on the OTW side, so Alex could now see everyone seated at the table; they no longer needed to crowd Sam to be seen by the webcam.

"Anyway," Sunil continued, "turns out they're a front company for the usual suspects: coal, oil, and gas. The guys you met? Also work for Hemmington Oil."

"Why am I not surprised," said Hana.

"You're kidding me!" Alex said.

"I triple-sourced it."

"I'm confused. Why would Big Energy set up an alternative energy company to compete with themselves?"

"To gobble up any government money for alternatives," Nigel told him. "And so people like you will go to them first."

"And they can buy you out—" Sunil began.

"Or bury me," Alex finished. "What an idiot. How could I not have seen that?"

"Don't beat yourself up," Hana told him. "You tried to do the right thing."

"Why is that so hard?" Alex lamented.

"Because of people like them," Nigel said. "Anything we can do to help get this out there, it's done. The sooner these people are fossils themselves, the better."

"I'll leak the Big Energy connection to the media," Sam said.

"I think you just did," Sunil reminded her. "We're still streaming."

Alex grinned. "I look forward to meeting everyone. But, to put it mildly, it's been kind of a rough day, so I'm going to try to get some sleep before Exeter." He yawned.

"That thing has autopilot?" Sunil asked.

"Primitive, but functional. I'll leave the satphone on." He duct-taped the phone to the instrument panel, making sure the camera had a view of him as well as a big portion of the sky outside. "Catch you at the airport. Wake me up if you see any more fighters."

"Mom called and left a voicemail," Samatha told him.

Alex leaned into the satphone camera. "Hi Mom, hi Dad! I'm right here. I'm okay."

"Go get your Zs," Sam said. "We'll keep lookout and meet you at the airport."

Alex pulled an iPad from his flight bag. Checking his GPS position, he engaged the autopilot and set the iPad's alarm. Then he pulled a baseball cap over his face and closed his eyes.

CHAPTER 24
TURBULENCE

SAMANTHA, NIGEL, AND THE OTHERS MADE THEIR WAY through a growing crowd at Exeter Airport. Sunil eyed the arrivals board as half the times switched to DELAYED. Approaching the doors to the light-aircraft arrivals area, they found a constable posted at every door. One of the officers moved to stop them.

"We're here to meet Alex Watson," Samantha said.

"Who isn't?" the constable said, blocking the doorway. "Sorry, press only."

Nigel flashed his OTW ID. The others did the same. The officer looked at them. "That's not press. Ohhh, I saw you lot on the telly. Keep up the good work then." He moved aside to let them pass, stopping others who tried to follow. "Sorry, press only."

Sam and her friends joined the press in a roped-off area overlooking the tarmac. The space was packed with local journalists, news crews, police vehicles, several fire engines, and an ambulance, all awaiting the accidental celebrity. The police had formed a barricade to prevent eager reporters from flooding the apron.

Sunil checked his iPhone, "Umm, guys? We have a bit of a problem."

ALEX SLEPT FITFULLY, ROCKED BY TURBULENCE. EACH time the Hawker jostled, he snored loudly.

"Alex, can you hear me?" It was Sam's voice, coming from the satphone. "You really need to wake up."

The plane jolted as if struck by something heavy, throwing Alex against the canopy. He woke with a start, rubbed his head, and looked ahead. He suddenly felt very small, like a man in a tunnel facing an oncoming train. The Sea Fury approached an endless wall of darkness that spanned the sky for miles in all directions. Alex sat paralyzed by the sight.

"Alex, dammit!" Samantha yelled through the radio.

"Yeah!" Alex came to life.

"You're headed right into a hurricane."

"Got that. Thanks. No rest for the weary." He untapped the satphone from the instrument panel and aimed it straight ahead, recording the looming storm.

"It's a big one. You'll have to go around or . . . turn back. Something."

Alex thought for a moment. "If I do that, I stay in international airspace. I'm not giving the U.S. another shot at me."

"That's crazy," Samantha told him.

"P-3s fly through hurricanes all the time," Alex said, attempting to calm her.

"Sunil says they have four engines."

"I'll be in and out of this thing before it knows what hit it."

Samantha said something back, but the satphone hissed static and her words were lost.

Using his satphone as a Wi-Fi hotspot, Alex pulled up the weather app on his iPad to track the storm. It was a massive Category 2, moving northwest at about thirty miles an hour. He was headed right through it. He wished he'd paid more attention to the weather conditions, but with all that had been going on, it'd slipped his mind.

The storm was hundreds of miles in diameter, with cumulonimbus cloud towers well over forty thousand feet—nearly a mile higher than the Sea Fury's maximum operating ceiling. In short, it was too big to fly around and too high to fly over. He could change course and fly southeast as the storm rolled the other way, but hurricanes were unpredictable, and had been known to change course—and the detour would add hours to his flight time. The longer he was in the air, the more vulnerable he was.

He decided his first inclination was right: he had to fly through it. He hurriedly prepped the cockpit, securing anything that might be jostled loose. He checked the seat belt and shoulder harness, and tried to brace himself for what was to come.

Just ahead, lightning flared like the wrath of God. Alex took the stick and plunged in. Bright flashes and earsplitting thunder assailed his senses as the storm swallowed the plane whole. The Sea Fury wobbled as the hurricane's rotating winds grabbed hold of it, pulling the old warbird into a new kind of battle. The airplane creaked and rattled in protest.

Alex wondered if the satphone feed was still working. It would be nice to know he wasn't facing this alone. "Anyone still with me?" he shouted over the sound of the wind and the prop. The plane caught a rogue downward airstream and was sucked into a nosedive. Alex responded with a reflexive pull on the yoke, and threw the throttle to maximum power to regain lost altitude. The maneuver increased airspeed but intensified the turbulence, throwing the plane into a spin.

"Alex? Alex!" Samantha's voice came through a faded connection. She sounded a thousand miles away.

He adjusted the rudder pedals and control column, attempting to balance the plane. Time slowed to a crawl as he struggled to pull out of the spin. Just when he thought it was hopeless, he regained control. But again, fierce winds knocked him off course. Could it get any worse?

The moment that thought entered his mind, it did. Golf-ball-sized hail pelted the canopy and dimpled the plane's metal body like a rain of rocks. Alex could feel the aircraft sliding a hundred yards sideways for every one it moved forward, like a lone swimmer in a raging river. He corrected course as best he could, fighting the stick. "Come on, baby. You can do this."

The plane powered forward, then dropped straight down. It bottomed out in an air pocket, slamming him into the seat. "We come out of this," Alex told it, "I'm going to call you Stormrider."

The plane jerked sideways and bucked like a wild bronco, enduring a beating that would have shattered a lesser craft. And when it seemed certain the storm would rattle it to pieces, an eerie, dead calm descended and a golden light suffused the plane. Alex gazed up into the glow of a cloudless sky.

A moment later, he snagged the satphone. "Hey, I think I'm out of it. Can you hear me?"

"Really?" Samantha said.

It was then that he noticed something odd about the clear blue sky: it was circular. Gazing at it was like looking up through a vast, cloud-walled tunnel. Alex lowered his gaze and looked ahead. "I take it back," he said. "I think there's more."

The plane crossed a vast cylinder of clear air—the eye of the hurricane—like a gnat in the Coliseum.

"What?" Sam asked, her voice growing faint again.

"I'm afraid the reports of my survival have been greatly exaggerated," Alex said into the satphone, wondering whether she could still hear him.

The hurricane wall in front of him churned counterclockwise. Awesome, beautiful, and inexorable. "In for a penny, in for a pound," he said to himself, and throttled up. The plane plummeted into the eye wall. Something smacked into the canopy and whipped away: a leafy tree branch.

"Land. This is good."

The plane was buffeted by microbursts—wild, localized air currents—and assaulted by more hail, even bigger this time. Hailstones battered the plane, cracking the canopy and tearing one of the flaps half off with a shriek of tortured metal. Alex struggled to see through the barrage. "Hail, not so good," he said.

He heard another shriek and looked back; the rudder was partially torn as well, the metal quivering in the wind. He picked up the satphone. "Ah, sis? I'm losing plane parts here."

"What? I can hardly hear you," Samantha said.

"The plane is coming apart! Did you hear that?"

"Alex?"

He looked around. Hail still pounded the canopy, opening holes now. Much more of this and the baseball-size stones would be bashing him to a bloody pulp. "I don't think I'm gonna make this," he said.

"*What?* Alex!"

He fought the controls. If he was going to live through this, he had to get out, right now. Catching glimpses of dingy sky, he aimed for it. The plane went into a dive, which only made the hail hit harder, causing the wounded flap to detach further. A giant hailstone smashed through the cracked canopy, bounced off the satphone—smashing it—and struck him a glancing blow on the head. He tried to hold on to consciousness, but lost the struggle and blacked out.

He woke to a deafening thunderclap as lightning arced past the plane, sizzling with power and lighting up the sky. He broke through the hurricane's outer wall in a steep dive and saw something dead ahead, tall and solid: a concrete lighthouse, racing toward him.

He grabbed the stick and tried to level out, realizing there was no way he could pull up in time. He turned the plane on its side, wingtip sparking off the concrete tower as a big wave slammed the lighthouse from the other side, higher than the plane. He leveled out in a wave trough, inches over the water, then pulled up hard, hoping the plane didn't come apart around him.

The sea reached up and tried to grab him, but by then he was high enough to avoid the bulk of it. The wave tip gave him a good swat, tearing the rest the flap off and adding salt water to the fresh that already soaked him to the bone. Only the crystal shield he'd built to protect the electric engine from the effects of Energy X kept the engine from getting wet and shorting out.

A darker darkness was visible in the gloom ahead: land. Alex made for it. If the lighthouse had been Wolf Rock Lighthouse, there should be a tiny private airport—called Land's End—just ahead. A moment later, it came into view on the left. The missing flap made it impossible to turn that way, so he circled the plane to the right and made his approach. The impact of the wheels touching down jarred the damaged rudder loose; it scraped down the runway after him.

Finally, the old Sea Fury rolled to a stop under gloomy skies. Alex leaned back in the seat and remembered to breathe, feeling the rain through the shattered canopy. He taxied off the runway, climbed down, and kissed the earth. Collecting the rudder, he put it beside the plane. Then he opened up the cowling and removed the EX battery, placing it in his flight bag. It was only a matter of time before someone spotted the old warbird, and he couldn't risk them finding Energy X in the bargain. He also took the EX power source from the wrecked satphone—where he'd installed it because the old plane had no charger.

He looked around the airport, which comprised a small parking lot, a few unassuming buildings, and a couple of hangars arranged around a stunted runway. For the moment, the place was deserted.

With the satphone smashed, he needed a payphone. He found one by the office, but it rejected his American quarters. Someone had left a bicycle near the office door. Looking around, feeling like a thief, he took it—but not before leaving a hundred dollars in its place, held down by a small rock.

Flight bag perched across the handlebars, he rode off through the rain.

CHAPTER 25
GROUNDED

INSIDE EXETER AIRPORT, A JANITOR LEFT A SERVICE hall and entered the observation area, locking a service door behind him. Distracted by the line of constables guarding the exit doors, he fumbled with his keys. Turning, he bumped into someone. "Excuse me, sir," he apologized.

"That's quite all right, mate," Phantom replied in a feigned Cockney accent. He palmed the janitor's keys, eyeing an airport security officer beckoning to a man with a briefcase.

"Sorry, sir," the cop was saying. "Random security screening." The man he'd stopped made no attempt to conceal his annoyance.

Phantom continued on his way as the officer patted down the civilian. He watched the janitor roll the cleaning trolley to a nearby men's restroom. Scoping the area, Phantom swiftly unlocked the service door and stepped through. Once in the hall, he found the door he wanted and joined the press outside. He squeezed through the mob of reporters until he spotted the target's sister, Samantha Watson. He watched as she answered her cell, said a few words and hung up. Then she and the other OTW people went back inside. He recognized their faces from the viral broadcast.

He made a quick call to Gretchen. "I need a trace on a call just ended, to Samantha Watson's cell at Exeter Airport. I want to know where the caller is. Track the phone from this point on. And I'll need a motorcycle."

He hung up and trailed Samantha's group inside. As he followed them into the building, he heard an airport security guard call out to him.

"Sorry, sir . . . . Random screening," the constable said politely.

Phantom pretended not to hear and angled past a shadowed pillar. He was armed, and there'd be no hiding that from a pat-down.

"Sir!" the officer called out.

Phantom slowed and turned, cupping a hand behind one ear. "Sorry, hearing's not so good," he said. Watching Samantha's group leave, he let the constable come to him.

"I need to do a quick search. Ask you a few questions."

Phantom scoped the area. "Of course," he said, doing his best impression of a cooperative citizen.

JACK AND PETE SAT IN G-TEK'S EXECUTIVE SUITE, watching newscasters fret over the unknown fate of Alex Watson, whose communications had stopped almost an hour ago. "With any luck," Jack said, "the hurricane will kill him."

"What if it doesn't?" Worry lines appeared on Pete's forehead.

"That's what the Phantom is for."

"And if he fails?"

"He never fails. That's why I hired him."

"Who names their kid Phantom, anyway?" Pete said, trying to lighten the grim mood.

Jack regarded him sternly. "The last thing he said was the plane was coming apart. Sounds like good news to me." He poured two drinks, and handed one to Pete. "It's like the president says. God is on our side." They clinked glasses and began to drink.

And then the CNN anchor interrupted the on-screen discussion. "We've just been informed that Alex Watson's badly damaged plane has been found at Land's End airport, on Britain's west coast. And while there's no sign yet of Alex Watson, it's clear he made it through the hurricane and was able to land safely. We'll continue to keep you updated on this developing story, and should have footage of the plane at Land's End shortly. Meanwhile, an airport constable has been found dead of knife wounds at Exeter Airport, where Alex Watson was scheduled to land before encountering the storm."

Jack set down his drink and killed the TV.

"I hope this Phantom guy is as good as you say he is," Pete said, downing the rest of his own drink.

"He's better."

FORTY MINUTES AFTER ALEX ENTERED THE STORM, HIS transmissions stopped. "I lost Alex," Sam told the others. She could hear her own voice trembling. "I think he might have crashed. We have to call the Coast Guard."

"Royal Navy," Nigel corrected. A couple of overzealous

reporters shoved their way from the back to reach the rope line, accidentally shoving Nigel aside. He grabbed onto Sam to keep from falling. "Sorry," he told her.

"I'm calling the navy," Sam said.

"They're not gonna mount a search in a hurricane," Sunil told her.

He was right. Sam let the phone drop to her side, then brought it up and called anyway; she had nothing to lose. But the rescue center confirmed Sunil's prediction, saying they could begin an air search only after the storm had passed. They asked her to call back then if the plane was still missing.

Sam hung up, despondent. She spent the next twenty minutes worrying, wondering—like everyone else who'd been listening to Alex via the OTW live feed—whether Alex would make it to Exeter. And then the cell phone rang in her hand.

"Hello?" Her brother's voice was the most welcome sound in the world. "Alex, thank God!"

"Is he okay?" Nigel asked.

Sam nodded. "Nigel and others are here with me," she told Alex. "Where are you?" She repeated his answer to Nigel. "Joppa Farm," she said.

Nigel punched that into a mapping app on his phone. "The cottage is closer. I'll send Hana. Should take her about thirty minutes to get there. We can all meet up at the cottage." He dialed Hana's number and turned away.

ALEX SLOWED HIS BIKE ON THE COUNTRY ROAD'S shoulder beside an old barn. He watched as a man walked his dog in the rain. Both wore raincoats. Mad dogs and Englishmen, wasn't that the saying? Alex dismounted and approached the pair. "Hi," Alex called out in greeting.

The man slowed, looking suspicious. He seemed to say "Hello" only out of deference to the British compulsion to be polite. He spoke with a distinctive Cornish dialect. His biscuit-colored English bulldog let loose a bark. Raindrops coursed through the animal's wrinkled face and over his Union Jack raincoat. "It's okay, Alfred," the man told him.

"My name's Alex Watson. I just crash-landed at that airport back there. Land's End, I think?"

"You mean St. Just?"

"I guess." Alex pointed back the way he'd come. "That one over there."

"St. Just," the man grumped.

"Anyway, I'm really glad to see you."

The man pulled his dog closer, as if to stand against an uninvited guest.

"My phone's dead, and I was hoping I could borrow yours to call a friend to come pick me up."

Reluctantly, the man pulled a cell from his coat pocket and held it out, palm-down. "See that it doesn't get wet," he instructed.

Alex pulled his jacket up over his head to form a makeshift umbrella, then dialed Sam's number and filled her in on the landing, the bicycle, and the borrowed phone. He had to ask Bulldog Man where he was.

"England," the man said, afterward mumbling, "Bloody Yanks."

Alex found a GPS app on the phone. "I'm at Joppa Farm," he told Sam.

"Wait, Nigel is looking up the map on his phone."

"Can you call Mom and Dad, tell them I'm okay?"

"Yeah. We're sending someone to pick you up. Hang tight."

Alex thanked her, told her how great it would be to see her again, and hung up. He passed the phone back to Bulldog Man. "Thank you very much. You just saved my life."

The man nodded, wiped off the phone, and dropped it back in his pocket. He grunted once, and continued on his way with Alfred.

Alex walked the bicycle to an empty roadside farmer's stand, which—now that he was thoroughly soaked—offered shelter from the rain. His wet clothes clung tight against cold skin. Hungry, worn-out, and chilled, he found himself fantasizing about a hot bath and a warm meal. After what seemed an eternity but was probably no more than half an hour, a distant rumbling grew nearer. At first he thought it was thunder, but the sound was too steady.

He watched the road as a small black dot came closer, becoming a black motorcycle with chrome mudguards and trim. It glided up beside him, something from another era. The letters on the gas tank spelled out VINCENT.

The black leather-clad rider scanned the area, helmet moving side-to-side. The rider's features were hidden behind a mirrored faceplate. Alex had assumed this was his pickup, but he felt a jolt of adrenaline when the rider's gaze fixed on him, and one hand reached inside the leather jacket. He would have run, had there been a place to run to.

And then the hand reappeared—holding a photo of Alex and Sam. The rider tipped up the faceplate—revealing a gorgeous young woman with features that were half Asian, half European. Alex remembered her from the OTW videoconference. "Hey," she said. "I'm Hana. Nigel sent me."

Alex grinned, despite being soaked to the bone. "Alex. Nice to meet you in person." He offered his hand, and they shook, leather glove on wet palm.

Hana handed him a spare helmet and nodded at the seat behind her. "It's not a Sea Fury, but it's almost as fast."

"This I have to see. Is this a real Vincent?"

"Of course. Black Shadow."

"Aren't they super expensive?"

"They are. This one belonged to my grandfather. He bought it before the price went insane, then gave it to me. I restored it."

Slinging the flight bag over his shoulder, Alex hopped on, and the bike roared off. The din from the engine would have been deafening, if not for the helmet. Hana was right about the speed; it ate up the road.

They sped through the lush Cornish countryside, rain beating on their helmets. They traveled through the small town of St. Just, then came out the other end on a country road that went on to parallel the shoreline.

A short distance before reaching the town of St. Ives—he could see the signs announcing its presence—Hana turned up a narrow, heavily wooded road. A few minutes later, the bike rumbled onto a small country estate. Hana held up one hand with three fingers extended as they pulled up in front of a Cotswold-style, thatched-roof cottage surrounded by flower gardens.

CHAPTER 26
THE COTTAGE

HANA LED ALEX INSIDE. THE MAIN ROOM HAD BEEN made over into a planning and communications center with whiteboards, maps, and computers. "So you're the boy genius," Hana said.

"That's what they tell me. Is there a phone around here?"

"Why?" Hana checked the security camera feeds and headed for the kitchen.

"I'd like to call my parents, let them know I'm okay."

"Bad idea."

"Excuse me?"

"Don't get out much, do you? Someone's trying to kill you, right? Whose phones do you think they'll be tapping? Your parents', your sister's, your friends.'"

"What about you?"

"They don't know we're friends."

"Are we?" The words spilled out of Alex's mouth before he could stop himself.

Hana stared at Alex. "Yeah. I don't pick up just anybody, you know."

"There was a man near the airport. I borrowed his phone and called Sam's cell."

"It's cool. Sunil gave us hackphones. The number you called only forwards to her phone, doesn't connect directly. All our phones change ID every twenty minutes. Or something like that. The phone you used might be traceable, but doesn't lead anywhere." She opened the fridge, cracked a Coke. "Want one?"

"Thanks. This whole someone-trying-to-kill-me thing is kinda new to me."

She tossed him the soda. He popped it open and sipped on it.

"We need you streetwise. I can give you a few pointers." She took a seat at the kitchen table. Alex joined her, taking in the furnishings. The table and benches seemed odd to him, like something from a public park.

"Country style," Hana said, picking up on his curiosity.

"So you're head of security," Alex said, changing the subject. "What do you do? I mean, if you don't mind my asking."

"I'm responsible for physical security at OTW offices and events. Though of course I can't really control the events with all those constables in the way."

"Why you?"

My father headed a minister's security detail, so I know the ropes. Also, I'm a second-degree black belt in Tae Kwon Do . . . and Nigel felt I had the right frame of mind for this."

"So you're going to keep me safe until Sam and the others show up?" Alex's sleep-deprived brain seemed to have hijacked his mouth.

"Me and the four ex-SAS guys outside."

"I didn't see anyone—" said Alex, realizing immediately how dumb that sounded.

"They wouldn't be much good if you had."

Alex mimicked her earlier gesture: one hand up, three fingers out. "What happens if someone drives in and doesn't flash the signal?"

"Bad things." Hana looked down at his feet. Alex followed her gaze, and saw a big puddle on the floor. Unlike Hana's leathers, his soaked clothes were flooding the kitchen.

"You'd better hit the bathroom," she told him. "Let me show you to your room. You have clothes?"

Alex indicated his flight bag. Hana led him through a hallway and up a flight of stairs.

"And by the way, that bike?" he said. "Isn't half as fast as my plane. Which, also by the way, someone needs to pick up or park or feed the meter."

"I'll look into it," she told him. They passed through a long hall, halting before the door at the end.

"How big is this place?" Alex asked.

"Big enough for us. They don't make them like this one any-more. It's old. I mean the structure is. But we cheated by putting up a few downstairs walls to add bedrooms and bathrooms. This is Sam's room." She opened the door.

The room had two matching windows, and French doors leading to a narrow balcony. The drapes were open, letting in plenty of light. There were two single beds on opposite walls, with identical nightstands, and a door in one corner opened into an attached bathroom. Samantha's belongings were neatly arranged on one of the beds. Her suitcase jutted out from underneath.

Alex set the flight bag down in the bathroom.

"So what else is in the bag?" Hana asked.

"You're not going to go all DHS on me, are you?"

She cut him a look.

"Exactly what you think is in the bag," he answered. She was obviously curious, so he opened the bag and removed the crystal box housing the main chunk of Energy X.

After a moment of stunned silence, Hana said, "It's beautiful. May I?"

He put the case gently in her hands, then grabbed a towel and made an attempt to dry his hair.

"It's a really bad idea to open that," he warned, as Hana's fingers wandered toward the crystal box's lid.

"Why, what happens?"

"Remember the Raptors? Bad things . . ."

AFTER SAM AND THE OTHERS RETURNED AND INTRO-
ductions had been made, everyone sat down at the oversized dining room table to eat. Three clean-cut men in military camouflage pants strode in with empty plates in their hands, muscles bulging through too-tight green shirts.

"Oh, hey. Let me introduce you," Nigel said.

"Alex, these are Simon, Oliver, and Duncan, our security detail. They walk on water."

"Only because it rains here all the time," Simon said.

Alex laughed and shook hands with each. "I thought Hana said there were four of you."

"Alastair's still on watch," Duncan told him. "We're just here to plate up and head out. Alastair will be along when we're back on post. We run two-man shifts that overlap at breakfast and dinner."

"You must be starving," Nigel said to Alex. "Dig in."

Alex eyed the shepherd's pie across the table. "How did this meal happen? I mean, who's the cook here?"

"Maggie," Sam answered. "She's the next best thing to a mom." She turned and called into the kitchen. "Come and join us, Maggie!"

"Be right there. Almost done slicing up the apple pie." Moments later, a woman with rosy cheeks and a happy smile emerged from the kitchen and sat with them.

"Thanks, Maggie," Alex told her. "This is some spread."

"You're most welcome, love." Even her voice was sweet and motherly. "I just stay for a slice of pie and a bit of company."

Sam slid the large casserole dish in front of Alex. "Guest of honor dishes first."

He dumped a heaping spoonful on his plate.

"We seem to be out of candles," Hana announced, turning the lights down and looking at Alex. "Perhaps we can find some other light source?"

Taking the hint, Alex retrieved the crystal box he'd shown her earlier and placed it on the table. After much ooh-ing and aah-ing and a barrage of questions, things settled down. Alastair appeared and departed, and then Nigel summarized the political situation as he saw it. "Big Energy is the number-one presidential campaign contributor," he said. "And what you have could wipe them out overnight. Bottom line, you're not going to get anywhere in the States as long as the current administration is in power. Or any administration like it . . . in my opinion."

"Sooo, what then?" Alex asked.

"Do it here," Hana said.

"Do it now," Sunil added, eagerness in his voice. Alex watched him slide some chili peppers from a saucer onto his plate. He thought it an odd accompaniment for a British meal, then noticed that Sunil had the only ones. Sunil caught his look. "It's the South Indian in me. I can't eat a meal unless it's super spicy. Care to try it?"

"Thanks, I'll pass," Alex told him.

"Actually, you'd most likely pass out," Sunil told him, switching from his English accent to a heavy Indian accent.

"It's true," Nigel confirmed. "He dared me once and, being the fool I am, I took him up on it. Seconds later my head was spinning, my tongue was on fire, and beads of sweat were dripping down my forehead. Hana called for an ambulance, but I was okay after drinking a pint of cream and sucking on a bucket full of ice cubes. The worst part was I couldn't taste normally for days."

Sunil snickered. Others shared a smile. Maggie finished her pie slice and excused herself from the table.

"Sunil, you were saying do it now?"

"Yeah. Forget about licensing it. Just set it up and make it work first, then the world will come to you."

"And don't let anyone know where or when," Sam added.

"A demo," Alex mused.

"Proof of concept," Nigel added.

"Once it's up and running somewhere, the genie's out of the bottle." Sunil mimicked flight, waving a hand in the air.

"Sounds good to me," said Patrick, who hardly said anything.

"If you have some test-city criteria, we're happy to do the research," Nigel told him. "Narrow down the choices."

Alex thought it over. "I want to start small. Power up a town somewhere."

"Why small?" Sunil asked.

"Easier, faster, less red tape."

"And the whole world won't know you're doing it until it's done," Sam said.

"Right," Alex agreed. "So no one can stop it. After that, we do something bigger."

"Have you thought about income?" Nigel asked. "What you're going to charge for this?"

"I have, actually. At first I thought I wouldn't charge anything."

"Whoa. You think energy companies are trying to kill you now . . ." Sunil said.

Samantha glared at him. "Is that supposed to be funny?"

"Just saying . . ."

Alex steered the conversation back on track. "Look. What's the number-one problem of every worthy cause on the planet?"

"Fundraising!" Patrick said immediately.

"Right," Alex confirmed. "What we have here is a wonderful thing, but it only solves one problem: energy."

"Big problem," Sunil put in.

"True. But we could charge a fraction of what the power companies are gouging the world for now and still make hundreds of billions of dollars," Alex explained.

"People would be happy to pay it," Patrick said.

"Okay, so," Alex said. "Using that money, we can fund a hundred other causes. A thousand. More even, at a level that's never been possible, and that the opposition can't match. This isn't just about changing the world. . . . . It's about changing everything."

There were nods of agreement around the table. Hana seemed more deeply affected than the others for some reason.

"Conscious capitalism. Best idea I've heard in a lifetime," Nigel said.

"We can even buy our own politicians," Sunil suggested. Samantha frowned at him.

Alex stood up and held out a hand—something he and Sam used to do as children, pretending they were musketeers. She stood and did the same, reaching halfway across the table to place her hand atop his. One by one, the others followed suit. The eerie blue glow of EX lit their faces from below, lending the impromptu ceremony an otherworldly aspect.

"Is someone supposed to say something dramatic here?" Sunil asked.

"'All for one and one for all,' if I remember it right," Alex said.

"Energy for all," Sam added.

"So," Alex said, taking back his hand. "Let's practice what we preach, get you off the power grid, and tell the utility company to take a hike."

"Here, here," agreed Nigel.

HOURS LATER, JUST AFTER DARK, ALEX AND SUNIL stood by the breaker box in the old garage beside the cottage. Alex fitted a new crystal box with an Energy X fragment into a recently added alarmed and triple-locked reinforced steel box beside the cottage's breaker panel, where he and Sunil had also added a bypass switch to disconnect the building from the utility company's power supply. When the switch was thrown, the cottage and its garage would become the first buildings in the world to be powered by EX.

Sunil regarded the tiny bit of Energy X inside its crystal cage. "That's all you need?" he asked.

"No," Alex told him. "That's way more than I need. But smaller pieces don't work at all. Like there's some kind of critical mass for power output."

"Weird."

"Yeah." Alex finished up. "Sometimes I think I should have called it Element Weird. And . . . we're done."

"Cool. Plug and play," said Sunil.

Alex turned from the box. "Okay. My presence has been requested out back for the Big Moment, so would you mind doing the honors and flipping the switch? I'll give you a shout when I'm there."

Sunil's face lit up. "Delighted. My own little part in history."

Alex made his way around the garage to the rear of the cottage, where the others had gathered on the stone porch, discussing the coming moment and all they hoped would follow. "Everyone ready?" he asked. Seeing that they were, he turned and shouted toward the cottage. "Kill it!"

Sunil threw the bypass switch, disconnecting the power company feed.

The cottage and the white tube lighting wrapped around its distant wood-rail fence went dark. Alex turned to the others and lifted a glass. "To first light . . . dawn of a new world." Everyone raised a glass and drank. Alex called again to Sunil. "Hit it!"

Sunil hit the switch connecting Energy X to the cottage. The house lit up like a Christmas tree, and the tube lights came back to life. Sam, Hana, Nigel, and Patrick applauded. Sunil rounded the garage clapping his hands.

"Congratulations," Hana said to Alex. Sunil showed him a selfie he'd taken with his cell phone, of the moment he'd thrown the switch.

"Keep that offline until we're ready," Alex cautioned.

Sunil nodded. "I'm going to put it in my autobiography."

They all sat in silence for a while, taking in the significance of a moment the world had yet to learn of. After a time, Nigel said, "You're about to be a very busy man, Alex. I think we're all about to be very busy."

Alex nodded, stifling a yawn. "Can I get some sleep first?" he asked, the last day and a half suddenly catching up with him.

"Right, sorry," Nigel said. "We're forgetting all you've been through."

Alex forced himself to stay awake for another round of congrats, said his good-nights, and turned to go, stumbling over a chair. Hana jumped up and hurried over. "It's been quite a day," she said. "Come on, I'll walk you up."

Sunil looked to Patrick. "I didn't get the personal concierge when I joined up."

"Were you driving a cool airplane?" Patrick asked.

"Mini."

Alex let Hana guide him inside and up the stairs. Now that the adrenaline of the day had worn off, he could feel his strength deserting him, and he moved like he was drunk. Hana flipped the light switch as they entered the room he shared with Sam.

"Cool," Hana said. "Free electricity on tap, courtesy of Watson Inc."

"We gotta find a better name," Alex thought aloud. "Something catchy."

Hana crossed to the small balcony and opened the French doors. "If you leave it open a few minutes, you'll smell moonflower all night. They bloom quickly on hot nights, sometimes so fast you can watch them open."

He joined her on the balcony.

"You know," she said, "we talk about changing the world all the time. No one seems to pay much attention. But this is different. Now the whole world wants to talk to you."

"What if I don't want to talk to them?" The words were out before he had time to think. He'd never been a particularly outgoing person, and his broadcast from the plane—though seen by millions—had seemed more like a conversation with friends at the time. He looked down over the waist-high railing. The patio lamp illuminated the heart-shaped leaves of the moonflower climbing the side of the cottage. Pollinating moths fluttered their delicate wings, hovering over the white blossoms. He could smell the flowers' heavy fragrance drifting into the room.

"This thing," he said. "This . . . Energy X is the star. I don't want to make it about me."

"You might not have a choice."

"I'm terrified of public speaking. Seriously. And that was before people started shooting at me."

"You're going to have to go all the way with this," she said, searching for conviction in his eyes.

"I know," he answered, his voice sounding distant, even to him.

They went back inside. Hana locked the balcony doors, drew the curtains, and checked the windows. "Teatime is 6 a.m.," she told him.

"We're playing golf?"

She mimicked sipping tea. "Teatime? You know, the British thing."

"Oh, oh. Right. Sorry. Earl Grey, like that." He would have blushed, but he was too tired.

"Like that. I'll see you in the morning."

"Morning. Right," he said, and navigated to the bed.

They exchanged good-nights and Hana left, closing the door behind her.

"*We're playing golf?*" Alex said. "What an idiot." He let himself collapse on the bed.

CHAPTER 27
SURPRISE!

HOURS LATER—HE WASN'T SURE HOW MANY—ALEX woke, feeling a cool breeze and smelling moonflower. Across the room, Sam's bed was empty. That was odd. Something else was odd, too, but he couldn't quite seem to focus on it. He closed his eyes again, enjoying the night breeze.

That was it. He'd watched Hana close and lock the French doors and check the windows. So where was the breeze coming from? He rolled over to check the doors—and found himself staring down the barrel of a suppressed pistol in a black-gloved hand. A dark figure pressed the cold metal against his skin.

Bang! Bang! Bang!

Alex snapped awake. There were no open doors, no shadowy gunman. Instead, there was sunlight peeking around the drapes, and a tap-tap-tap on the door. Sam's voice called through it from the hall. "Alex? Are you decent?" He checked the time on the alarm clock: 2:10 p.m. Had he really slept for fifteen hours?

"Alex?"

"Coming," he answered. He swung out of bed and answered the door. Samantha walked in. "Hey sleepyhead," she told him, adopting a proper British accent. "Top o' the mornin' to ya. How are you feeling, young chap?"

"Smashing, darling," Alex yawned back at her.

"I have a surprise for you."

"The good kind, I hope."

"Definitely."

Alex returned to the bed, sat down, and fell backward. "Or maybe I should sleep straight through to tomorrow. I'm half-way there already."

Hana tapped on the open door. Alex sat up as she entered with two cups of tea on a tray. "Teatime," she said. "Fortunately we Brits have several, so if you miss one, there's always another. We're a nation of tea junkies." She set the tray on the nightstand. "Made from the best leaves grown in the Sri Lankan hills of Nuwara Eliya."

"Thanks, Hana," Alex said, taking a cup. "You made this?"

"Woman of many talents," Sam told him.

Alex took a sip. It was fantastic. "Now that's a great cup of tea," he announced. "Excellent, in fact. My morning ritual is a strong cup of coffee, but if I'd known tea could taste like this . . ."

"Thank you. I botched a few tanker trucks full before I got it right."

Alex nearly sprayed a mouthful of tea when he laughed.

"The gang's downstairs for a late lunch," Hana told him. "Care to join us?"

"Will that be catered as well?" Sam asked with a grin.

"Not a chance," Hana replied.

"Give me ten minutes," Alex said.

"I'll tell the others. Enjoy." Hana departed, closing the door behind her.

"I think she likes you," Sam whispered when she left. "And she's very particular about who she likes."

"Really."

"She's only tough on the outside."

Alex nodded. "So what's this big surprise?" he said, changing the subject.

"Well if I told you it wouldn't be a surprise, now would it? Come down and see. You said give you ten minutes." She glanced pointedly at her watch. "You're down to nine."

Alex sprang up and made a show of rushing into the bathroom.

SIX MINUTES LATER, ALEX WENT DOWNSTAIRS. Rounding the corner, he nearly crashed into someone. "Whoa," said a familiar voice. It was James. For a moment, Alex was speechless. "Surprised?" James asked.

Alex found his voice. "Dude! You're here!"

"Not much gets by you," James told him.

Alex pulled him into a man-hug. "It's good to see you. When did you get in?"

"Sam picked me up at Exeter while you were comatose. At least, that's how she described it. Ah, speak of the devil."

Sam caught sight of them from another room and headed their way.

"Thanks for that call," Alex told James. "You saved my life."

"I'm just sorry I got you into this mess in the first place."

"Good intentions . . ." Alex said as Sam walked up.

"We all know where that road leads," she said. "Now, let's get you two a proper English lunch."

They made their way to the kitchen and joined the others. James had already been introduced to everyone, so talk quickly turned to the intrigues surrounding Alex's blue rock. "Did you get my voicemail?" James asked Alex.

"When did you call?"

"Same day I called and told you to run. Early morning."

Alex shook his head. "Must have been after my run-in with the hit man, or whatever. My cell's in a ditch off Brevard Road."

"So you don't know about my little run-in with the NSA."

"*NSA?*" Alex and Sam said at the same time.

"That's what they said, anyway. Smashed in my apartment door and took me to some secret interrogation place."

"No way," Sam said.

"They're not fooling around," Sunil said. "You're a wanted man."

"I still can't get over feeling that this is all my fault," James said. "I was just trying to make things better."

"Forget it," Alex told him.

"As far as making things better, though," Nigel added, "you came to the right place. We'll be happy to put you to work."

"Ready and able," James told him. "What's next?"

"Alex was talking about powering up a town," Hana said.

"And I still want to do that," Alex said. "But I've been thinking to do something else first. More personal. Something everyone can relate to—a car, maybe."

Hana slid an iPad mini from a pocket and ran a Google search.

"Something classic might be good," Nigel said.

"Something modern," Sunil countered.

"It should look like something special," Sam mused aloud.

"What she said," James added.

Hana stepped close to Alex and held up the iPad screen. It showed a sleek, futuristic car with seductive lines. Alex thought it looked like something a superhero would drive. "Perfect," he announced. "What is it?"

Hana passed the iPad around. "The Lightning."

"Ampere's new electric car," Sunil said. "Too cool."

"I read about that," Patrick told them, nodding. "Is it available yet?"

"It debuts at the London Auto Show," Hana said.

"Which is when, exactly?" Alex asked.

"Two days from now," Hana told him.

"We'll never make that," Patrick lamented.

"Actually, Nicholas Miles wrote us a sizable check last year," Nigel told them.

"Ampere's CEO?" Sunil asked. "Why don't I know that?"

"He wanted it discreet. We've never spoken, but I'll see if I can reach him." Nigel snagged his cell phone and headed outside to make the call.

"That'll make a splash," Sunil said. "The car's already got a huge marketing machine behind it. Nicholas's a billionaire."

"I should start researching towns," Patrick said. He finished his tea and followed Nigel outside.

"And I have to unpack," James said. "Which room is mine, again?"

"First door on the right," Sam told him.

"Ignore the boxes," Sunil added. "We were using it for storage."

The group broke up, getting ready to return to work. Sam looked to Alex and grinned. "When did you become Mr. All-the-Right-Moves?" she teased.

Alex shrugged helplessly. "Am I?"

"So far," Hana said, moving to the next room.

Alex wasn't sure whether that was a double entendre, but it sounded encouraging.

CHAPTER 28
SHOOTER

THE NORMALLY SEDATE, SMALL-TOWN LAND'S END Airport had become a media ground zero overnight. Even after dark, stragglers from the press remained, hoping to get a glimpse of Alex's suddenly famous plane, or even score an interview with Alex himself. Thus far, they'd had to content themselves with speaking to airport employees and an unsuspecting local man out for a stroll with his raincoat-clad dog.

A cleanup crew worked to clear debris and broken branches left by the passing storm, and construction workers had stapled plastic over a missing portion of the office roof, which now rested beside a tree a hundred yards off.

Following a phone call and a payment from OTW, the Sea Fury had been moved inside a hangar, which was now guarded by an off-duty constable who walked endless circles around the building, warning off the occasional reporter or local spectator. Most of them had already been told to bugger off, so there wasn't much else to do.

Had he chanced to look up on this particular circuit round the hangar, the constable might have observed Phantom clinging to a rainspout, looking back down at him with a gun in his hand. Instead, he swung the beam of his flashlight back and forth before him as he walked, seeing nothing but grass and tarmac.

Phantom tracked the cop until he rounded the next corner, then holstered his gun and continued his climb. Once on the roof, he made his way to the nearest skylight and looked inside. The plane sat as if waiting for him, illuminated by a dim light to one side. He padded softly around the skylight, viewing the interior from every angle. He saw no one inside.

He did see what appeared to be a ladder ascending one wall. Turning, he made his way to the spot on the roof where the ladder should emerge. He found a hatch, used a mini-torch to burn away the lock, and slipped inside.

Moments later, he reached the plane and opened the cowling. He found a brand-new electric engine—but where was the power source? He followed the wires to the place where the batteries should be, but there was nothing there. Certainly nothing like the photo he'd been sent of the blue-glowing rock. Other than the engine itself, the only unusual thing was a collection of overlapping clear panels lining the engine compartment. It felt like some kind of industrial sheet-crystal. Fishing a digital camera from a pocket, he began snapping pictures.

A FEW HOURS LATER, PHANTOM STEPPED INSIDE Gretchen's apartment and set down his motorcycle helmet. Gretchen sat in a dark corner with her reading glasses and half a dozen computer monitors. "The OTW people are not using traceable phones," she reported. She tapped a pen on the desktop as she spoke, a sign she was as frustrated as he was.

Phantom paced the room. "What about the live stream?"

"Another dead end: a repeater in an abandoned building."

"Where's their headquarters?"

"Mail is sent to a London post box, which is also their business address."

"Property records?"

"Checking that now . . ." she swiveled her chair, fingers returning to the keyboard. "It doesn't look promising."

Phantom stopped pacing. "Traffic cams," he announced.

"What?"

"Traffic cams and ALPRs—automated license-plate-recognition cameras. They're all over London and the major highways. They keep that data forever. Can you hack the system and run a search?"

"Probably," Gretchen boasted, propping up her reading glasses. They were too big on her; no sooner had she pushed them up than they began their slow and inevitable downward slide. She tapped away on multiple keyboards.

"Check cars registered to the OTW people. If that doesn't work, check the airport cams to see what they were driving. They left just after I called you."

Gretchen worked her computers. Coded searches ran on multiple screens. Photos of cars and license plates flashed by too rapidly to follow. "May have something here," she said.

Phantom watched as she brought up a map, the car's route highlighted in green.

"Facial recog match says Nigel Schaefer was in a black Astra that left the airport and traveled west on A30 to A3074. Then disappeared here." She tapped the screen with her pen.

"Can you enlarge that?"

She made the image bigger. "They left the dual carriageway here."

Phantom eyed the spot where the green line representing the car's route ended. "A few miles south of St. Ives. Search traffic cams, crime cams, anything you can." Scooping up his motorcycle helmet, he headed for the door. "Send me a map with gas stations, grocery, and liquor stores," he said as he left.

Four hours later, he called Gretchen from Cornwall. "Do you have anything for me yet?" he asked.

"Give me another ten minutes. I'll call you back."

Phantom hung up and waited, bike parked beside a country road. Ten minutes later, Gretchen called back. "I checked cell tower logs, looking for phones traveling the same route as the car at the same time. Only one went all the way. I can tell you where it stopped." She gave him the GPS coordinates.

"Stay close to the phone," he told her. "I'll call if I need anything else." He hung up. Consulting a GPS app, he spun the bike around and powered toward his destination as the first signs of dawn appeared around him.

He went off-road as he neared the location, guiding the quiet bike over wooded terrain. When he felt he was close enough—two hundred yards—he drifted to a stop and hid the bike in a stand of dense brush. He went ahead on foot to scope the area, carrying binoculars and a popular book on birdwatching. A short time later, he spotted the car, parked near an old stone cottage on the far side of a meadow.

Going back to the bike, he wheeled it closer, with the engine off. Holstering the SIG P226 pistol beneath his untucked shirt, he removed the hard-shell travel case from the back of the bike and assembled the rifle inside, adding suppressor and scope when he was done. He pulled on camouflage gear over his street clothing, painted his face, and made his way into position, across the meadow from the cottage, with an angle on the front door.

Rifle on its bipod before him, he watched the house through binoculars. One of the OTW people was on the porch, talking on his cell phone. Phantom saw him hang up and go back inside. Several others were visible inside the house, including the target's sister—which he thought boded well.

NIGEL SMILED AS HE WALKED IN FROM THE PORCH.

"Uh-oh," Sam said. "Nigel's smiling. That means we're going to be busy."

"Good news with the Lightning guys?" Alex asked.

"I spoke with their VP of marketing," Nigel told them. "Supposedly he's kicking it upstairs . . . What's wrong with being busy, anyway?"

"Nothing. Busy is good," Sam acquiesced.

"Fingers crossed, huh?" Alex said.

"Sounds promising," Patrick added.

Alex regarded his own wrinkled clothing. "I only brought one change of clothes. Is there somewhere I can shop for new ones?"

"No worries," Nigel told him. "There are plenty of stores on High Street in the St. Ives Town Center. I'm sure Hana would be happy to take you shopping." Nigel winked at her.

"I'm not much of a shopper, but I know where the shops are," Hana said.

"Love to come along, if I'm not imposing," James said. "It's my first time out of the country . . ."

"Sure," Alex told him.

"Okay, three of us," Hana announced. "Anyone else? Going once, twice . . ." She held up the radio. "Guardian, we cool?"

"How did you get so paranoid?" Patrick said.

Hana ignored him. Simon's voice came over the radio. "All clear, Darkrider."

"*Darkrider?*" Alex said.

"She likes to ride her bike at night," Sunil explained. "Really fast."

"Simple pleasures," Hana conceded, leading the way to the front of the house. She opened the door and stepped out, then moved aside to make room for Alex. As he came up beside her, sunlight glinted off something in the trees across the meadow.

Her foot was already tripping Alex, hands pushing on his back as she yelled "*Down!*" She heard a wet *thwap* and felt blood spray across her face just before they hit the ground behind the low stone wall that surrounded the house. There was no sound, which meant the shooter was using a suppressor. She looked to James, who stood in the doorway, looking down at Alex's blood on his shirt. "Inside!" she told him, watching as he stumbled back through the doorway and fell out of sight.

Simon and Oliver materialized out of nowhere, seeking a target, seeing nothing.

Hana got on the radio. "Shooter across meadow from front

door. Alex is down, don't know how bad." She tore his shirt open and looked at the ragged hole in his shoulder.

Alex felt himself panting like a dog. His chest felt like someone had jammed a red-hot poker into it. "How bad?" he managed to ask.

Hana gazed down at him. She looked scared, but all she said was, "I've seen worse."

Simon caught Oliver's eye, indicating a section of brush in the trees. And then one of the bushes stood up. At least that's what it looked like. The shooter was wearing a netlike garment covered with local foliage. The gun must have been covered as well, because Simon didn't see it. "*Ghillie suit! Twelve o'clock!*" he yelled.

Oliver opened fire with a handgun. His bullet whizzed past the man. Simon cut loose with his MP7 submachine gun, but the bush sank to the ground, becoming impossible to distinguish from the surrounding foliage. Leaves jolted from a different spot as the attacker's gun *coughed* softly. Oliver spun to the ground as Alastair and Duncan rounded the corner from the rear of the cottage.

"Over there!" Simon pointed.

They hesitated momentarily, then heard the shooter plunging away through the woods. Alastair and Duncan gave chase while Simon tended to Oliver. He'd been shot in the chest.

In the woods, the pursuing SAS men paused, seeking a target. But the brush was dense and the ground uneven. They caught glimpses of the quarry, but their bullets arrived too late. Whoever this was, he was no amateur.

Alastair pointed to his own eyes, asking silently: See him?

Duncan shook his head, heard another metallic *cough*—closer this time—and saw Alastair sink to the ground, clutching his gut. He waved Duncan on: Go get him.

Duncan moved forward, using trees for cover. Coming to a small rise, he saw the running bush some distance off and opened fire. The shooter grabbed his leg and fell, shooting back almost before he hit the ground. Duncan dropped low as bullets hammered into tree bark just above him.

Seconds later, he heard running, and chanced a look. The shooter had ditched the ghillie suit and was struggling toward a small rise. Duncan brought his subgun up, loosing a three-round burst. Blood misting in the air around him, the shooter tumbled off the far side of the rise.

Phantom abandoned the rifle and dragged himself toward the bike, now mere feet away. Bullets hammered into the engine as he reached for it. He rolled over, hand reaching for the gun at his side. But it was too late: a hard-looking man in camouflage pants and shirt had him dead to rights, holding an MP7 at CQB position. "Give me a reason," the man said.

AS GUNSHOTS REVERBERATED THROUGH THE WOODS, Hana shouted into the cottage from her position beside the wall. "Alex and Oliver are shot!" she yelled. "We need ambulance and police!" She turned back to Alex, keeping pressure on the wound. His eyes were closed. She checked his pulse: still there. "Hang in there, Alex," she told him. "We haven't gone shopping yet."

Inside, Nigel was already on the phone. Hana saw him peer

out the door, looking ill. "At least three people shot," he said into his cell.

Three? Hana saw someone's feet in the doorway: James. He hadn't been looking at Alex's blood on his shirt; the bullet must have passed through Alex and hit him as well. Which meant there was another hole in Alex's back. She rolled him over and pressed her other hand to that wound. She peeked over the stone wall; the shooter had apparently fled. Simon still knelt over Oliver, cell phone in one hand. "Need some help out here!" Hana called into the cottage.

Patrick swept the dining table clean as Hana and Nigel set Alex on top of it.

"What can I do?" Sam asked, sounding panicked.

"Plug the holes," Hana said, pointing to a basket of clean linen napkins. They used them to stanch the bleeding as best they could while Nigel, Sunil, and Patrick pulled James away from the door and tended to him.

"Towels! Need towels!" Hana said urgently. "And something to tie them on with!" The napkins just weren't enough. Sunil ran for the linen closet. Sam started to pull a blood-soaked napkin from Alex's wound, ready to replace it with a fresh one. "No, leave it on," Hana told her. They packed more on top of it.

"Blood just keeps coming out of his chest," Nigel said, kneeling over an unconscious James.

"Keep pressure on it!" Hana told him. "Pack it with linens and cinch a towel over it until the medics get here." Sunil arrived with a pile of fresh towels and a tangled mass of extension cords. Hana directed the makeshift dressings as gunfire continued outside and the wail of sirens rose in the distance. Patrick hurried around, locking doors while Sam kept yelling Alex's name and trying to shake him awake.

Alex's eyes fluttered open, and he blinked a few times. "Man, that tea's got some kick," he said weakly, and tried to sit up. Halfway there, he started to lose consciousness.

"You've lost a lot of blood," Hana told him. "There's not enough to go around when you sit up."

"Then I won't do that." His eyes tracked onto the others, working on the floor beside the table. "James too?"

Hana nodded. "Bullet went through you, he was behind you."

"How . . . is he?"

"Not good," Nigel announced, standing. "Weak pulse. Unconscious."

"Gotta get him . . . hospital," Alex said, fading again.

"They're coming," Sam told him.

"Am I gonna die?"

"Eventually," Hana told him. "But not today."

"There was a little pause there," Alex pressed. "Before you answered. Like you're not sure maybe."

"I'm sure. You're not going to die."

"You know they always say that to people who are going to die, right?"

Despite the circumstances, Hana found herself grinning.

"Sounds like the shooting has stopped," Nigel said. "I'm going to check on Simon and the others." He looked around. "Where's Patrick?"

"Locking doors and windows, I think," Sunil told him.

Nigel picked up the radio. "OTW One to SAS One," he said.

"Go ahead," he heard Simon reply.

"What's your situation?"

"Threat neutralized but two men down."

"Medics on the way; I'm coming out." He turned to Sunil. "We've got four people shot, maybe five. Call emergency back and let them know we're going to need more medics out here."

Nigel stepped outside. Oliver's too-still body lay nearby, chest covered with red-soaked dressings. Simon knelt beside a bandaged Alastair, who wasn't moving. Duncan, by the look of it, had just punched a fifth man in the gut. He fell face-first to the ground, his hands cuffed behind him. Oddly, there were no guns in sight. "What's happening?" he asked Simon.

"Did my best to patch up Oliver, but . . ." He shook his head. "Tried to help Alastair here, but it's not looking good." He tilted his head toward Phantom, as Duncan jerked him up by his cuffed wrists. "That's our shooter. How is it in there?"

"Alex lost a lot of blood, but he's talking. James is out, shot in the chest. Still with us so far."

Simon nodded. "I told emergency the shooter's been captured so the bobbies don't come in looking to kill someone."

"Good idea."

The first emergency vehicles rolled into view. Nigel ran to meet them at the access point from the main road. Two ambulances sped to the cottage; the other stayed on the main road. Police vehicles spilled officers onto the drive. Officers hurried to meet Nigel. "I'm Officer Jones," said the first to arrive. "What happened here?"

"Four shot and injured. Suspect right there," Nigel pointed to Phantom, who was trying to stand on his uninjured leg. "Shot in the leg, I think." More officers arrived and listened in as Nigel summed things up.

"Did he say anything?" Officer Jones asked.

"I don't know. Our security lads are the ones who nabbed him. You might want to ask them. He was trying to kill Alex Watson."

"The bloke on the news? The American?"

"Right, he's inside."

"Can we speak with Mr. Watson?"

"The man just took a bullet. Can we get him to the hospital first?"

"Oh, of course. I didn't realize. Fine. He can tell us if this is the same chap who attacked him in the States." Jones signaled the other officers to secure the scene.

Nigel watched as the medics spread out. He saw Sam in the doorway, beckoning them inside. "Where will they take the wounded?"

"Your people will go to St. Michael's Hospital in Hayle. We'll have the suspect taken to West Cornwall Hospital in Penzance, under police custody, of course. We'll have more questions for everyone here."

"Anything we can do," Nigel told him.

THE FRONT YARD SOON TURNED INTO A POLICE CONVention. Simon and Duncan stood over their tarp-covered comrades. Officers led the shooter to the back of a squad car. He looked like he'd gone ten rounds with Mike Tyson.

Officer Jones ignored his ringing cell while he interviewed Simon and Duncan. He gestured toward Phantom, whose leg was being bandaged. "Any idea how he got those bruises all over him?"

"He seemed a bit clumsy after he was shot in the leg," Duncan related. "He fell."

"Several times," Simon agreed, pressing a handkerchief against his own bleeding arm. "Mostly on his face."

Jones talked to himself as he wrote on his iPad. "Suspect noted to be clumsy." He stared at Duncan's arm. "You should get that looked at."

"They're busy with people needing real help. I'll live."

A patrolman approached, holding out a cell phone. "HQ on the line, sir. Say they've been trying to reach you."

Jones took the phone and listened as Hana stepped from the cottage and walked past, a bag on one shoulder. "Very well then," he said into the cell. He stopped writing and handed back the phone. "It seems Scotland Yard is taking over," he announced. "They'll have a man here shortly. I'm afraid he'll be asking all the same questions."

Hana saw James and Alex in the same ambulance and marched over. Sam was already there. She found Alex still lucid, and James coughing blood.

Alex laid a hand on James's arm. "Hold on, James, we're going to the hospital now. Fix us right up, you'll see." The medics hooked them both up to EKGs and IVs.

"I need to ride with my brother," Sam told one of the medics.

"Look, miss, you can't ride in the back," the man told her. "There's no room and it's against regulations."

"Where are you taking them?"

"St. Michael's in Hayle."

"But—"

Hana planted a helmet in Sam's hands. "We'll be there before they are."

The doors thunked shut and the ambulance sped off down the country lane. Hana mounted the bike with Sam behind her as an officer hurried their way. "Here now, you two are witnesses!"

Hana started the engine.

"We'll still be witnesses at the hospital," Sam told the cop.

Before he could reply, Hana dropped the bike into gear and roared off—swerving to avoid an arriving Scotland Yard car. Sam held on for dear life.

CHAPTER 29
ICU

ALEX WOKE IN HIS HOSPITAL ROOM, BANDAGES AND A dull throbbing ache where his chest met his shoulder. Hana stood beside him. She took his hand.

"Welcome back," she told him. "Sam went for coffee. The others are still back at the cottage, helping the police."

"Thank you. I remember you . . . helping."

She nodded.

"How's James?" he asked.

"He's in ICU."

"When can I see him?"

"That's up to the doctors. You need to rest."

A nurse barged in. "It's good you're awake," she said to Alex. "Your friend James is asking for you. He's insisting. His doctor says he's in critical condition, but we're making an exception for you to come see him. I'll wheel you to ICU. Let me get a wheelchair." She hurried off, returning a few minutes later with the promised conveyance. Unhooking Alex from the IV, she helped him into the chair.

"Do you want me to come with you?" Hana asked.

"No, I'm good, thanks," said Alex.

"I'll let Sam know." She offered a smile as they departed, but there was only one reason she could think of that they'd break policy to let Alex see James, and it wasn't a good one.

The nurse sped Alex through the halls, navigating obstacles with an ease borne of much practice. Before long, they were in the ICU ward, where she wheeled him though double doors and parked him next to James's bed. "I'll leave you two alone," she said, before drawing the privacy curtain and padding off.

James was on a ventilator, surrounded by monitors, tubes, and wires. Alex stood up, adjusted the sling on his arm, and hobbled to his bedside. James's eyes opened, and he smiled weakly.

"Good to see you, champ," Alex said, placing a hand on James's shoulder.

"Nice of you to visit," James croaked around the ventilator tube. "What's your damage?"

"I'll be all right. You took a bullet for me. The second time you saved my life this week!"

"Technically, the bullet went through you before it hit me."

"Minor detail," Alex replied.

"Docs don't think I'm gonna make it," James rasped.

"What do they know? You're a fighter."

"Look after my dad for me. Tell him I'm so sorry. Tell him I love him."

Alex nodded, feeling the tears flow. "I love you, man," he said, hearing the quaver in his voice.

"I love you too."

"You're gonna pull through."

"You've been a real good friend to me, Alex. Like a brother." James paused to catch his breath. "Don't let these assholes stop you. Make the world a better place." His lids fluttered and his eyes rolled back until only the whites were showing. Monitors started screeching. A mob of hospital personnel burst in and gathered around James, working madly. The nurse who'd brought Alex there reappeared, helped him back into the chair and wheeled him from the room. From the look on her face, Alex knew there wasn't much hope.

BACK IN HIS HOSPITAL BED, ALEX STARED AT THE CEILing, not really seeing it—or anything else. James, the best friend he'd had since grade school, was gone. On some level, he couldn't help but feel it was his fault, even though he knew that wasn't true. Thoughts of grim vengeance filled his mind and threatened to crowd out all else. He struggled to keep the darkness from taking over completely only because he knew James would see that as letting the bad guys win, by making Alex like them. James would say the best vengeance would be destroying what they and everyone like them held most dear: their companies. "Just make this work," he would have said, "and the bastards will probably kill themselves."

Hana and Samantha returned, bearing coffee. Alex got a glimpse of Simon and Duncan in the hall, apparently standing watch. Samantha set one of the coffees down beside the bed. "I'm so sorry about James," she said, wiping away tears. She gave him a hug, careful to avoid his injured shoulder. "How's his dad doing?"

"It was a hard phone call. He's lost everything, there's no one for him now. Can you call Mom and Dad and ask them to visit him, keep him company?"

"I already did. They've asked him to stay with them for a while."

"The people we're dealing with have to go," Alex said. "Whether we can get them prosecuted or not, we have to crush them. Grind them into the dirt until they don't have the power to do anything like this ever again."

"Just keep doing what you're doing," Hana told him, "and their stockholders will hang them."

"Better yet," Sam said, "they'll abandon them. Dump their stocks."

"Whatever we're going to do," Alex said, "we need to do it fast. Because they're not going to stop. But once this is out there and working? I become irrelevant. At that point, killing me makes no difference. It becomes a risk with no reward."

"I'll twist Nigel's arm," Hana said. "See if he can speed up the research for a test town."

Alex's doctor came in. "How is he?" Sam asked.

The doc looked to Alex. "You seem to be out of the woods, so far as any immediate danger is concerned."

"I feel fine," Alex said. "Except for the shoulder. When can I leave?"

"We'd like to keep you here for observation. Another forty-eight hours, say."

"Is that normal?" Samantha asked.

"No, but . . . being a celebrity, we can't have you walking out of here with an infection or something."

"Wouldn't reflect well on the hospital," Alex said.

"Not to put too fine a point on it. Also, you have an appointment with Scotland Yard."

"When is that?" Alex asked.

"Now, actually."

A soft knock sounded and the door opened, admitting a Scotland Yard detective. He looked like he was dressed for a business meeting.

"He's cleared," Simon called in before the door closed.

"I should hope so," said the detective. He moved to shake Alex's hand.

"Kevin Young, Scotland Yard."

"Alex Watson."

"Well, down to business. We don't know much about the shooter. Nothing at all, actually, other than the fact that he was good enough to find you and take out two SAS men."

"What!" Alex said.

"Two of your four security escorts were killed. You didn't know?"

"No . . . *No!*" He looked to Sam and Hana. "Why didn't you tell me?"

"We were going to," Hana told him.

"We thought you'd had enough grief for one day," Sam added.

Alex looked to Detective Young. "You should know that the shooter has some connection to G-Tek in New York. I'm sure they hired him."

"What makes you certain?"

"Because they're not G-Tek. They're a front company for Big Energy, and what I have will end them. Also, my friend James told me he overheard the CEO and their lead attorney talking about sending someone after me the same night I was first attacked. His call saved my life."

"James Campbell?"

Alex nodded.

"Makes sense," Detective Young continued. "Of course, proving that is something else . . . I have been authorized to offer you protective custody."

"Thanks, but I'm a little leery of governments right now, no offense. Perhaps you've seen the video."

"None taken, but we're not the United States."

"Thanks, but I'll pass just the same, for now. What's happening with my would-be assassin, if you can say?"

"We're having a hard time IDing him. He's a ghost: no prints or DNA sample in any of our databases, and no DNA hits on relatives. He carried no ID or passport, and the motorcycle he rode was recently purchased from a private owner."

"So he's not new at this," Hana concluded.

"It would appear not," said Detective Young.

"He's the same man who tried to kill me in Asheville, in the States."

"Are you positive?"

"Yes. I got a good look at his face when I was being put in the ambulance. Where is he?"

"His leg was treated at a hospital in Penzance. Right now, he's being transported to a secure facility in London."

CHAPTER 30
DANIEL MOORE

AT THE COTTAGE, POLICE CONTINUED THEIR SEARCH of the grounds and nearby woods, and seemed to have an inexhaustible supply of questions for Nigel, Sunil, and Patrick—who were alternately told they could go about their business and pummeled with inquiries. Once the entrance and dining area had been thoroughly photographed, they were given official permission to clean up the blood.

Soon after, an unseen searcher rifled through Alex's room, looking for the blue rock. It had to be there somewhere; Alex hadn't had time to move it and—so far as he could tell—no one else had been in the room since the shooting. There was just no place else it could be. And yet after three separate searches of Alex's room, the other upstairs bedrooms, and even the bathrooms, it was simply nowhere to be found.

AFTER THE SCOTLAND YARD MAN DEPARTED, ALEX looked around in a panic. "Energy X! I left it in my room."

"Relax, tiger," Hana told him, tugging at the strap on her back-pack. "Have the old blue magic right here." She opened the top and showed him; she'd put his whole pack inside hers.

INSIDE G-TEK'S EXECUTIVE SUITE, JACK WOKE TO A TAP on the door. He rolled out of bed, feeling like he hadn't slept at all. He found Pete looking much like himself: rumpled and unshaven. "Something you need to see," Pete told him.

They moved into the office, which smelled of day-old takeout. Pete snagged a remote and cranked up the volume on the TV, catching the BBC newscaster in midsentence.

"—who haven't yet heard, Alex Watson has been shot outside a small home in Cornwall, just south of St. Ives, apparently used as headquarters by Occupy the World. There's no word yet on Mr. Watson's current condition, but we do know there was a gunfight at the location that killed three others. Two of those three were former SAS men working a security detail at the location. The third fatality was apparently Mr. James Campbell, an American friend of Alex Watson who arrived in the UK just this morning. An unidentified fourth man was also shot, and was taken into custody by Scotland Yard."

"Well, that's messy," Jack said. "But with any luck, Watson won't make it out of the hospital. Do we have the rock?"

"Still waiting to hear back on that. Can any of this come back to us? Phantom entered the country on our jet."

"Unless he used his real name or is still carrying the same passport, not a problem," Jack assured him. "You worry too much."

On the television, the BBC newscaster continued. "James Campbell, who is among the deceased, is or was until very recently an employee of New York-based G-Tek, which is, as viewers may recall, the same company Alex Watson suggested might be linked to the earlier attempt on his life. Recent revelations by Occupy the World have uncovered that the so-called 'green energy company' is actually controlled by a group of conventional energy companies—"

"You were saying?" Pete remarked.

Jack's desk phone buzzed. He pressed the intercom and put it on speakerphone. "I thought I told you to cancel everything," he told his assistant.

"Sir, you have an important visitor waiting in reception. He doesn't have an appointment."

Resisting the temptation to tell her to instruct the guest to get lost, he asked, "Who is it?"

"He says he's with the FBI."

"Give us a moment," Jack said, his blood running cold. He killed the speakerphone.

"Don't say too much," Pete advised. "If you're unsure about an answer, look to me and I'll nod or answer for you."

Jack swept takeout containers into a wastebasket, switched off the TV and buzzed his assistant back. "Send him in." The doors opened, admitting an intelligent-looking man in his thirties. He had dense hair and thin brows. Jack rose to meet him as the door shut behind him. "Jack Miller," he said, extending a hand.

"Special Agent Daniel Moore," the man said sternly, shaking Jack's hand.

"This is Pete Bowman, the company's chief legal counsel."

Agent Moore shook with Pete as well, and looked around. "Nice office."

"It's really a second home," Jack said. "We spend so much time here. Please, have a seat. Can I get you anything?"

"No, I'm good, thanks." He took a seat before the desk.

"What can we do for you, Agent Moore?" Jack asked.

"What do you know about Alex Watson?"

"Not much, really. We had a brief meeting with him. But other than that, just what's been on the news."

"There were two assassination attempts within a forty-eight hour period. Three men were killed in the most recent incident in Cornwall, and two police officers in North Carolina."

"Yes we just saw that on the news. Terrible thing. I hope Mr. Watson is all right."

"I can't share that information. I can tell you the Bureau is working with Scotland Yard to identify the responsible parties."

"Did you have any questions?" Pete asked. "Meaning no disrespect, but Jack does have a large corporation to run."

"What was your meeting with Mr. Watson about, and who was present at that meeting?"

"We bought a six-month research lease on his alleged energy source," Jack told him. "I was there, Pete, Alex of course, and a former intern of ours, James Campbell."

"Who's now dead."

Jack nodded. "We just heard."

"Who asked for the meeting?"

"It was James's idea, and I suppose Mr. Watson's. We didn't solicit the meeting."

"So why did Mr. Watson come to you?"

"He was looking for a platform to launch his . . . power source."

"And did you come to an agreement?"

"Yes. As I said, the lease."

"When was the last time you saw James Campbell?"

"I'd have to check, but . . . I think a few days after the meeting. After that, he didn't show up for work. We assumed the job was more than he was prepared for; we lose a lot of interns in the first few weeks."

"I'll be blunt. Did either of you have anything to do with James Campbell's death or the attempts on Alex Watson's life?"

"Of course not!" Jack protested.

Agent Moore looked to Pete. "No," Pete told him.

"It doesn't even make sense," Jack added. "We're obviously interested in his power source, because we licensed it for a research phase, but if we want to buy it or extend the license, we can't do that with him incapacitated or, God forbid, dead."

"I don't think either of us will be answering any more questions without a court order and another attorney present," Pete announced.

"Relax, gentlemen. This is not an interrogation. Just collecting statements for the investigation." Agent Moore stood. "It might interest the two of you to know that I spoke with Mr. Campbell before he left for the UK. He said he was working late and overheard the two of you discussing things I'm pretty sure are illegal." He took a moment to savor the expressions on the faces before him, then said, "I'll show myself out."

CHAPTER 31
THE INCIDENT AT ST. JAMES'S PARK

A YOUNG HIPSTER SAT IN A BATTERED CAR PARKED ON Dacre Street in London, a short distance from the Broadway intersection. He eyed the fistful of cash thrust through the window by the stranger's gloved hand. The hooded sweatshirt and huge sunglasses worn by the stranger made it impossible to see facial features.

"And that's all I have to do?" the hipster asked.

THE ARMORED POLICE VAN SLOWED IN HEAVY TRAFFIC along Broadway near St. James's Park. Two officers sat in the front, eyeing diners in the "EAT" restaurant across the sidewalk. Two burly officers rode in the back, cradling submachine guns and keeping watch. The unwilling object of their attention was Phantom, clad in a green-and-yellow jumpsuit. Hands and feet shackled, he sat with his back to the front divider.

The van's driver eased forward, approaching an intersection. His partner checked his watch. "We're close. With any luck, we can wrap this by dark. Fancy a bite over there?" He jerked his head toward the restaurant.

"I do."

Just before they reached the intersection, a battered car jumped from the curb and cut in front of them. The van's driver stomped the brake, avoiding a collision by centimeters. "Bloody hell!"

"Watch him!" his partner said. Before he could say more, the passenger-side window shattered. A hooded figure with large sunglasses tossed an object inside. Something ricocheted off the windshield and landed on the dash. It looked like a small handle. The first object came to rest on the floor. *"Grenade!"* the passenger yelled, and both men bailed out the driver's door, running flat-out.

Hoodie climbed in the passenger side, slid across, and took the wheel. The hipster backed out of the way, and the van rocketed forward in a screeching turn onto Dacre Street. Pedestrians fled before it. Hoodie fastened the seat belt.

The guards in the back fought to keep from bouncing off the walls. The voice of the van's former driver sounded over their radios. "The van has been hijacked! We are not in the van! We are not in the van!"

Phantom had pitched onto the floor, apparently by accident. Neither guard took notice of the fact that he'd braced both feet firmly against the front wall, just below the bench he'd been sitting on.

Halfway down the block, the van jumped a curb and flew head-on into a brick wall. Airbags deployed up front, saving the driver. But there were no airbags in the back. Both guards went airborne and crashed into the front divider. The first broke his neck on impact; the second broke half his ribs and started spitting teeth.

Phantom, who alone had been prepared, pounced on him in a heartbeat, ripped away the guard's sidearm, and grabbed the keys to his shackles. Freeing himself, he shot out the lock on the back door and kicked it open. He seized the second guard's pistol and two spare magazines, then leapt into daylight. Bystanders froze in their tracks. Phantom saw Hoodie walk through shadows, ditch sweatshirt and shades, emerge as Gretchen in a business suit, and smooth her hair.

Seeing police in three different directions, Phantom opted for the fourth—which had been his plan from the start. He limped for the tube station, then half fell down the steps when he got there. He caught himself on a wooden framework bracing one wall, where repairs were being done during the day. A gaping hole in the wall beckoned with its darkness, and Phantom slipped inside.

Three constables rushed down the steps after him. He let the first two pass. The last he struck in the throat with one of the pistols. The constable gasped for breath as Phantom dragged him into a darkness from which he would never emerge, snapping his neck to stop the noise.

A moment later, the surviving officers from the van pounded down the steps into the tube. After they'd passed, Phantom stepped from the shadows, wearing the dead officer's uniform. He made his way down to the platform.

Behind him, police searching the tube station spotted a very still form in a green-and-yellow jumpsuit. They wasted two minutes yelling commands before they ventured into the shad-ows, handcuffed the figure, and turned it over—at which point someone recognized the body as one of their own.

One of the surviving officers pointed. "There! On the plat-form, Westminster bound!"

PHANTOM HEARD THE CALL GO OUT ON HIS POLICE radio; they knew he was in uniform. He saw a stopped train boarding passengers. Merging with the crowd, he squeezed his way onto the train. Turning, he saw a dozen officers racing toward him. But the doors snapped shut in their faces, and he watched them slide sideways and out of sight as the train pulled away. The victory was temporary; he had perhaps a 50 percent chance of making the next station—Westminster—before it, too, was lousy with police.

Moments later, the train reached the station and screeched to a stop. The automatic doors slid open, spilling passengers onto the platform. Phantom scanned the area; it was crawling with plainclothes officers. All exits were covered.

Drawing one of the pistols, Phantom whipped his arm around a young woman's throat and shoved her out of the train before him. The woman struggled madly, elbows jabbing into Phantom's ribs. He showed her the gun, and pressed the muzzle against her head.

"Stop moving," he ordered, "or you'll never move again." The woman stilled. The crowd parted around them as he guided his hostage toward the escalator. Oddly, some ran just far enough to reach cover, then stuck their cell phones out to record the scene.

Once it became obvious they wouldn't be taking him by surprise, the plainclothes officers drew their guns. Their shouts echoed through the station: "Scotland Yard! . . . Drop your weapon! . . . You're surrounded!"

"Stay back or I'll kill her!" Phantom responded. For a moment, no one moved. Then Phantom took another step toward the escalator. The officer at the bottom yelled down, "Release her and we can talk!"

Phantom kept moving forward. The woman he held sobbed hysterically, shaking so badly she was hard to hold onto. They edged past the officer who'd spoken last, Phantom unflinching before him, and backed onto the escalator.

Constables gathered at the base of the escalator, watching as Phantom reached the top. Once there, he dragged his hostage off the stairs and looked around. He didn't think much of whoever was in charge of this operation—first for letting him get this far, second for having absolutely no one waiting upstairs. Unbelievable.

He shoved the woman to the ground, ran from the station, and jumped into the nearest taxi.

The cabbie looked at him in the mirror, taking in his police uniform. "Well, this is a first, constable. Lost your way, 'ave you?"

Phantom pointed a gun at his face. "Drive! South to Croydon." The cabbie hit the gas so fast Phantom nearly shot him by accident.

Thirty minutes later, the taxi dropped Phantom at a payphone north of Croydon. The area was deserted. The cabbie raced away, minus his car radio and cell phone. Phantom called Gretchen at a prearranged number; she was waiting with a clean car four blocks away. A short while later, a car approached. The high beams flashed twice in the darkness. She swung to the curb, picked him up, and followed the road signs taking them out of London.

An hour later, they reached her apartment on the outskirts of Reading. Once safely inside, she grabbed the first-aid kit and set to work on his leg. "If this gets infected, you'll need a doctor," she told him.

Phantom nodded, drinking whiskey to dull the pain while she cleaned the wound and applied a fresh dressing.

CHAPTER 32
TATER DU

ALEX BLEW OUT A SIGH OF FRUSTRATION. "LOOK, SAM, I'm okay. Really." He pulled his arm from the sling and flexed his bicep, trying to conceal the agony this caused. "See?"

"If we're going to do this," Hana said, "it needs to be now." She held up the clipboard at the base of the bed. "The doc's next visit is in ten minutes."

"I don't know . . ." Samantha hemmed.

"Look," said Alex. "He's just being cautious because I'm some kind of celebrity. Which is the point: the whole world must know I'm here by now. How safe can that be?"

Sam looked to Hana, who nodded her approval of Alex's plan.

"Why don't we bring my guards in?" Alex said.

Hana opened the door and beckoned the SAS men inside.

"Hi, Simon, Duncan," Alex said. "I'm so sorry about Oliver and Alastair. They were good guys. I know those words don't mean much, but . . . I wish I'd had time to know them better."

Both men held their emotions in check. It seemed an effort. "They will be missed," Simon told him. "But they didn't die in vain. It was for an honorable cause. You make good on that, and their sacrifice means something."

"Count on it," Alex told them. "And thank you. I never really got a chance to say that."

Simon nodded. "It's what we do."

After a moment of silence, Alex said, "I want to leave here right now. Just go. No security. What do you think?"

"You're a bloody big target sitting here with the media outside," said Simon.

"You should have security," Duncan urged.

Alex looked to Hana. "I'll have her." The SAS men exchanged looks.

"Speaking of which," Alex said to Hana, "how did you know I was about to be shot?"

"I saw a glint in the brush, like sunlight off glass or metal."

"Rifle scope," Duncan guessed. Clearly, Hana's stock had just gone up.

"All right," Simon said reluctantly. "It's your life. But we're on call if you need us. How will you leave?"

While Alex explained, Hana excused herself, saying she had to visit the ladies' room. Instead, she found a payphone and made a quick call. "Be ready at eight," she said when she was done. She returned to the room and gave Alex his backpack. His things—including Energy X—were inside. "Ready to rumble?" she asked.

Moments later, she and Alex rode up the ramp from the underground parking garage, crossed the lot, and left the grounds. Despite a growing media presence outside, no one paid much heed to the two helmeted riders.

Hana took them southwest on Carnsew Road and onto the A30. The evening sun was low, making for a scenic ride on winding country lanes, and a glittering sea when they reached the coast. They followed the road to the English Channel, passing the city of Penzance.

Alex leaned forward, yelling to be heard over the bike and through two helmets. "Where we headed?" he asked.

"Someplace illuminating!" Hana yelled back.

The old bike powered forward. Alex held onto Hana and took in the sights, enjoying the fresh sea air. After a time, Hana slowed, then pulled up beside an English pub with picnic tables outside. The building was old and squat, with wide red shutters on mahogany window frames. A weathered sign by the door read LAMORNA WINK PUB.

Hana doffed her helmet and shook out her hair. Alex would have removed his helmet as well if she hadn't stopped him. He nodded, wondering what he'd been thinking. The whole world knew his face now, and they were supposed to be traveling discreetly. Hana held up two fingers. "Back in two minutes," she told him.

Alex gave her a thumbs-up and sat sideways on the bike, watching the locals at the picnic tables. There were several families, kids running around making noise to one side. He noticed one man who didn't seem to fit. Large and belligerent-looking. When Alex's eyes met his, the man stood and walked toward him, reaching under his denim vest. There was nowhere for Alex to go. Then the man's hand reappeared—holding his wallet. He lumbered past Alex and went inside.

Hana returned just after and stuffed a takeout bag in one of the bike's leather panniers.

"That was fast."

Hana picked up her helmet. "I called it in earlier, told them when we'd be here."

"I still don't know where we're going."

"You'll see. It's not far now." They mounted up and sped from the lot, the back wheel kicking up stones. Soon Hana had them on a serpentine road, leaning into curves as the blacktop blurred past.

"Do we want to slow down a little?" Alex yelled.

Instead, Hana twisted the throttle. The bike leaped ahead. Alex held on tighter. They topped a small hill, after which Hana slowed their speed—though not by choice; just ahead, the road narrowed to a worn footpath, bordered by tall grasses and overgrown shrubs.

Hana guided them onto the path, descending a steep slope to an old stone lighthouse by the sea. A battered sign read TATER DU LIGHTHOUSE, which Alex thought an odd name for a landmark. A short distance from the lighthouse's whitewashed walls, the greenery ended abruptly at a hundred-foot cliff that dropped into the Atlantic.

Hana picked the lock on the lighthouse door, making it seem so easy Alex thought a professional thief would envy her. "Why do you know how to pick locks?" he asked.

"Childhood hobby. I also rig a mean IED."

"You're joking."

Hana smiled to herself, but didn't reply. She pushed the old door open and rolled the bike inside.

Alex scoped the building's bleak interior: round concrete wall, decrepit generator, empty battery racks. A rusting iron stairway spiraled upward. "Charming," he said.

Hana retrieved the takeout bag and nodded toward the stairs. "It is. Come on." Alex followed her up. She paused to lift the trapdoor at the top, then climbed through. Alex went after, emerging onto the interior catwalk, a platform that supported a huge, seven-foot lantern. Hana closed the trapdoor behind him.

"Right," Alex said. "Don't want to be falling through that."

Hana placed her hands over his eyes from behind. "Turn around slowly," she told him. He did. Hana turned with him. When she took her hands away, Alex found himself staring out through a great, curving wall of glass at a spectacular sunset. Pink cotton-candy clouds floated in a hazy orange sky. Below them, shimmering waters were set ablaze by the setting sun. It was as if Mother Nature wanted to make up for yesterday's hurricane. "It's beautiful," Alex breathed. "How did you find this place?"

"I took a wrong turn and wound up here. Can you believe it? I come here sometimes when I need to think."

"No one comes here?"

"It's been shut down for years. It was built to run off diesel, but they hauled that stuff out of here. There was talk of converting it, but they ran out of money."

They circled the catwalk, and stopped facing southwest. "See down there," Hana told him. "You can just about make out two rocks. They show better during low tide. That's a sub-aqua dive site. They launch dive boats from Penzance."

"How do you know that?"

She looked at him.

"What?" he asked. "You dive too?"

"Life's meant to be lived. I want to do it all."

"Ever been in a light aircraft?"

"Not yet."

"I'll take you up sometime, if we get a chance. The views are fabulous."

"I'd like that. You hungry?"

"Starving."

She handed him the takeout bag, grabbed a couple of folding chairs and a collapsible table, and took them outside, onto the "widow's walk" that ran around the lighthouse's exterior. Alex followed, a gentle sea breeze caressing his face. He leaned cautiously over the railing. He could almost look straight down the cliff face. The short bay below was empty, leaving them alone with the ocean.

The two of them sat down to eat, enjoying what Alex thought must be one of the best views in the country.

Later, after the departing sun had left them in darkness, Ilana watched as Alex tinkered with the wiring behind the lantern, working in the glow of an old flashlight. "Did I ever thank you for saving my life?" he asked.

"Not that I recall."

"Thank you for saving my life."

"You're welcome."

"Really, that took guts. You could have been killed yourself."

"I never thought about it."

"And who sees a glint in the woods and thinks, 'sniper,' anyway?" Alex asked. "There something you're not telling me?"

"My father was a maintenance contractor in Iraq, my mother a teacher. We were there during the war. I was eleven. It took us six months to get out. People who didn't pick up on things like that didn't get out. I saw a flash like that half a second before my sister was killed. She was right beside me."

Alex paused in his tinkering. "I'm sorry."

Hana nodded. "I guess you could say she saved your life."

Alex went on with his work, hooking the crystal-boxed EX fragment from the satphone up to the big light. He guesstimated the proper resistor thickness; fortunately, he kept an assortment of small crystal boxes and resistors with the rock. "Your parents okay?" he asked.

"Yeah. We made it out. A lot of people didn't."

"Still doesn't answer the question: why risk your life for me?"

"If we win this, there won't be any more wars for oil. Or oil companies to push governments into them. Besides, I fancy you."

"Really?"

"Really."

Even without looking, Alex could tell she was smiling. "Then let's make this dinner and a show," he said, finishing up. "Stand over there, please." He pointed to a spot on the widow's walk. She moved to the spot. "Here?"

"Right. Now close your eyes, tight. I think it only fair to warn you, I can really light up your life."

He hit a switch, and the seven-foot lamp ignited like a blinding sun, right in front of Hana. It made her look ethereal, angelic. Alex strode into the light to join her, until they both seemed clothed in light. He moved close, took her hands, and kissed her. She kissed him right back.

The light began to rotate beside them, white beam reaching out for miles, carving the night sky in half.

Hours later, they woke to the rose-pink light of dawn dancing over the old lighthouse's whitewashed walls. The sea air was rejuvenating, making Alex feel like a new man, energized and ready to take on the world. Of course, he reflected, Hana may have had something to do with that as well. He held on as she piloted the bike up the hill, leaving the lighthouse behind. When they reached the top, he heard her cell beeping. She ignored it.

A short time later, they pulled up outside the Lamorna Wink Pub. "Your phone was beeping," he told her.

"I'll see who it was. There's no reception past that hill by the lighthouse, so they could have called anytime last night or this morning. Keep the helmet on."

"I know the drill," Alex told her as she checked her phone. "It was Nigel," she told him. "No message." She looked around, spotted a payphone, and removed the battery from her cell. Catching his look, she said, "I don't like to use these for outgoing calls. Or at all when things are dicey, but we should check in now and again."

"I thought Sunil made the phones secure."

Hana shook her head. "How did they find us at the cottage, if not through a phone?"

"I don't know."

"Until we know, better safe than sorry."

They walked to the payphone. Alex lifted the visor on his helmet and watched Hana dial Nigel's number. He gathered from what followed that his doctor was unhappy about his sudden departure from the hospital. Hana listened gravely for a moment, then held the phone out to Alex. She helped him off with the helmet, and made a point of standing between him and any passersby, so no one had a chance to recognize him.

Nigel filled him in on Phantom's London escape and the police fatalities. Maybe Hana wasn't paranoid after all. "There is some good news," Nigel told him afterward. "We managed to get hold of Nicholas about converting the car." Alex listened as Nigel went on, then thanked him and gave the phone back to Hana to say her goodbyes. She hung up and looked at him. Despite the grim news about his would-be assassin, he couldn't keep a mischievous glint from his eye.

"What could you possibly be happy about?"

"You know that company we talked about, with the electric car?"

"The one you want to convert, yeah."

"We're on for the London Auto Show."

"That's fantastic!"

"The CEO is flying in tonight. We get to use his place until he gets in. He's assigned an engineer to help us. And it's not just the car." He glanced around, as if fearful of being overheard. "There's also a motorcycle."

Something sparkled deep inside Hana's eyes. "There's a bike?"

CHAPTER 33
LONDON AUTO SHOW

THEY FOLLOWED GROSVENOR ROAD ALONG THE RIVER Thames with its bridges, balustrades, and streetlamps. People hustled along the promenade, and traffic was already gridlocked. Hana wove smoothly through most of the traffic, the wind whistling past their helmets until they arrived at the Savoy.

Alex scanned the lobby as they went inside; he'd never been in any place like this. He waited for Hana by the elevators. He'd traded the helmet for a baseball cap pulled low over his eyes, but still felt conspicuous. Maybe he just felt out of place; he wasn't sure. He watched Hana pick up an envelope at the desk and rip it open as she walked his way. She dumped out the key inside and held it up. "Penthouse," she said. "More formally known as the Personality Suite River View."

Moments later, they entered the suite. It was lavish and spacious: the kind of place, Alex thought, where you could stay for one night—or buy a car instead. A very nice car. Window walls offered stunning views of the city outside. The interior featured two bedrooms, marble floors, Italian linens, and bright Swedish furnishings that looked like they'd just come off the showroom floor. "So this is how the other one percent lives," Hana said.

"Careful there," Alex cautioned. "I may soon be one of those people."

"You'll never be one of those people," Hana told him. They moved to the windows and gazed out. Waterloo Bridge spanned the Thames on their left, while the huge London Eye Ferris wheel spun around just across the river. They could see Big Ben and Parliament in the distance.

"You might go a little easy on Nicholas," Alex said. "He's doing the right thing."

"I know. I'm just so used to dealing with bad people. Why are we doing this again, the show?"

"To demonstrate a practical, everyday use for Energy X."

"By powering two vehicles with something that could power a city."

"Small detail. We want to make an impression. If people see they may not have to put gas in their cars ever again, whose side do you think they'll be on?"

"Good point."

Alex checked his watch. "So, it's another hour before this engineer shows up . . ."

"Long enough," Hana said, and kissed him.

NIGEL, SAMANTHA, SUNIL, AND PATRICK ATE BREAKFAST in the living room, uncomfortable with the thought of using the dining room table Alex had been bleeding on the day before.

"They should be in London by now," Sam said.

"I don't like that Hana's not using her mobile," Nigel said. "If we need to get hold of her . . ."

"So she thinks they found the cottage by tracing our phones?" Patrick asked.

"The phones are solid," Sunil insisted. "They must have found us some other way."

"Not that I doubt your phone hacks," Sam told him, "but what other way? We need to find out. And I don't like Alex being in London when we know the shooter escaped there."

"It's not like they're going to bump into each other at the tube station," Patrick said. "No one even knows Alex is in the city."

"No one knew he was here, either," Sam pointed out.

"Hana's a tough cookie," Nigel said. "She doesn't miss much."

"Will Alex be part of the auto show?" Patrick asked.

"That would be so cool," Sunil said.

"No, he'll just do the conversions," Nigel answered.

"We don't want him any more exposed than he has to be," Sam added.

"Miles plans to announce a joint venture with Alex and OTW," Nigel told them. "When he introduces the vehicles."

"The whole world's going to be looking at this," Sunil mused. "I mean, everybody. This is major good."

ALEX WAS PULLING ON THE FRESH CLOTHES HANA HAD ordered delivered to the room when the penthouse doorbell chimed. He moved to the door, looked through the peephole, and saw a red-faced man gasping for air as if he'd just run a marathon. He was dabbing his forehead with a white cotton handkerchief.

"Who is it?" Alex asked, fairly certain he already knew, but wanting to be sure.

"I am the engineer," the man said with a thick German accent. "Nicholas Miles said you are expecting me, yes?"

Alex opened the door. "Yes," he said, regarding a bespectacled man of proper manners, much girth, and little hair. "Alex Watson."

"Yes, I know. You are famous now. I am Gustav, Ampere's chief automotive engineer. I am famous in a smaller way."

They shook hands, and Alex invited him inside. Gustav puffed into the room with an oversized laptop case that appeared to be bursting at the seams. He wheezed like an asthmatic, and for a moment Alex wondered if he might be having a heart attack. "Are you all right?" he asked. "Can I get you something?"

"Water would be nice, *danke*. Is long walk here, no?"

It hadn't seemed long to Alex, but then he wasn't carrying Gustav's weight. He found some fancy bottled water in the fridge, and handed one to Gustav as Hana appeared from one of the bedrooms, hair glistening from a just-finished shower.

"I hope I'm not interrupting anything?" Gustav said.

"You're fine," Hana told him, then introduced herself and shook hands. "When do we start?"

"You have the power source with you?" Gustav inquired.

Alex fetched his pack and removed the clear crystal box housing the largest piece of Energy X. Gustav squinted at the intense blue light. For a moment, it seemed he forgot to breathe. When he recovered from the sight of it, he said simply, "Would now be too soon?"

"Now would be perfect," Alex told him.

X

A BLACK LIMOUSINE WITH TINTED WINDOWS TOOK them to the Canary Wharf district, where preparations were underway for the show's next-day opening. Alex had been afraid the limo would be conspicuous, but he saw a dozen just like it, and no one was looking at any of them. The newest, sleekest cars in the world were being arrayed on sidewalks, lawns, and inside window-walled buildings. Automotive journalists, photographers and curious onlookers gathered outside temporary barriers, hoping for an early look at the cars of the future.

The limo glided to a stop before a glass-fronted tower with the first-floor windows covered from the inside. "This is it," Gustav said.

Alex tugged down on the brim of his hat and stepped from the car with Hana and Gustav. Alex saw that the building's entire ground floor was walled with reinforced architectural glass, tinted a light turquoise. This, combined with the cold, clean lines of the structure, gave the tower a futuristic feel. The doors were roped off and guarded by large, efficient-looking men in suits. Gustav nodded to them and breezed past, saying only, "They're with me." Alex and Hana hurried through the door after him.

Inside, a partition had been angled across the doorway to keep those outside from peering in when the door was open. Once they rounded this, the reason for the secrecy soon became apparent. While the cars they'd seen thus far were very nice, the cars before them now were absolutely stunning. This was the heart of the show: space-age designs, exotic materials, and outlandish supercars resting on a vast tiled floor polished like a mirror. Engineers and mechanics tended the vehicles, making sure all was in readiness for the show's opening.

Alex couldn't help but stare at the cars—the new Bugatti in particular—but Gustav passed them by without a glance. Whether this indicated a genuine lack of interest or a carefully cultivated intimidation tactic aimed at the other support teams—not one of which failed to note his presence—Alex wasn't certain. He quickened his step to keep up.

"You realize the properties you describe are quite impossible," Gustav informed him as they approached an oversized stage.

"It's also aerodynamically impossible for bumblebees to fly," Alex noted. "And yet they do."

Gustav smiled. "This is true," he said as they climbed the short steps to the stage, a section of which had been walled off with rolling panels bearing the Ampere logo. A young security guard sat in a chair beside this; he looked up from an automotive magazine at their approach and leapt to his feet. "Gustav! I mean, Mr. Hoffman. It's you."

"It is indeed," Gustav told him, basking in the adulation of an obvious fan.

"This is a real honor." The guard fumbled for a pen and held out the magazine, open to a page bearing Gustav's photo. "Would you mind?"

"Not at all," Gustav replied, signing his photo on the magazine page. He handed it back, he shook the guard's hand. "My associates here will be helping me with some last-minute adjustments." The man's eyes flicked over Alex and Hana for perhaps half a second. "If you would be kind enough to see to it that we have a bit of privacy and are not disturbed . . ." Gustav concluded.

"Yes, sir. Absolutely. I'll just be . . . right over there. If you need me, I mean."

They watched as he picked up his chair and moved offstage, set up beside a service door, and returned to his magazine.

"Engineers are the rock stars of the auto-show circuit," Gustav explained, and led them around the partition. "May I present the Lightning and the Thunderbolt," he announced, voice brimming with pride.

The prototypes were breathtaking: a matching convertible "Lightning" car and a "Thunderbolt" motorcycle with sensuous lines so sleek they seemed to flow from another dimension. Both vehicles were silver, and the car featured a see-through hood. The best phrase Alex could think of to describe them was frozen motion; even when still, they gave the impression of speeding forward.

"They're beautiful," he said.

Gustav watched Hana run a hand over the bike, as if he feared she might damage it. "My instructions are to observe and assist," he told them, "to provide any needed information, and to shoot you if you damage the vehicles." He did not smile as he said this.

Alex indicated the sling on his arm. "Someone beat you to it," he said.

Gustav laughed. "So they did."

Hana swung a leg up and straddled the bike.

"Please. Don't do that," Gustav urged.

Hana grinned and dismounted. "They're both gorgeous," she told Gustav as he snatched a cleaning cloth from a pocket and wiped down the spots she'd touched. Alex and Hana shared a smile.

"I'll need the power specs," Alex said, "so I don't overload the engines."

Gustav hauled an iPad mini from his overstuffed bag. "What exactly is this Energy X?" he asked, bringing up the specs.

"I don't know."

"You've tested it?"

"Of course."

"And you still don't know."

"Nope."

Gustav grunted and showed Alex the specs. "Impressive," Alex said.

"I've worked on these vehicles for four years," Gustav told him.

"Then another few hours won't hurt, right?"

"Hopefully not."

The next several hours were spent modifying car and bike to accept their new Energy X power sources. Gustav had already prepared the crystal boxes in accordance with Alex's emailed instructions, as well as several crystal resistors of various thicknesses for each. He'd also had the Lightning's engine compartment shielded.

Initially skeptical, Gustav became an instant convert when Alex handed him a power-energy meter and quickly opened the lid on the box containing Bloo. The meter maxed out immediately, as Alex had known it would. Thunderbolt and Lightning's headlights lit up, despite the fact that their batteries had been disconnected, and a murmur of dissatisfaction sounded from the room beyond the partition as the big room's lights flickered briefly. After a brief pause, Gustav had pronounced, "This changes everything." From that point on, he couldn't be helpful enough.

As day wore into evening, the other teams in the showroom finished their work and departed. The young guard was only too happy to go out and bring them back a meal, for which he was handsomely tipped. Later, a work crew appeared with mannequins dressed like race-car drivers and supermodels and placed them in designated spots on the main floor. "Someone's idea of a theme," Gustav said as they watched from the stage during one of their brief breaks.

Once the work crew left, the lights were dimmed to near-darkness, and the whole vast room took on the appearance of a futuristic cave with still-life figures and darkly gleaming cars. With no one keeping watch, Hana slipped off the stage and went exploring, while Alex and Gustav labored under work lights behind the partition.

Every now and then, Gustav would peer into the dimness, watching as Hana tried out the driver's seats in various unaffordable vehicles. "I can't be responsible for any damage your young lady friend may inflict," he said to Alex at one point.

Alex didn't respond. He was too busy test-fitting the crystal boxes in place: one beneath the Lightning's transparent hood, the other just over the Thunderbolt's taillight. "Almost finished," he announced, straightening. "Now we just knock a few ten-gram pieces off the rock and adjust the resistors to match the desired power output. The thicker the crystal over the hole, the less energy makes it out of the box."

Gustav scratched the bald part of his head. "It's that simple? No heat buildup, no converter?"

Alex shook his head. "There's no off switch on this baby; power flows directly into the wires, 24/7. That's why we need the isolation switches."

"Where do you think the energy comes from?"

"No idea. Channeled from another dimension for all I know. Or care. For now, it's enough that it works." He lined up three crystal boxes on the rolling workbench beside the car: the one housing Bloo, and the two empties brought by Gustav.

From the showroom floor, Hana could see the blue glow reflecting off the ceiling.

"We have to make the transfers quick," Alex said, "or we'll wreck everything in the building with an electrical circuit."

Gustav swallowed hard and nodded.

"I'll do the transfers, you close the boxes, okay?"

Alex readied his pocketknife and slid aside the cover from the big box. The stage lights came to life as Alex sliced off a tiny piece of the fist-sized EX rock and dropped it into one of the smaller boxes. He and Gustav closed their boxes at the same time. "You okay?" Alex asked, noting Gustav's sudden pallor. He seemed panicked at the thought of destroying a few million dollars' worth of automobiles in a matter of seconds. Gustav nodded.

They repeated the process without mishap, and Gustav seemed to recover somewhat.

Alex put Bloo back in his pack and zipped it shut. "I'm going to double-check the output on these before installing them," he said, indicating the two smaller boxes.

Gustav appeared to weigh his reply, then said, "I must visit the men's room. Too much schnitzel, I'm afraid." He gestured toward the wheeled partitions as he left. "We can remove these once the power sources are in place."

Hana watched him say something to the young guard by the door and disappear from view. She moved onto the stage and stood beside Alex, then sat on the bike again. "When the cat's away," Alex said.

OUTSIDE, A DARK-GREEN 1970 BARRACUDA RUMBLED up to the service entrance. Phantom stepped from the passenger side, limped to the door, and picked the lock as Gretchen drove away. This job was dragging on, and that was never good. His source had assured him the target would be here. Then again, the source had said the same thing about the Savoy, and that hadn't panned out.

Admittedly, he'd underestimated the target, and he was angry—mostly with himself. He'd never been much for excuses, or for emotional investment—but this was becoming personal, and every evasion by the target felt like a fresh slap in the face. He needed to finish this. Tonight.

The lock surrendered at his practiced touch, and he focused on the task at hand. He drew a pistol and suppressor, fitted them together, and made sure there was a round in the chamber. With one last glance at the alley behind him, he slipped inside the building.

ALEX FINISHED WITH THE CAR AND CLOSED THE HOOD. He rolled the partition aside, killed the work lights, and carried the new EX fragment to the bike. Its eerie blue glow cast Hana in an otherworldly light and, for a moment, it was easy to imagine they were the only two people in the world. When he was close enough, Hana leaned over and kissed him.

As she seemed disinclined to move, Alex installed the box with Hana still astride the bike. As he rose and looked toward Hana, he saw the service door open, the light from the hall beyond silhouetting a figure in the doorway. It wasn't Gustav. He saw the guard rise quickly. There was a flame-colored flash, illuminating the face of the figure in the doorway: the man who'd tried to kill Alex, holding a gun with a too-long barrel.

Alex froze, heart pounding in his chest. "Don't move," he whispered, his face mere inches from Hana's. He watched over her shoulder as the guard crumpled to the floor and Phantom stepped into the room. The door swung closed behind him, and the dimness returned.

Hana's eyes flicked to the side, but she didn't turn her head.

"It's him," Alex breathed. He didn't have to explain who. "I don't suppose you brought a gun," he whispered.

"This is Britain."

"Tell that to him."

"He's going to see the glow."

She was right. The Lightning's engine compartment blocked the light from five sides, but the clear hood meant EX's signature glow was visible on the ceiling. And the rolling workbench beside the Thunderbolt bike was the only thing blocking its light from that side. The moment the killer's eyes adjusted to the gloom, he couldn't help but see them both, outlined in blue. It was only a matter of time.

Phantom stepped away from the door. The room was huge, with dozens of cars and scores of mannequins scattered among them. Still half blind from the brightly lit hall, he peered into the gloom, waiting for his night vision to kick in. It took longer than it used to.

Alex lost sight of the killer when he slipped into shadows, but picked him up again when he stepped closer. Moving with excruciating slowness, Alex reached past Hana to the workbench, fingers closing around a wrench. He looked to Hana, then flicked his gaze from the bike to the streetside windows, and back again. She nodded, thumb hovering over the starter button. He slowly brought the wrench back to his side.

Something caught Phantom's eye: movement. He spun around, gun held out before him, every sense alert. Part of the ceiling over the stage appeared to be . . . glowing blue. He started toward the stage. One of the mannequins moved, and something glinted through the air, straight for his head.

The instant the wrench left his hand, Alex grabbed his pack and swung onto the bike behind Hana. He felt the Thunderbolt hum to life beneath him and held on with both hands, gritting his teeth at the pain in his shoulder. Then the world spun as the bike turned, melting rubber across the polished stage. He had a quick impression of the killer ducking and the wrench shattering a windshield beside his head. Then the bike launched off the end of the stage, skipped across the Bugatti's hood, and hit the floor. The tile was so slick the bike almost went out from under them, which was a good thing, because bullets streaked through the space where they'd been, punching holes in the Bugatti.

Hana pulled it out and raced for the nearest window. A mannequin head exploded beside them, glass flying everywhere as they ducked low and their attacker tried to shoot them through the windows of the cars they passed.

Seconds later, they smashed through the huge covered window and plunged blind into the street. Glass and paper fell away, revealing some kind of delivery truck, right in front of them. Hana swerved so hard Alex was sure he'd fly off the bike and under the truck's wheels. And then they were clear.

Headlights flicked on beside the building as they passed, and the roar of an old engine drowned out the bike's electric hum. Alex twisted around to look behind them. A Barracuda slewed onto the street in pursuit, accelerating so fast it had to be a Hemi or nitrous. Farther back, he saw another car skid onto the road, flashing silver in the streetlights: Lightning. He tapped Hana on the shoulder and yelled, "Trouble!" She nodded and turned hard onto the next street as gunshots sounded behind them, echoing off the skyscrapers all around.

Alex glanced over his shoulder as the 'Cuda skidded around the corner, barely making it. The Lightning came close behind, cutting a tighter line. Hearing car horns, he looked ahead and saw traffic. Hana wove a serpentine path through modern compacts, while the 'Cuda plowed through them, tossing them aside like fleas off a dog.

The 'Cuda screamed closer. An arm hung out the driver's window, aiming a gun. But the car was sideswiped as the driver fired. The bullet shattered the bike's taillight. Hana cut right, crossing traffic, and rocketed up another street. The cars behind them suddenly slowed, headlights winking out. Dark skyscrapers lit up as they passed, then fell dark again. Alex craned his neck and looked down; the bullet or shrapnel had smashed a hole in the crystal box above the taillight.

With no electronic components to fry, the 'Cuda kept coming—as did the Lightning, with its shielded engine. Alex saw a ramp ahead on the right, leading up. "Ramp!" he yelled.

At first he thought Hana hadn't heard him, because she

took the bike to the left instead, crossing several lanes. But she was just baiting their pursuers; at the last second, she swung back, darting between cars and flying up the ramp. Weight and momentum working against it, the 'Cuda couldn't get back across fast enough to make the ramp.

The Lightning lived up to its name, angling up the ramp after them. There was little traffic here, and Hana twisted the throttle open, the speedometer climbing past 180 miles per hour. It was strange to hear no rumbling engine, just the soft hum of the bike and the roar of the wind.

Thunderbolt and Lightning raced along the elevated roadway. Alex caught a glimpse of the speedometer, pushing past 220 miles per hour—and still the car kept pace. He felt something whiz past him and saw a rip appear in Hana's jacket collar. There was blood on her neck, but the bullet had just grazed her.

She aimed the bike at an off-ramp and barely made it. The Lightning followed, sparking off the railing. Hana braked hard and swerved onto another street. Unable to slow as quickly as the bike, the heavier Lightning overshot the turn and had to swing back, giving them some breathing room. Hana veered off the road, over the sidewalk—and down the steps into the tube station.

When they reached the platform, there was nowhere to go. Travelers regarded them oddly, some taking videos with their phones amidst the mad ruckus. Looking back, Alex saw headlights on the stair wall. A loud din, then the Lightning materialized, immediately trailed by a path of destruction and panicked would-be tube-goers. He pointed over Hana's shoulder, toward their only option: the tracks. Hana nodded, dropped the bike into gear, and launched the bike off the platform. Alex nearly fell off when they hit the track bed. Hana gunned the motor, starting a bone-jarring ride into the train tunnel.

Hana looked back as the Lightning flew off the platform at an angle, landed roughly, then raced down the tube-shaped tunnel after them.

"Look out!" Alex yelled as a train rounded the curve ahead, coming straight at them. There was no way the bike could pass beside it. Hana twisted the throttle, speeding up instead of slowing. Just ahead, the tunnel widened to two tracks. If they could get there before the train . . .

The conductor blasted the horn, a deafening sound in the narrow confines. Hana aimed the bike at the quickly shrinking gap ahead. Just when Alex thought they'd surely crash and die, she dodged onto the second track. The bike jinked sideways as the train barreled past, catching Alex's sleeve. For an instant, he thought he'd be pulled from the bike—but his jacket ripped and they were free.

PHANTOM SAW THE BIKE DODGE THE TRAIN AHEAD and knew he could never do the same. He tried to turn the car around, but there wasn't room. The front end caught on the rounded wall. The car flipped and spun, wedging upside down between the walls, five feet off the ground. He found himself hanging upside down in the seat, looking at the oncoming train.

He unbuckled the seat belt and fell to the tracks. He could see the blue glow through the buckled hood. So close. He glanced at the train again, then reached up into the engine compartment.

His fingers closed around the glowing box and he wrenched at it with all his strength, knowing there would be no second chance. He felt the mount give, and it was his.

The train's wheels screeched on the tracks, trying to stop, but there was no room. Phantom ducked under the car and hugged the wall beside a support beam. The wall was curved, but so was the train. Still, if he could make himself as flat as the beam . . .

The train smashed through the car beside him, obliterating it. The engine tore a chunk out of the wall beside his head before the train shoved it farther down the tube. It sounded like the end of the world. And then the train was past, leaving him with the glowing blue box. He dropped it in a pocket and followed the train. When it finally ground to a halt and the passengers stepped off to gawk and make their way to the next station, he joined them.

ALEX SAW A STATION COMING INTO VIEW AHEAD. PART of the platform had been jackhammered away, and construction equipment had been parked on the rest of it. A huge banner on the wall read STATION CLOSED FOR REPAIRS. A pile of dirt and rubble sloped down from the chewed-up platform, and Hana gunned the bike up this and stopped on level ground. "You okay?" she asked.

"Never better," Alex replied. "You think the train got him?"

"Let's not hang around to find out." She took them up the stairs, through the yellow CAUTION tape and onto the street in an upscale shopping district, the stores closed for the night.

They glided down the road, shop windows lighting up as they passed, then falling dark again. Hana's cell rang. She picked it up.

"I thought you took the battery out?" Alex said.

"I put it back. I was about to call Nigel when this happened."

A loud rumble sounded ahead, and the 'Cuda slewed into view, screeching around a corner. Bullets flew out the window. Hana dropped the phone. Alex snagged it from the air as she turned the bike and powered up an alley. The 'Cuda followed, driver reloading.

"A little busy now!" Alex yelled into the phone. He thought he heard helicopter blades in the background.

"Alex? This is Nicholas Miles. Gustav tells me you're touring London in my prototypes."

"Not exactly." Gunfire sounded from behind as Hana veered onto the next street.

"I'm over the city right now. In a helicopter. How can I help? Both vehicles have GPS, but I've lost the car."

"Can you pick us up? We're being shot at!"

There was a pause on the line. He heard the 'Cuda leave the alley behind them, then a gunshot. One of the side-view mirrors shattered. Hana dove into another alley, blocking further shots.

"Can you make it to Lloyd's?" Nicholas asked over the phone.

Alex leaned up and yelled to Hana. *"Airlift! Lloyd's?"* She nod-ded. "We're on!" Alex said into the phone. A bullet ripped the cell from his hand. Another hit the bike. The engine stuttered, but Hana kept pushing it, using corners to break the line of fire. Then the engine cut out entirely and left them drifting. Hana restarted, getting a burst of speed—then nothing.

Alex looked up at the sound of rotor blades beating the air, and saw the chopper pass overhead as buildings lit up and went dark around them. The break in the crystal case over the bike's taillight was in the rear wall, so the chopper was in no danger.

Alex heard the Cuda gaining behind them, but the gunshots had stopped. He hoped that meant their pursuer was out of bullets. A silver tower rose in front of them: the Lloyd's building, with its famous glass-walled exterior elevators. The engine caught again. Hana hit the building's stairs at an angle and they left the ground, crashing half through the nearest elevator wall. Alex reached out and slammed the button for the top floor.

The elevator started up as the 'Cuda screamed toward them. They could only watch as it hit the stairs at the same angle they had—and left the ground, as they had. Alex could see the driver—a blonde woman—clearly. Her hands gripped the wheel as the car grew larger and smashed into the elevator's bottom corner, ripping half the floor away and disappearing beneath them.

The top of the rising elevator car pulled away from the building, tilting out over space. Bright blue lights flashed in the distance, coming closer as the helicopter circled overhead. Its rotor wash caused the elevator to lurch farther outward. They were too heavy. "Shove the bike out!" Alex yelled. Hana's look told him that wasn't happening, and he wasn't sure he could manage the bike's weight with his injured shoulder. They were both gazing up at the chopper when the 'Cuda's driver pulled herself up through the floor.

Alex felt a sudden gut-kick, followed by a fist crashing into the bullet wound in his shoulder. The pain from the latter was staggering. Hana backhanded Gretchen in the throat, a glancing blow. Gretchen backed into Alex, and he felt himself falling. He threw both arms wide, catching himself before plunging through the damaged floor. Feet dangling in midair, he grabbed onto a section of broken handrail.

Gretchen drew a blade, but Hana closed before she could use it, locking up the knife arm and bashing it against the wall. Gretchen kneed her in the stomach, but Hana held on, raking her attacker's arm across the jagged glass of the shattered wall until the knife fell away and tumbled into space.

Gretchen kneed her in the gut again, bending her over. Alex could see the next knee strike would be to Hana's face.

He reached out and wrapped an arm around Gretchen's right foot. Hana pulled back and kicked her in the chest. Alex let go of the foot and watched as their attacker fell backward over the bike and plummeted thirteen stories.

Hana grabbed his hand and helped him up. The floor shifted under them and started making a grinding noise. The bike rolled toward the edge, stopping when the crystal box over the taillight hit metal—and broke apart completely. The Lloyd's building lit up beside them, and Alex heard the chopper engine falter above them.

Moving as fast as he could, he snatched the EX fragment from its shattered container and thrust it into the box in his pack, alongside Bloo. He slid the lid into place, blocking the blue stone's output. The building went dark again, and the helo's engine regained its smooth roar.

The elevator creaked to the roof as the chopper touched down. Nicholas and two other men ran over to help. "The bike!" Hana yelled over the rotors. Working together, they grabbed hold of the bike and rolled it up the sloping floor. They had it most of the way onto the roof when the elevator car sheared from its track and fell away. Hana nearly went with it, but Alex grabbed onto her and Nicholas onto him.

Battered and bleeding on the 'Cuda's crushed hood, Gretchen saw the elevator coming. She tried to move, but her body wouldn't cooperate. All she could do was watch it fall and welcome the blackness.

On the roof, Nicholas asked Alex and Hana if they were all right, then introduced himself. He was in his thirties, with Scandinavian good looks and a South African accent.

"Sorry about the prototypes," Alex said.

"No worries," Nicholas told him. "If we can get the traffic-cam footage, we'll be the hit of the show!"

"Is Gustav okay?" Hana asked.

"Upset but fine. He'll get over it."

The sound of sirens penetrated the roar of the rotors. "What about the police?" Alex said.

"No time! I'll talk to them later!" He gestured toward the chopper.

"We *must* take the bike," Hana insisted.

Nicholas and his crew looked from Hana, to bike, to chopper, and finally to Alex, who shrugged. "No way that fits inside," said one of the crew.

Hana pointed at the chopper's belly. "What's that?"

The others looked. Nicholas smiled. "Cargo hook!"

They found a braided steel cable in the tool compartment, wrapped it around the bike frame, and slipped both ends over the cargo hook. Two minutes later, they were airborne, passing high above arriving police cars. One of the crew used a first-aid kit to bandage Hana's neck. "So," Nicholas said, "where do you want to go today?"

"Not sure," Alex replied. "Can we borrow your phone to find out?"

"You bet."

Hana used it to call Nigel.

"By the way," Alex said, "thanks for saving our lives."

"All part of the job," Nicholas quipped. "May I see the cause of all this mayhem?"

Alex took the crystal box from his pack and handed it to him.

Nicholas regarded Energy X in silence for a moment before speaking. "So this is the future."

"We hope so."

"And you've no idea how it does what it does?"

"None. But I do know it's a million years old. Literally. So running it down seems unlikely."

Nicholas returned the box, a little reluctantly it seemed.

Hana hung up Nicholas's cell and handed it back. "We have a destination," she announced.

A SHORT TIME LATER, THE CHOPPER EASED DOWN IN A seaside clearing, setting the bike down first and landing beside it. Alex and Hana thanked Nicholas again and hopped to the ground. Hana gazed longingly at the Thunderbolt. Nicholas stepped to the ground, unclipped the cable from the cargo hook, and climbed back inside.

"Keep it!" he called out, and the chopper roared back into the sky.

Hana beamed gleefully.

Alex looked around. "Where are we?" he asked.

"Welcome to St. Ives."

A pair of headlights flicked to life and drew closer until an antique pickup truck came into view and stopped beside them. It was so old Alex wondered how it could possibly still run. The door squeaked open and a grizzled, tweed-garbed old man with bushy brows got out. He looked healthy for a man of his obvious years. Hana introduced them, telling Alex this was Nigel's father, Grant. "He has a home on the seafront, not far from here."

"I'm hopin' you'll be safe there," Grant said with a Cornish accent, opening the truck's tailgate. He slid down an old board as a ramp for the bike.

Alex gazed out at the inky ocean, moonlight reflecting off the wave tops. Alex and Hana pushed the bike up the ramp into the truck bed, and Grant tied it down with practiced hands. He seemed a man of few words.

"Samantha said you worked for *National Geographic*?" Alex said, thinking to start a conversation.

"Used to. Retired."

"Grant's on the St. Ives town council," Hana said, fixing Alex with a meaningful gaze. "He makes important decisions."

"Important in a small town don't mean much anywhere else," Grant replied, finishing up and closing the gate. "We'd best be on our way, then."

The three of them climbed into the cab, and the old truck bounced along the beach until it reached a paved road. They took this for a short distance, paralleling the night-black sea, then pulled up the drive of a well-lit bungalow. A short hedge surrounded the property. Exterior floodlights revealed walls painted teal blue, large skylights in a gray slate roof, and a wrap-around two-level deck. It was a short walk to the water, and the nearest neighbors were barely visible.

"Make yourself at home," their host told them. "I'll put a kettle on. There's an open patio in back. Perfect for lovebirds."

They circled the house to the back porch as Grant went inside, enjoying the view as the moon broke free of scudding clouds and cast its silver light across the water. "You know, St. Ives wouldn't make a bad candidate for conversion," Hana said after a moment. "And we've got the head of the town council right here . . ."

"Should we make an executive decision?" Alex suggested.

Moments later, the patio door slid open and Grant emerged with tea. "This should calm your nerves a bit. Had a bit of a rough day from what I hear . . . . Anyway, bed's made up for you, room's on your left when you come in. So when you're done out here, lock up before you turn in. It's late for me, so I'm off to bed."

"Thank you for letting us stay here," Alex said.

"Mmm. Any friend of Nigel's is welcome here. Good night, pleasant dreams, all that." He went back inside.

When the inside lights went off, Alex said, "Let's sleep on it. I don't remember St. Ives being on Nigel's list. Oh, and I have something for you." He pulled a necklace from his pocket—a tiny, glowing bit of Energy X inside a small, faceted crystal case on a black leather cord.

Hana's eyes lit up. "It's beautiful! Thank you."

"I thought you might like it."

She gave him a kiss. "When did you find time to make that?" she asked.

"Here and there. I finished up at the hotel, while you were in the shower." He reached out and placed it over her head. The cord rested lower than the bullet wound on her neck, so it wouldn't chafe. Hana put her arms around him and pulled him close.

CHAPTER 34

ST. IVES TOWN COUNCIL

ALEX WOKE TO THE SWEET AROMA OF ENGLISH TEA and the sound of waves lapping at the beach. He rolled out of bed, followed the scent, and ended up in the dining room with Grant and Hana. Walls and shelves bore photos of Grant and his *National Geographic* travels, along with souvenirs from exotic destinations around the globe.

"Good morning," Alex said, sitting beside Hana.

"A good morning it is, young man. What's your pleasure, PG Tips or Yorkshire Red? Me, I go with the Yorkshire, but everyone else in England likes PG Tips."

"I'll have what you're having," Alex said, inhaling the aroma. Their host seemed a bit more talkative this morning. Maybe he was warming to them. Then again, maybe he just ran out of good cheer by nightfall. Alex poured from the indicated teapot and offered a toast. "To a less exciting day." He blew on the steaming hot brew and took a sip. Grant's tea did not disappoint. "I love it," he said. "It's got some kick to it."

"Anyone up for poached eggs and baked beans?" Grant asked, rising. They told him they were famished, and he set off for the kitchen.

"How's your neck?" Alex asked.

Hana tapped the bandage with a finger. "Could have been worse."

"Tell me about it."

"How's the shoulder?"

"Still there."

Grant returned with two plates and silverware.

"That was quick," Alex said.

"Made this earlier. I'm up at dawn."

"You're not joining us?" Hana asked.

"Already ate. I'll be running off to work now. Important decisions to make and all that." He gave them a wink.

"Thanks for the hospitality," Hana said.

"Don't mention it. Good to have some young folks in my old house for a change. I'll be back around four." He tugged on a tweed hat and paused with his hand on the door. "If the house is still here," he said, and stepped outside.

Alex looked to Hana, not understanding.

"I think he means if no one blows it up because you're in it," she explained.

"There is that," he said, sampling the baked beans. "Any chance we'll be found here?"

"Not if we lie low. Nigel and I talked about this place without mentioning any names, so even if someone was listening in, they'd be clueless."

"Good. Now that we're alone . . ."

"Yes?"

"We need to talk about how these guys know our every move. Even we didn't know we'd be at the auto show until yesterday."

"Phone tap, phone trace?"

"I'm not convinced of that. Not if Sunil's as good as you say he is. And these guys showed up too soon after you put the battery back in, so it's not that . . . Who knew we were at the auto show?"

"Gustav knew—and disappeared just before all hell broke loose. Nicholas knew, probably others at Ampere."

"They knew about the hotel but not the cottage. . . . We have to consider the possibility it's one of us."

Hana thought about it. "I suppose it's possible. At least we know it's not me."

"Do we?"

"You're serious?" Hana said, indignant. "I saved your life."

"What better way to get close to me, earn my trust?"

She slapped him, hard.

Alex cupped her face in his hands and kissed her. "That's the reaction I was looking for."

"Want to see it again?"

"Pass. Thanks, though. I know it's not Sam."

"Okay, who else? I know it's not Nigel."

"Because . . ."

"Because I know. The cause is everything to him, and you're good for the cause. He'd probably take a bullet for you himself."

"Which leaves Sunil and Patrick," Alex said.

"Let's say I buy your theory. How do we find out who it is?"

The room fell silent while they thought about it. Then Alex

said, "I have an idea. . . . We bring Sam and Nigel out here, without telling the others. We have the SAS boys hide two locked boxes near the cottage, then call Sunil and Patrick separately and tell them I hid EX before I was shot—"

"—and ask them to get it," Hana finished.

"One of them will call us when they find the box," Alex said.

Hana nodded. "And one of them will call someone else."

AN HOUR LATER, NIGEL AND SAM WERE AT GRANT'S bungalow, having told the others they needed to buy supplies for Alex's next project. Nigel had assigned Sunil and Patrick separate tasks at opposite ends of the property so the calls would come when they were apart. Alex, Hana, Sam, and Nigel sat around the dining room table. No one was happy at the prospect of discovering a traitor in their midst, but it had to be done.

"Everyone ready?" Alex asked. The others nodded. Using Nigel's cell, Alex sent Sunil into the woods, and told Patrick the box was in the garage. When it was done, Sam said, "You realize if they both call us, we'll have no idea how our info is leaking out."

"Unless it's someone at this table," Nigel added. No one said anything after that; they just waited.

IN THE TREES BEYOND THE COTTAGE, SUNIL CHECKED the rock formation Alex had sent him to, going over it twice before spotting the box. He looked around, then pulled out his phone.

At the same time, Patrick dug through boxes, old tools, and

car parts in the garage, finally coming up with the locked box Alex had described. He made a quick call on his cell.

INSIDE GRANT'S BEACH HOUSE, NIGEL'S PHONE RANG. Every eye in the room fixed on the cell as it vibrated across the table.

STILL IN THE TREES, SUNIL HUNG UP THE PHONE, TUCKED the box under an arm, scoped his surroundings again and hurried toward the cottage.

Patrick pocketed his cell and put the box on the backseat of his car in the garage. He opened the garage door, slid behind the wheel, and turned the key. The engine didn't start, didn't even crank. He pumped the gas pedal and tried again without success. Then his eyes caught movement beside the car: it was Duncan, lowering himself from the rafters overhead. Face painted black to match the shadows he'd come from. The ex-SAS man fixed him with the most predatory stare he'd ever seen.

AT THE BEACH HOUSE, ALEX HUNG UP THE CELL. "THAT was Sunil," he announced.

"So it's Patrick," said Nigel. The phone rang again.

"Or not," said Hana.

Alex picked up, listened for a moment and hung up. "That was Duncan. Patrick dialed a number in New York and tried to run with the box."

"Wow," said Samantha.

"I just can't believe it," Nigel added.

"We need to get Sunil out here," Alex said. "Have him put the cottage back on the grid and bring the EX power source with him. Also, we need to speed things up. We're here now; Sunil will join us. Nigel's dad heads the town council. Hana and I were talking last night, and we think we should convert St. Ives."

"It's a very small town," Nigel said, "and the council can be ornery."

"Small means fast," Alex said. "We convince them, and it's done."

"Instant proof of concept," Sam agreed. "The whole world will know it works, that this is real."

"The place will be a tourist mecca," Alex added. "People will come from all over the world to see the first town run on Energy X."

"The town does have financial challenges," Nigel told them. "They can barely pay the power bill."

"Perfect," Sam said. "I mean, not that they can't pay the bills, but that we can fix that. It should be a slam dunk."

"A what?" Nigel asked.

"An easy sell," Sam explained. But Nigel seemed unsure. "What?" Sam asked.

"It's just that the St. Ives town council is run by old-timers and they're a bit set in their ways," Nigel said.

"Well, we'll just have to make them see the light," Alex said. He took EX from his pack and set it on the table. Its glow washed over them, filling the room.

Later that afternoon, Grant arranged for an impromptu council meeting. As expected, the council was unsurprisingly skeptical of the idea, even after repeated assurances that the conversion would cost the town nothing. The council members, few of whom were under seventy, were somewhat suspicious when Alex said the town should remain wired to the power-company grid.

The turning point came when a particularly contentious member asked why, if they'd never need outside power again, they should keep the connection. "Because," Alex told them, "this installation will generate many times more electricity than St. Ives can possibly use. The law allows you to send any excess energy into the grid, and the power company is legally obligated to buy all of it."

A quiet murmur spread through the council. "You mean they'll be paying *us?*" someone asked.

"St. Ives and OTW will split the proceeds, but yes. In fact, with any luck, we'll bankrupt the power company." And with that, there was no further opposition.

OVER THE COURSE OF THE NEXT WEEK, A CREW OF electricians installed the bypass and power-return hardware. There was the occasional question as to what exactly would be powering the town. These were met with talk of a planned wave-power generator to be installed the following year. The foreman seemed to have his doubts that such a scheme would work, but a job was a job, and he saw that his crew did their part well. Alex and Sunil made the final connections.

Sworn to secrecy until the official announcement, the council called a public meeting in the town square and invited local media as well—all without revealing the purpose of the meeting. "An important announcement about the future of St. Ives" was all they said. National and international media would be on the scene soon enough; this was for the people of St. Ives.

At the appointed time, shortly after dark on a Monday—Sam's idea, both for visual effect and to give the media a full workweek to spread the story—the town square was filled to capacity. The mayor, a corkscrew-haired old lady with the energy of an eighteen-year-old, stepped onto the small stage, accompanied by the deputy mayor—a thin, gray-bearded, delicate-looking man. The two of them were about to become global celebrities.

Alex felt he should speak, if for no other reason than to help draw media attention to the project. At the same time, he had no desire to hog the spotlight or give his persistent would-be assassin time to catch up with him. In the end, he'd asked the mayor to do a quick introduction, after which he'd speak briefly for the townsfolk and the cameras—and then leave the rest to Nigel, Sam, and Sunil. He'd already recorded a longer talk to be sent out with the press release the moment he left the stage.

"Good evening and welcome," the mayor said into the microphone. "We are graced today with an historic juncture. Starting today, St. Ives will be a household name throughout the world, thanks to the man it is my great pleasure to introduce to you tonight—Mr. Alex Watson."

Alex took the stage. The curious murmuring was replaced by a stunned silence. For a moment, Alex stood silent as well; he'd never liked public speaking, even before small groups. Now the whole town was right in front of him, and millions more would be watching online and on TV. He tried not to think about it, and focused on what he wanted to say.

"I imagine many of you know me," he began. "And, through OTW's broadcasts, what I mean to do. The world has to change. Energy X gives us the means to do that. A better world starts right here in St. Ives, tonight. Your town is the first to be powered entirely by Energy X. From now on, the power company will pay St. Ives for generating power, instead of the other way around."

The crowd was caught between disbelief and gratitude. "Let's see it then!" someone shouted.

"You got it," Alex shouted back. "Let there be darkness!"

On cue, Sunil killed the lights in the square. Truth be told, most of the town had been smoothly switched over and was already running on Energy X, but the cameras needed something dramatic.

Alex drew EX from his pack and held it out before him. Seeing the blue glow of the rumored power source in front of them, the crowd gasped. "Let there be light!" Alex called out. Sunil threw the switch to convert the rest of the town, including the lights in the square, which snapped on around the crowd. "You've just made history," Alex announced, "by converting to 100 percent clean energy."

A ripple of wonder passed through the crowd, smiles lighting every face. Alex slipped EX back into his pack. "I'd like nothing more than to stay and answer questions," he said. "But as you know, I have my own personal hitman, who's no doubt on his way here right now. So I'll leave you in the capable hands of OTW chair Nigel Schaefer and OTW public affairs head Samantha Watson. I really can't say enough good things about their organization—or the wonderful town of St. Ives. Thank you."

Applause rose from the square, becoming thunderous. Alex waved, left the stage, and disappeared into the town hall. Hana was waiting on the far side, and the two of them were gone long before any curious reporters could circle around the buildings forming the town square.

JACK AND PETE WATCHED ALEX'S RECORDED PRESS release on the executive suite's TV. "The reason I videotaped this statement is because someone's been trying to kill me," Alex said to the camera. "Over this." He held up the crystal box with Energy X glowing inside. The lights around him dimmed to black, to give viewers a better look at the rock. Its glow turned his face an eerie blue. "I call it Energy X," Alex said. "But, hey, every new technology has its critics, right?

"Things evolve. Dinosaurs gave way to mammals, just as traditional power sources will give way to this. The town of St. Ives is now completely powered by Energy X. I'd also like to announce something else . . ."

"There's more?" Pete said, not knowing what came next but dreading it just the same.

"The formation of EXpower," Alex continued, "a company dedicated to powering the world. Cheaply. Reliably. Eternally. The company will make a public stock offering in the next forty-eight hours." On the screen, Alex seemed finished, then added, "By the way, if you're currently invested in any kind of oil, gas, coal, or nuclear power—now might be a good time to sell." Alex winked at the camera.

"Oh. My. God." Pete said.

Jack swept a paperweight off the desk and hurled it into the TV. The screen didn't shatter, but it did split into several jagged shards, hissing and sparking. Several of the sparks landed on the $32,000 Oriental rug, setting it alight. He had to jump up and stamp the flames out with his feet.

CHAPTER 35
THE MYSTERIES OF ENERGY X

LATER THAT NIGHT, NIGEL, SAM, AND SUNIL MADE THEIR way to Grant's beach house, where Alex and Hana were already waiting. Grant was staying with a lady friend for the night. The group watched the BBC recap of the night's announcements.

"Like Mr. Watson's encounter with American fighter jets and his dramatic pursuit through the streets of London," the BBC anchor said, "his video press release went viral just moments after its release—"

Alex killed the TV.

"Hey!" Samantha said.

"I'm tired of being the center of attention," Alex said, looking flustered.

"Well, you'd better get used to it," Sam told him. "It's going to be like this for a while. Energy X needs a face people can relate to, and that's you."

Alex looked around for support, but found none. "She's right," Nigel said. "Like it or not."

"When did you tape that?" Hana asked.

"Last night," Alex told her. "Upstairs, while you were fixing Nicholas's bike."

"My bike," Hana corrected.

"Forgive me. By the way, isn't your bike—I mean your *other* bike—still at the Savoy?"

"It's coming here tomorrow. We on schedule with that, Nigel?"

"Yes," Nigel replied. "I saw an email earlier. Andrew hired a lorry and should be here by tomorrow afternoon."

"Who's Andrew?" Alex asked.

"He works in our London office," Nigel said. "Manages our finances."

Sunil changed the subject. "You know you can't form a company and do an IPO in forty-eight hours, right?"

"Technically correct," Alex agreed. "Practically irrelevant. I cut a deal with Nicholas. We're renaming a private company he already owns and was planning to take public this week. So all we had to do was amend the IPO."

"Works for me," Sunil said. "So I guess it's a done deal. We take this public, investors give us the money to expand, and EX rules."

"Maybe. There is a problem no one really knows about yet . . . We don't have enough."

"Enough what?" Nigel asked.

"Enough Energy X. What I have is enough to power the U.S., or a few other countries, but this bit I brought with me? Is all there is. Ever."

No one spoke for a moment. "How sure are you?" said Sunil at last.

"Well, it's not from Earth, there's nothing here like it, and we don't know where it came from."

"Ouch."

"How do you know there's not more?" Sunil asked.

"Umm..."

"You mean maybe that's not the only piece that fell?" Hana said.

"Right," Nigel put in. "It could have been something like a meteor shower."

"Or a big rock that broke up on entry," Sunil said.

"In which case it could be scattered across half the globe," Samantha added.

"Or at the bottom of the ocean," Alex said. "But you're right: I don't know for sure."

"Why not?" Sunil asked.

"Other than frying electronics, I haven't found a way to detect it at a distance."

"Radiation?" Sunil said.

"Nothing I could find in a college physics lab. And I can't really show my face anywhere else or let this out of my sight."

"What about Nicholas?" Hana suggested. "Give him a piece, have him put his people on it. You *are* business partners now."

All eyes turned to Alex. "Good idea," he said. "We can ask them to do a full-spectrum analysis, see if it emits anything we can pick up at a distance."

"So, what's our next move?" Sam asked. "After contacting Nicholas?"

"For OTW?" Alex said. "Ride the publicity. Use it to help get your message out there."

"What about you?" Sam said.

"I'm thinking to hole up for a day or two. Brainstorm a bit, see what I come up with. It's only a matter of time until the press realizes Nigel's dad is on the town council and people start banging on the door. Anyone know a place with no distractions?"

No one seemed to have a ready answer, except for Sunil. "I haven't been undistracted in years," he said.

"I know a place," Hana offered.

"I'll grab my bag," Alex told her.

"You mean right now?"

Alex returned with his backpack. "Why not? The more I move around, the safer I am—and the rest of you, too." He looked to Nigel. "I need a favor."

"Name it."

"Take the EX sample Sunil brought from the cottage and take it to Nicholas at the Savoy. Personally. From your hands to his. I'll give him a call, let him know you're coming and what we need."

"Right-o."

Sam packed some sandwiches she'd picked up earlier and put in the fridge, along with a couple of tall aluminum flasks filled to the brim with ice-cold water. She drew Alex into a hug. "Be careful," she told him.

Outside, he watched as Hana pulled a tarp off the Thunderbolt. "You painted it black?"

"Is that a problem?" Her tone made it clear she would brook no resistance in this matter.

"No, I just . . . didn't recognize it."

"That's the idea, since half the known world now knows what it looks like."

Which was an excellent point: Nicholas had milked CCTV

footage of the chase for all it was worth, and a mirror-finished silver bike was hard to miss. She'd even added a padded metal box to hold a new crystal box in position over the replaced taillight. Painted black, of course.

They climbed aboard the bike, pulled on their helmets, and rode off.

PHANTOM SAT ON A ROYAL-BLUE PARK BENCH IN THE heart of Victoria Park, near the pond with the fountain. Children screamed and ran to and fro, throwing balls and playing with their dogs. In the distance, an afternoon cricket match was underway. Phantom took bread slices from a brown paper bag, ripped them into pieces, and tossed them on the ground, watching pigeons vie for morsels and thinking of Gretchen.

Also on the bench, but not so close as to seem familiar to casual passersby, was a long-haired teen with an open laptop. He worked the keyboard with fast, scrawny fingers, squinting through thick glasses.

"Can you hack it?" Phantom asked, not looking at him.

"Might take a few hours."

Phantom tossed another handful of bread, then got up and walked away, leaving the bag behind. The kid slid it over to look inside. He found a short stack of American hundreds buried under bread slices.

THE THUNDERBOLT SLASHED DOWN A RURAL ROAD, with no sound save its odd electric hum and the air rushing past. Suddenly the humming stopped, leaving only the wind.

Hana tried to restart, but the bike drifted to a stop. She and Alex dismounted. "I thought you repaired the damage," Alex said.

"I did."

"Well, we're not out of gas."

Hana checked the wiring. Alex opened the crystal box and looked inside. Energy X was there, but the blue glow was gone. He stared at it for a long time, the color draining from his face.

"What is it?"

"Can I see your necklace?"

She pulled the crystal pendant from beneath her shirt. The tiny bit of Energy X inside had gone dark.

"What's going on, Alex?"

"I don't know," he said gravely. "It's never done this before." He asked for the new phone Sunil had given her at Grant's house. He turned it on, held it over the crystal box on the bike—and opened the box. The phone kept working. He switched it off again, handed it back to Hana, and closed the box.

Alex unzipped his backpack and looked inside as Hana stepped close. His once-glowing chunk of Bloo looked like an ugly lump of coal. "It's dead. And I don't know why."

"You said it would last forever."

"This can't be coincidence. I get hold of it and then it dies? There's something I'm not understanding here . . ."

"Maybe it's just this piece?"

"Call Nigel, ask him to find out if St. Ives is still running. We also need to check the lighthouse, and the piece with Nicholas."

She filled Nigel in on the situation, then put the call on speaker so Alex could listen in. "It's mass hysteria," Nigel told them. "BBC News is all over it. Here, listen."

He must have held the phone up to a TV or computer

speaker, because the next thing they heard was a BBC newscaster. "The town of St. Ives was left completely without power
today when the 'EX system' installed by Alex Watson suddenly
failed for unknown reasons."

"What's going on?" Nigel asked.

"Do you know if the lighthouse is still working?" Alex said.

"My guess is no," they heard Sunil's voice say.

"We can send Duncan or Simon to check it out," Nigel said.

"Please. Just so I know. And check in with Nicholas."

"As soon as we get off the phone. My father and the whole
town council are calling me; what are we going to do?"

"I have no idea," Alex told him. "Let me think for a while. I'll
call you when I come up with something."

"Don't take too long. The media are killing us with this." Nigel
hung up.

JACK AND PETE WATCHED CNN ON A BRAND-NEW
thin-screen TV on the office wall. The newscaster's words were
encouraging. "Energy-company stocks, which had fallen drasti-
cally in the wake of EXpower's IPO announcement, rebounded
sharply within minutes of the news from St. Ives."

Jack eyed the two Energy X samples on the conference table:
one taken from the laptop Alex had left with them, the other
express-shipped by Phantom, who'd taken it from the crashed
Lightning. He rose and poured them each a drink. He and Pete
finished them in one go. "So it's over?" Pete said.

"No. It's not over. Get Justice on the phone. See if they'll put
out an Interpol warrant."

"For what?"

"Manipulating the stock market. Endangering national security. Fraud, if he goes through with the IPO. Do it now, while we've got this slippery bastard by the balls."

ALEX AND HANA WALKED THE SHOULDER OF THE SAME road they'd just been riding on, rolling the bike between them. The area was rural; occasional barns and other weathered structures dotted rolling hills.

"I can't believe it's all gone," Alex said.

"You'll think of something," Hana told him, trying to be encouraging. "We need to hole up someplace where you won't be recognized."

Topping the next hill, they came across a decaying building with a sign so worn it could hardly be read: TREVOR'S MACHINE SHOP. The windows were boarded up, and tall weeds grew in front of the swing-out garage doors. Alex looked around; there wasn't a soul in sight. "How do you feel about breaking and entering?" he asked.

"As long as it's for a good cause."

Hana picked the lock on the chain that ran through the garage-door handles. Alex helped her swing one door open against the weeds. Despite outward appearances, the gloomy interior was full of tools, workbenches, and shelves that sagged with oils and chemicals. There was even an old gas welder in a corner.

"This'll do," Hana decided.

They wheeled the bike inside, pried the boards off the back windows for light, and pulled the garage door shut again. Alex then ran the chain back through the handles for appearances' sake, and climbed in the window. Hana called Andrew and told him to bring her Black Shadow bike to the machine shop, and to pick up a few days' supplies for her and Alex. "He should be here in a few hours," she said after hanging up.

"We're going to have to leave the new bike here, or have Andrew pick it up," Alex said absently. His mind was clearly grappling with bigger problems. Hana thought it sweet that he would even think of her dilemma with the bike, given everything else that was going on. "You worry about powering the world," she said. "I'm going to work a little project. Since we are in a machine shop."

"What project?"

"You'll see when I'm finished."

"Assuming I'm still around. The good folks of St. Ives are probably readying their pitchforks and torches right now."

Alex pondered his Energy X problem while Hana busied herself in the shop. The electricity was off, so she was limited to hand tools and the welder as she constructed a metal frame. She paused to share the meal Sam had packed them, then returned to her task.

SEVERAL HOURS AFTER COMMANDEERING TREVOR'S machine shop, they heard a car pull off the road and park behind the shop. Alex peered out the back window. "It's Nigel," he said.

"What's he doing here?"

Alex shrugged and called out the window. "Go around front and unwrap the chain."

He watched as Nigel stalked from sight. A moment later, the door creaked open. "What the bleeding hell is going on?" Nigel demanded.

"Hello to you, too," Hana told him, doffing her welder's mask.

"Wish I knew," said Alex, feeling more helpless than he'd ever been in his life.

"The St. Ives Town Council is throwing a fit. Nicholas hasn't yet backed out of the IPO, but he's not happy."

Alex started to say something, but Hana spoke first. "Alex will sort this out. Just give him some time." Before he could reply, Hana peppered him with questions. "Did you bring my bike and the supplies, and what happened to Andrew?"

"Yes, yes, and I told him I'd come instead." They stepped outside and walked around back, then wheeled Hana's old bike down a ramp from the back of Grant's pickup and grabbed a duffel from the cab.

"Thanks," Alex told him.

"You fill the tank?" Hana asked.

Nigel nodded. "Where are you going, anyway? There's nothing out here."

"That's the point, isn't it?" Hana argued.

"We have to fix this," Nigel kept on. "We look like idiots."

"I'm aware of that," Alex said, looking in the bag. "Thanks for the supplies."

Nigel seemed ready to snap out a reply, then changed course. "Sorry," he said simply. "The stakes are really high on this one."

Hana pointedly rested a hand an Alex's injured shoulder. "I think he knows that."

"Right. I'll tell everyone not to panic."

"Do as you say, not as you do?" Hana said.

"Something like that. You want me to take Thunderbolt?" Hana shook her head. Nigel shook hands with Alex, gave Hana a quick hug, and was on his way.

"Give me a hand with this, would you?" Hana said.

They hauled her freshly painted tubular frame to the Black Shadow. Hana tightened a few adjustable joints with locking wing nuts, and used the padded clamps she'd welded to the new frame to attach it to the bike frame. The other side she clamped to Thunderbolt's frame. Hana's creation joined the two bikes like twins, three feet apart.

"A dually?" Alex said. He clipped the duffel on top of the new frame, slipped his pack over his good shoulder, and held the door open while Hana started the Black Shadow and guided the double-bike outside. After locking the doors and reboarding the windows, they mounted bikes from different centuries and powered away, leaving the old building behind.

PHANTOM AND THE TEENAGE HACKER SAT IN A COR-
ner booth on the lower level of a bustling, seventies-themed Piccadilly café. Though past lunchtime and too early for dinner, the dimly lit place was packed. Rock music played on the speakers, and the walls were littered with period memorabilia. The chubby waiter who'd served them was dressed like Elvis. Phantom drank tea, while the kid slurped a strawberry shake.

"I got it narrowed down to five," the hacker said. "Gotta be one of them." He spun his laptop around. Phantom saw five blinking yellow dots on a map of England: one in London, one in the southwest, and three elsewhere. The one in the southwest moved slowly eastward.

"Can you send the live feeds to my phone?" Phantom asked.

"I can do that." The kid turned the laptop around and started typing.

Phantom pushed his napkin across the table and left. The kid peeked underneath: another stack of hundreds.

Making his way toward the stairs leading up to ground level, Phantom saw a large biker type rise from the last booth and look from Phantom's face to something over his shoulder and back again. There was a TV on the wall behind Phantom. Tuning out the surrounding din, he heard a newscaster saying Scotland Yard had released a photo of Alex Watson's would-be killer. He didn't need to turn around. What he did need to do was stick a knife in the biker's gut and prop him up so he looked like he was dozing for the next few minutes. Seconds later, it was done.

THE TWIN BIKE TRAVELED A WINDING ROAD THROUGH open country. After the silence of the electric bike, the rumble of the Black Shadow's engine now seemed odd. With the noise and the three-foot distance between them, conversation was impossible, so Alex just took in the sights while wracking his brain for an explanation of what he now thought of as "the EX problem."

Eventually, the ruins of an old castle came into view, conjuring up images of knights and damsels. They made their way to the hilltop and the castle—of which very little was left—and hid the bikes beneath a stone arch. "Ruins," Alex said. "Appropriate. What is this place?"

"Okehampton Castle. It was built in the eleventh century, to keep the locals from revolting. Then it was a hunting lodge. Then Henry the Eighth executed the owner and it became a bakery. Now it's just for tourists. But no one comes this time of year."

Ancient steps led them up an enormous mound to a towering stack of medieval stonework that had once, perhaps, served as the keep wall. They sat at its base, on rocks hewn a thousand years before. In the distance, they could see the rooftops of Okehampton village jutting through old-growth trees. A gentle breeze carried the fragrance of lemon-scented fern and other flowers. It was a perfect summer afternoon: blue sky, green hills, ancient ruins.

"This place reminds me of Japan," Hana said. "Not the look; the feel. Like it's been here forever. Timeless. It gives you a sense of where you came from."

"You were born there?"

She nodded. "Kyoto."

Alex looked around. "I can't say it reminds me of anything. America's new. We have no idea where we came from. Which is probably why we don't have a clue where we're going."

Hana grinned. "Doesn't stop you from being in a hurry to get there."

"Exactly."

"What are we going to do?" Hana asked.

"I was hoping maybe you had some ideas."

They laughed nervously.

"That's not really funny, is it?" Alex said.

THE NEXT MORNING, HANA WOKE IN A SLEEPING BAG Nigel had included with their supplies. A clinging fog covered the now-ghostly landscape. She found Alex sitting cross-legged on the hill, the fist-sized EX rock in one hand. "Did you sleep?" she asked, yawning.

He shook his head. "Couldn't stop thinking. Happens sometimes. That's usually when I get my best ideas." He rubbed tired eyes.

"Any of those coming now?"

"Just one: we're screwed. We don't know what EX is, how it works, why it works or—more to the point—why it doesn't work. So how can we know how to fix it? We've got the future right here, if we can just turn it back on. I don't know, maybe we're just not smart enough to figure it out."

"Well, what do we know?"

"Nothing."

"You said it couldn't be coincidence."

"Right. The thing's been around for eons. It didn't just happen to go on the blink after I picked it up."

"Then you'll figure it out." She leaned in and closed her eyes, offering a kiss. Her throat was blue.

"Get back!" Alex almost shouted, pushing her away.

"*Excuse me?*" The blue glow on her throat disappeared.

"Lean forward again, like we're going to kiss," Alex said.

"Fat chance."

"Oh. Sorry, just . . . It's for science."

She leaned in again. The rock in Alex's hand began to glow.

"Now lean away."

Hana leaned back, and the glow disappeared. "What—"

"Your necklace," Alex said. He reached out and tugged on the leather cord, lifting the crystal pendant with its tiny slice of Energy X from beneath her shirt. When he moved the rock toward Hana, rock and necklace glowed. When he moved them apart, the blue light faded to nothing.

"That's it!" Alex said. "There's some kind of critical mass required. When I kept slicing samples off the main piece, it got too small to power the others. And when I bring these two back together, it's big enough."

"But the piece in the necklace is shielded by the crystal."

Alex placed Bloo back in its own crystal-shielded box and repeated the experiment; once again, both pieces glowed—though with both pieces shielded, they had to be almost touching. "What does that mean?" Hana asked.

"It means the pieces are emitting something that's not stopped by the shielding. Not completely. And who knows how far it carries when there's no shielding. So Nicholas may find a way to detect EX at a distance. Keep these here, close together. I'll check the bike." He hurried down the hill and opened the box over the Thunderbolt's taillight. Inside, the EX fragment glowed brightly. He hurried out from under the arch, ready to give Hana a big thumbs-up, but the drifting morning fog was so thick at the base of the hill he could no longer see the top. Instead, he shouted as loud as he could, "It works!"

He charged back up the hill and arrived out of breath. Hana greeted him with a hug. "I knew you'd figure it out," she said.

"That makes one of us. I'm going to have to borrow your necklace."

"My necklace or power half the world. Hmm. Tough choice."

"Thank you. Text Nigel, see if St. Ives is back up."

Nigel texted back: "checking." Then: "Power box glowing. Switching over . . . WORKS! Will have Sam tell media. Dad wants to know if it's going to stay on this time."

Alex took the phone and texted Nigel: "Yes! Tell Nicholas the

IPO is on." He gave the phone back to Hana. She held it up and swung it around. "I had five bars a minute ago. Now there's no signal."

"Meaning what?" Alex asked.

"Paranoid version? Someone's blocking it. We need to get off this hill."

"Back to the bike," Alex said, keeping his voice low. He dropped the necklace into the crystal box with Bloo, and put them both in his pack. They started back down.

"If it is him, how did he find us?" Hana whispered. "Patrick doesn't know we're here. No one does."

When they reached the bike, Alex tilted the Thunderbolt's seat up and removed a small chip, holding it up. "Nicholas's GPS, remember?" He dropped the chip on a rock and ground his heel on it.

"Let me grab my sleeping bag." Hana stepped away.

Alex clipped the duffel bag to the twin-bike frame. He turned to look for Hana, but couldn't see more than ten feet. He called out softly. "Hana?"

There was a scuffling sound, like shoes on a rock. "She's right here," a male voice answered.

Alex moved to one side and said, "How do I know?"

"Just go!" Hana's voice said.

Alex moved again, to keep Phantom guessing about his location. "What do you want?" he said to the fog.

"Same as always," Phantom said. His voice seemed to be moving as well, but not very far. If he was holding Hana, that would limit his motion. Alex padded back to the bikes and removed the box from the Thunderbolt. "Let her go," he demanded, moving again. "I'll give you the rock."

"Let's see it," came the voice from the fog.

Alex moved close to the sound, and saw a thick shadow in the mist. He crept closer and made out two shapes, welded together. One was too tall to be Hana. Taking careful aim, he hurled the EX fragment he'd taken from the bike, still inside its case. The rock's blue glow arced through the fog and crashed into Phantom's head.

Alex rushed forward, shoving Phantom to the ground and grabbing Hana. He kept going, pulling Hana with him. A suppressed gun coughed twice behind them. One of the bullets skipped off a stone wall by Alex's head.

"Slow down," Hana whispered. "Less noise."

They circled back to the bikes, making as little noise as possible. "What about Energy X?" Hana asked.

"I'd rather have you. Get on." Alex mounted the Thunderbolt as Hana jumped on the Black Shadow. The second the old beast rumbled to life, Phantom would know exactly where they were. "Ready?" she whispered. Alex nodded. Hana kick-started the bike and twisted the throttle hard.

Immediately, they heard bullets ricochet off the arch. But their attacker was on the far side of it now and would have to climb the wall or find the arch in the fog and pass through it before he could get another shot at them.

Hana angled away from the arch, found the road by memory and went as fast as she dared in the ground-hugging fog. If there were more shots, they didn't come close.

CHAPTER 36
THE MESON COUNT

THEY EMERGED FROM THE MIST AS THE ROAD CLIMBED, some distance from the castle. Alex signaled for Hana to pull over. "Where's the nearest place we can get lost?" he asked. "Someplace big."

"Exeter."

"Can we get someone to grab EX from the lighthouse and bring it to us there?" Hana made the call, then removed the battery from her phone. They raced along the A30. Thirty minutes later, they reached the city's outskirts. They stopped at a phone booth to check in with Nigel and tell him about their latest encounter with Phantom. Nigel told them the lighthouse fragment was on its way to Exeter, but he needed to know where to deliver it. He also said Nicholas had left a message, asking Alex to call him. Alex thanked Nigel and dialed Nicholas.

"Glad the rocks are up and running again," Nicholas said. "I'm kind of jammed, so I'll cut to the chase. These things are meson emitters."

"That's weird," Alex thought aloud. "But potentially useful . . . .
Didn't I read you have some kind of cosmic ray detector in orbit,
looking into deep space?"

"I do."

"I don't suppose you can turn that around and point it at the
Earth?"

"It's my satellite. I can damn well do anything I want with it."

"Great. If you find something emitting mesons, chances are
it's another EX rock."

"Or an atom smasher."

"Can you lend me an engineer?"

"Just tell me where."

Alex turned to Hana. "We need an out-of-the-way place with
a lot of electronic components."

"New or used?"

"Doesn't matter."

She gave him a location. He passed it along to Nicholas, told
him what the engineer should bring and hung up, then dialed
another number. "We need to get everyone together. Now."

A HALF HOUR LATER, THEY STOOD INSIDE A WARE-
house-sized, indoor-electronic salvage yard, littered with every
electronic device imaginable. Alex was fairly certain they'd find
everything they needed here. The only downside was that the
place reeked of fried electronics—like fifty tons of shorted-out
batteries.

It took another two hours for everyone else to arrive: Sam,
Nigel, and Sunil with the EX fragment from the lighthouse. It

was after all a weekend, so they should have the place to themselves. Alex filled in the others about their latest run-in with Phantom and Nicholas's discovery.

"Right," Nigel said, "so . . . what are we doing here? It's a bit of a risk bringing everyone to you. If we'd been followed . . ."

"The best way to end the threat is to turn on the world with EX. To do that, we need more than what we have. If Nicholas's satellite gets a hit, we need to be ready to follow up immediately. The satellite can give us a general search zone. But wherever that is—assuming we're that lucky—it's going to be up to us to go in and find it. "

"Okay . . ."

"And to do that, we're going to need some kind of portable meson detector."

Someone pounded on the closest door, making them jump. Sunil moved to look through the peephole. "It's some fat guy with a briefcase," he told the others. Hana joined him, looked through the hole, then opened the door, admitting Gustav.

"Thanks for coming," she told him.

"I go where I'm told," he said, stepping inside with an equipment case. He took in the new surroundings with unspoken disapproval.

"Sorry to leave in such a hurry last time," Alex said.

"Four years of engineering destroyed in moments," Gustav recapped.

"Magnificent machines," Alex said, hoping to change the mood.

"Ja. They were."

"We still have Thunderbolt."

"Ja, Nicholas told me it is yours to keep now. We are working on newer models."

Alex introduced him to the others. Gustav seemed polite, but unimpressed. He opened his case, which had several padded compartments, withdrew a glowing crystal box, and placed it on a sorting table. "That is the bulk of the sample you sent to Nicholas. We kept a tiny bit for continuing research."

"Thank you."

Gustav nodded and seemed to mellow a bit.

Alex slipped the returned EX fragment into the box holding the main piece, and gave Hana back her necklace. Gustav reached into his case again and came up with a small, folded foam sheet. He opened it, revealing a fragile-looking panel wired to a control board. "You asked for a meson detector," he said. "I give you: a meson detector."

Everyone leaned close. Sunil whistled softly. "Wow. What does one of those cost?"

"A lot," Gustav replied.

All eyes turned to Alex. "I was hoping you and Sunil might help us build an airborne platform to carry this. I dabbled in drones a bit back home, but it took me forever. We need something up and running now."

"You built a *drone?*" Sam said.

Alex held his hands out, a foot apart. "Little guy," he replied defensively. "To keep an eye on the house." He looked to Sunil and Gustav. "So—what do you think?"

Sunil gestured toward the stadium-sized sea of junk around them. "We're in the right place," he said.

"Where do we work?" Gustav asked.

"Here," Alex told him. Sunil smiled. "Maybe we can draw up some quick plans?"

For some reason—creative differences, perhaps—Sunil and Gustav worked separately, then presented completely different plans an hour later. The rest of them gathered around to look. Gustav's drone was sleek and beautiful, like something from a science-fiction movie. Sunil's looked like it had been cobbled together out of a garbage heap. Eyes lingered over Gustav's sketches.

"That's very nice," Sunil said.

"It's gorgeous," Hana added, heads nodding around her.

"Thank you."

"Umm, one question," Sunil said. "How are we going to build it?"

"Like any other project. We vet the plans, send them to a fabrication shop, test a few copies to refine the design to the next generation—"

"Do you have any idea what that will cost?" Sunil interrupted.

"No. Why?" Gustav seemed genuinely puzzled by the question.

"Because we can't afford it," Sunil said.

"More to the point, we don't have the time," Alex added.

"What do you do when you don't have a part?" Sunil asked Gustav.

"Call down to the machine shop, have them make one."

"Here's a thought: exclude it from the design."

"Budget has never been a concern."

"Obviously."

"I'm afraid we'll need to use what we have here," Alex said, trying to keep the peace, "and be up and running sometime today." Gustav grunted noncommittally, and they got down to work. Sunil and Gustav merged their designs and worked on building prototypes, while the others acted as scavengers, gathering whatever parts were deemed necessary and helping to test for functionality.

Several models were test-flown; some crashed, two self-destructed, and one stubbornly refused to take off. Half a day later, they settled on a four-rotor design with a central payload space. It looked clumsy, but was stable in flight.

Using a remote, Sunil danced the finished drone around the ceiling girders, then brought it down to hover over the table. Gustav slapped a palm down on his sketches, to keep them from blowing away. Sunil landed the drone on the table. After triple-checking all the components and running another test flight with a newly installed camera and transmitter, they carefully fitted the meson detector into place.

IN THE G-TEK OFFICE SUITE, JACK AND PETE DISCUSSED their latest acquisition: the EX fragment Phantom had just recovered in the UK. "What are we going to do with it?" Pete asked. He gestured toward the other fragments on the conference table; one from Alex's laptop, the other taken from the EX-powered car in the tube tunnel.

"Drop them in a volcano, fire them into space. As long as they're gone. We need to recover the rest of it, get things back to normal."

"Let's just hope there isn't more of it out there."

Jack's cell rang. He checked the number. Earlier, a source inside Nicholas Miles's Ampere company had told them that after speaking with Alex Watson or OTW, Nicholas had tasked one of his satellites with scanning the globe for meson sources. Jack had then had the EX fragments tested, and discovered they were meson emitters.

Jack's source didn't have access to Nicholas's satellite feed, so Jack had called in a favor and persuaded an ally to duplicate Nicholas's search with their own satellite. Their number was on his cell screen now. He took the call, spoke briefly, and hung up, looking to Pete. "There's more," he said.

They arranged an emergency videoconference with Hemmington Oil CEO Larry Price and COO Becky Lewis. Hemmington was the largest G-Tek investor and had to be kept in the loop.

"More bad news?" Larry asked. He didn't bother with a greeting.

Jack tried to sound upbeat. "Good news this time," he said. "We now have three fragments in our possession, and that source I told you about has located what appears to be a much larger piece. Bigger than the one Alex Watson has now."

"Making it an even bigger threat," Becky said. "Tell me how that's good news."

"We have an opportunity here. If we can get there before he does . . ."

"This mess started with you," Larry told him. "You clean it up."

"I'm going to need some resources, people on the ground."

"Whatever it takes," Larry said, and cut the connection.

Jack called for a chopper on the roof and put a jet on standby, wishing he'd never heard of Alex Watson.

SUNIL FLEW THE FINAL DRONE, USING AN IPAD MINI AS a remote. The drone's feeds showed on both his and Gustav's iPads. "Verify no system errors," Gustav announced, running a diagnostic.

"Meson detector . . . on," Sunil said. The others gathered around the twin iPads, watching the real-time video feed from the drone, overlaid with a faint map and GPS coordinates. Several blinking blue dots appeared, close together.

"There it is," Sam said.

Sunil hovered the drone over Alex's pack, then flew from one side of the building to the other, and back to hover above them. It never lost track of the EX fragments in the pack.

"Try moving EX instead of the drone," Sam suggested. Alex jogged away with the pack; on the iPad screens, the blue dots moved away. Sunil sent the drone after Alex. "I'd say it's working," he told the others. Gustav nodded. Sunil held up a hand. It took Gustav a moment to get this, after which he gave his fellow engineer a high five.

"What's the detection range?" Sam asked as Alex returned.

"Difficult to say," Gustav told her. "Mesons are extremely short-lived."

"But they travel like a bat out of hell," Sunil added.

"It should suffice for our purposes," Gustav began, then checked his ringing equipment case and pulled out a satellite phone, answering the call and listening. "Yes, I'll do that," he said, and hung up. He started a video chat on his iPad, holding the device up for everyone to see. Nicholas gazed back at them from the screen.

"Good news and bad news," Nicholas told them. "The good news is, there's more. We picked up quite a few hits."

"You mean there's a lot of this stuff?" Sam asked.

"Not exactly. After accounting for the pieces with you, St. Ives, and three pieces in Manhattan—"

"Those last will be the stolen bits," Hana said.

Nicholas nodded. "We're left with one more hit. Judging from the meson count, it's bigger than the one Alex already has. Much bigger."

A ripple of excitement spread through the group.

"And the bad news?" Nigel asked.

"Tell me it's not at the bottom of the Atlantic," Alex said.

"That might have been easier," Nicholas told them. "It's in Zimbabwe."

"Aren't they in the middle of a revolution?" Sam asked.

"Unfortunately. And short of a few cargo-carrier contacts, I have no connections there whatsoever."

"I don't get it," Sunil said. "If this new piece is so big, why did St. Ives and everything else stop working? If Alex is right about critical mass, then even with his piece cut down, the bigger chunk should have kept the others running."

"Distance might be a factor," Nicholas offered.

"Or the new piece is somehow shielded," Alex theorized.

"But then we wouldn't have detected it, right?" Nigel asked.

Gustav shook his head. "Mesons will go through anything. Even if Energy X's power output won't."

"Thank you," Alex said to Nicholas. "This is just what we needed."

"It's not ours yet," Nicholas reminded him. "I did the easy part."

Alex thought for a moment, the rudiments of a plan coming together in his head. "You have cargo contacts here, too?"

"I do."

"I'm going to need to get in touch with them. And do you have anyone in South Africa? Someone who could maybe build something and get it across the border?"

Nicholas nodded. "Probably, depending on what it is. You understand once you're in-country, you'll be on your own over there."

"Actually," Nigel said, "that may not be entirely true. I've spoken with Patrice Mahna a few times."

"The rebel guy?" Hana asked.

"Right. We're by no means tight, but he has no love for oil companies, I can tell you that. Thinks they're the root of all evil."

"Aren't they?" Sunil asked.

"Certainly in his country," Nigel said. "The country's swimming in recently discovered oil, and they pretty much own the president. Anything that's bad for them is good for Patrice."

"The enemy of my enemy . . ." noted Nicholas.

"Exactly," said Alex. Stepping away from the others, he told Nicholas what he needed.

HOURS LATER AT HEATHROW AIRPORT'S CARGO TERMI-nal, a large crate was loaded into the back of a green cargo plane bound for Africa. Inside the crate, Alex, Hana, Sunil, and Gustav sat on the padded floor, secured to the padded walls by foam-filled harnesses. A small LED lantern swung from the ceiling. The drone rested on a foam cushion between them. Nigel and Sam had stayed behind to handle PR and attempt to reach and—if possible—negotiate some on-the-ground assistance from the rebel leader, Patrice Mahna.

The crate thunked down in the plane's hold, rocking them in their harnesses. Sunil spilled his potato chips. "If I get seasick, does that mean I'll get airsick?" he asked.

"You could have told us about that before," Hana said.

"I didn't think of it. I never fly."

"What happens if Nigel can't cut a deal with Patrice," Sunil asked, " or can't reach him at all?"

"We grab the rock and split," Hana said matter-of-factly. "Kick him and the country some kind of bonus afterward."

"You mean just take it?"

"You want to hand it over to a dictator backed by oil companies? Besides, we can't exactly hang out in a war zone with the most valuable thing on the planet, can we?"

"Right."

Alex looked to Gustav, who'd been silent since entering the crate. "Thanks for coming along," he said. "You didn't have to do that; this is our madness."

Gustav sighed dramatically. "Our destinies seem intertwined." He shrugged. "Besides, how many people know how to repair a meson detector?"

CHAPTER 37
GETTING AWAY WITH MURDER

SCOTLAND YARD INSPECTOR KEVIN YOUNG TOOK THE call from FBI Agent Moore in his office. They'd been working the Alex Watson/G-Tek case together—Moore handling things on the American side—since shortly after the attack at the OTW cottage. Moore had initially thrown himself into the investigation, but lately Moore's emails had been sporadic and less helpful, and Young wasn't quite sure what was going on.

After exchanging a few pleasantries, Moore sighed. "I have to tell you, even if we can make a perfect case, we may not get these guys behind bars. I'm already getting hints from superiors, asking if I'm sure about this, what my career plans are, things like that. Jack and Pete are so well connected, it's scary. I've tried to press ahead, but it's clear there's not a lot of interest over here. Long story short, even with dead cops on two continents, I'm not sure this'll fly."

So that was it, Young thought: politics. He hadn't been subject to the same pressures on his side of the pond because the G-Tek execs weren't here, only the assassin—who, even if he was captured alive and decided to talk, likely didn't know for certain who'd hired him in the first place. At any rate, it seemed the larger investigation was going to go the way of the post-crash Wall Street "investigation." Which was to say, there would be no prosecutions.

He thanked Moore for being honest, the two of them griped a bit about meddlesome superiors, and he hung up the phone. It was disheartening, to say the least. Still, nothing stopped him from pursuing the cop-killing hitman or stirring up a bit of dust himself.

NIGEL AND SAMANTHA BUSIED THEMSELVES IN THE OTW's London office, fielding calls about Alex and the recently revived Energy X while finalizing plans for OTW's Canary Wharf rally. Andrew called them into the next room, where most of the staff had gathered around the TV, watching a news report. "Again, the rumors are unconfirmed at this time," the newscaster was saying. "Conventional energy company stocks have been on a roller coaster ever since the unveiling of the so-called Energy X, with the troubled G-Tek's prices swinging wildly.

"Today's report that G-Tek's CEO has been under investigation by the FBI—a report confirmed by an unnamed source in Scotland Yard—has sent G-Tek prices into free fall. Analysts fear the rest of the industry may follow. There's widespread speculation that investors newly leery of traditional energy stocks will instead invest heavily in the upcoming EXpower IPO offering..."

Nigel offered Sam an uncharacteristic high five, while the rest of the office whooped and cheered.

CHAPTER 38
BLUE GOLD

INSIDE A SHIPPING CRATE HIGH ABOVE THE ATLANTIC, Gustav's satellite phone rang, waking him. He checked the unfamiliar number, frowned, and tapped Alex. "It's for you," he said, and went back to sleep.

"This is Alex."

"This is Patrice Mahna," said a heavily accented voice. "I understand you have a proposition for me." There were engine sounds in the background. "I don't know what you think I can do for you, but I'm not in a position to do very much. In a few months, things may be different."

"I can make them different," Alex said. "Right now."

"I'm listening." More engine sounds, and men yelling in the background.

"I can power your country. Forever." Alex surprised himself. He'd never had the opportunity to utter words like that.

Sunil, wakened by the call, made no secret of listening in.

"Enough electricity to make you a first-world country," Alex continued. "Even sell power to your neighbors. And you can kick the oil companies out on their asses."

Sunil cupped his hand and whispered in Alex's ear, "Commission. Commission."

"We'd take a commission from that. But what you use is free," Alex told him.

There was a pause. "And in return you want what?" Patrice asked.

"Heavy equipment and transport."

"What kind of equipment?"

Alex thought for a moment. "I need to dig up a big rock and get it out of the country."

"And where exactly is this rock?"

"I don't want to say on the phone."

"When are you coming? I will have someone meet you."

Alex checked his watch. "I'm guessing another five hours or so." He gave the name of the airport. When asked which flight, he smiled and said, "Give me a number to call and I'll let your man know when we're on the ground. I'm a little cautious lately."

A rough laugh answered him. "Welcome to my world," Patrice told him, and gave him a number. "I cannot guarantee your safety, but I will do my best to protect you while you are here."

"That's good enough for me," Alex told him.

"Then I look forward to meeting you," Patrice said. The sound of gunshots came through the phone, and the call ended.

"Something wrong?" Hana asked.

"Nothing... We just... need to be careful when we get there." He started wondering how deep the meteor was buried, how long it would take to get it up, what kind of equipment would be needed . . .

Hana nudged him and winked. "It'll work out. War zones are in my blood."

Five hours later, Alex called the number given him by Patrice, and told the man who answered which plane they were on, which crate they were in, and whom it was addressed to.

Thirty minutes after that, they landed at Harare Airport. The cargo door took several minutes to hum open and clank down on the tarmac. Alex felt the crate slide along the floor and down the ramp, where something pushed them to one side. Voices surrounded the crate, and for a moment Alex was sure they were about to be busted by customs. But then the crate was lifted, moved, and dropped onto something higher—a truck bed, maybe. Hopefully.

A metal gate slammed and an engine started. The smell of diesel seeped inside the crate, and they started to move. So. . . a truck—but whose? Something hit the crate in several places, making it squeak. After a moment, Alex realized someone was prying up the lid. Daylight seeped in as the crate's top inched up on one side—followed by blinding sunlight as the lid was thrown back.

When his eyes adjusted, Alex saw a half dozen unfriendly black faces, all squinting down at him through rifle sights. The men wore camouflage fatigues. He had no idea whether they were government troops or rebel soldiers.

Sunil ventured a wave and a friendly smile. "I sure hope these are the right guys," he said.

One of the men barked orders in Shona, and the soldiers

lowered their guns. Alex and the others climbed out from the crate while the truck cut through a bumpy field. Once the crate was empty, two men lowered the rear gate and shoved it out. Young boys appeared almost instantly to salvage the wood.

Someone parted the canvas at the front of the truck, revealing the cab. The driver was dressed in civilian clothes, but looked like a soldier. The passenger wore a brown suit and gold-rimmed glasses. His hair was short, kinky, and peppered with gray. He looked like a college professor somehow dropped into the middle of a revolution. "Patrice sends his regards," he said in perfect but accented English. "I am Clemence. Pleased to meet you."

"Good to meet you, too," Alex said.

Clemence smiled. "Not all of us wear jungle fatigues. I am Patrice's science advisor. I majored in geology at MIT."

Alex shook hands as the truck wobbled along the uneven road riddled with potholes.

"You will have to forgive my friends. They see everything as a threat. White men in particular. For the most part, they are right. So—what exactly are we looking for?"

Hana lifted the necklace from beneath her shirt and held up the glowing crystal.

"Incredible. I have never seen anything like it. How big is the one we're looking for?"

"Don't know exactly," Alex told him. "But we're told it's pretty big. Not sure how deep, either."

"The soil here is not too difficult. We will look at the site and I will arrange the equipment." Alex showed him a map with the target area circled and GPS coordinates scribbled in red.

Clemence produced a handheld GPS unit and punched in the numbers.

"Do we need some kind of contract?" Sunil asked.

Clemence smiled and shook his head. "Not necessary. Your word is good enough for Patrice."

"Really?"

"Yes. If you break it, he will have you all killed."

Conversation was somewhat muted after that. Alex and the others gazed out the back as the truck bounced along a series of rural trails. Morning sunlight filtered through high-branching, flat-crowned trees, offering some refuge from the tropical climate. Still, the heat disagreed with Gustav, who constantly dabbed his face with a handkerchief.

Alex caught glimpses of wildlife in the forested areas between villages. At one point, they rounded a sharp curve and passed a group of young boys busy picking up small objects from the roadside. The boys smiled and waved as they passed. "What are they doing?" Hana asked, waving back.

"A truck rolled there yesterday, spilling a load of corn," Clemence said. "They're scavenging what's left." Some time later, Clemence checked the GPS unit. "Almost there," he announced. "Once I've evaluated the site, I'll have a better idea what kind of equipment you'll need. We'll bring it in by truck."

"How long will that take?" Hana asked.

"We should be digging in twenty-four hours. It's a rebel-controlled area; the government never comes here."

Sudden gunfire sounded outside, and the truck skidded to a halt. The soldiers in the back readied their rifles. *"Throw your weapons out of the truck or die!"* a deep voice commanded.

Blinded by the truck's walls, it was impossible to know how many men they faced, or where they were. "How many?" the lead soldier called to the front.

"Too many," Clemence replied. One by one, the soldiers dropped their guns over the tailgate.

"*Get out of the truck!*" the same voice shouted. "*One at a time.*"

They had no choice but to obey. Jumping to the ground, Alex saw several dozen government soldiers, led by a large, bald, scarfaced man. A battered pickup truck blocked the road ahead, obviously just driven from the trees. They'd been ambushed.

Clemence moved to stand beside Alex. "It would seem you were expected," he whispered.

"*No talking!*" Scarface yelled. He stepped close, looking over Alex and his companions. "You meet the strangest people in the jungle," he said. Then he pulled out a radio and started talking in Shona. Moments later, Alex's crew and Clemence were separated from the others, searched, and herded into the bed of the pickup truck. Alex's backpack was taken, as was the drone.

Other trucks were parked farther back in the trees. The rebel soldiers were loaded onto one of these. The government troops piled into the other vehicles, and the whole convoy continued down the road, the truck they'd come in bringing up the rear.

Scarface rode in the pickup's cab with the back window open. For the next thirty minutes, he ranted about Alex and the others sneaking into his country, wanting to stop the oil and ruin everything. Despite the seriousness of the situation, Alex found himself wondering if the man would ever shut up. He was actually relieved when the convoy finally rolled to a stop at the foot of a small hill.

The government troops herded Alex and the others from the truck and up the hill. Topping the rise, they found themselves overlooking a rocky valley. There were trucks, tents, and a hundred or more government soldiers. Heavy equipment was parked beside mounds of freshly dug earth, and an ancient crane spooled cable into a deep hole. "How did *they* find it?" Sunil asked.

"I expect the same way we did," Gustav answered. "Using a satellite."

Scarface and his men marched them down into the valley. Workers shouted at each other to be heard over the dilapidated crane's motor. The rebel fighters were taken in another direction, while Scarface led Alex's group toward the hole. The cable stopped spooling, and the noise from the crane lessened. Two men in suits walked out from behind it. "Hello, Alex," Jack said. "Glad you could make it. You remember Pete."

Though not surprised to find Jack and Pete behind this, Alex wondered why they'd come in person. He supposed they didn't trust anyone else. "And our mutual friend," Jack continued as a third man limped around the crane. Alex found himself gazing into the eyes of the man who'd tried to kill him—and had killed his best friend instead. Unthinking, he lunged forward, only to be brought up short by Scarface's hand on his collar.

"You should let him go," Phantom said. "Get this over with."

"You two can get reacquainted soon enough," Jack said. "But since you came all this way, I thought you might want to have a look at what you came for. He signaled the crane operator. The noise started up again as the cable tightened and began to rise. A moment later, a black rock the size of an SUV rose into view and stopped, gripped by a mechanical claw. The surface glowed blue through cracks in the black coating.

Alex gazed at the rock in awe. If his little piece of Energy X could power a country, this could power the world, and then some. Forever. He saw Scarface jiggling a radio, which had suddenly stopped working. Wondering why it had worked before, Alex bent down and scooped up a handful of excavated dirt.

"Crystalline," Clemence observed.

"The impact crystallized the rock around the meteor," Alex said. "It could only be detected from above." Alex let the soil slip through his fingers.

"Very good, Mr. Wizard," Jack said. Scarface handed him Alex's pack. He looked inside. "Thanks for this."

Alex looked at the meteor. "What are you going to do with it?"

"I can't decide," Jack told him with a smile. "But probably drop it in a volcano."

Alex nodded. "Has it occurred to you that destroying something that contains enough energy to power civilization for centuries may release all of that energy at once—vaporizing the entire planet?"

Jack's smile faltered. "I'll look into that," he said, regaining his composure. "Either way, this is the last time that rock will see the light of day." He looked to Scarface. "Put them in the big tent."

Scarface and several of his men escorted Alex and the others to a large, dingy tent and put them inside. There was a big folding table, ringed by fold-up chairs. "Make yourself at home," Scarface joked. He walked out a moment later, leaving two guards behind.

Phantom entered soon after, Alex's pack on his shoulder, bowie knife in one hand. "Where are all the pieces?" he asked.

No one answered.

Phantom circled the table. Reaching Hana, he whipped the blade up under her chin. "This is the last time I'll ask nicely," he said. "Where's the rest of it?"

"St. Ives," Alex said to buy time, wracking his brain for a way out of this.

"Not for long. We know there's more than that."

"The pieces you have. The motorcycle . . ."

"I wish I could believe that," Phantom said. He pressed the blade against Hana's throat. Alex saw a trickle of blood leak onto the blade. Alex got up, intending to make a grab for the knife. One of the guards hit him with a rifle butt, and he crashed onto the table instead.

In the same heartbeat, machine gun fire sounded outside. Phantom threw himself to the ground as bullets ripped through the tent wall. The rounds passed over Alex and the others seated at the table, but riddled the two guards, who were standing. Alex snatched the pack from Phantom, who rolled under the wall and was out of the tent in seconds.

There was shouting outside in at least two different languages, and the world erupted in gunfire.

"Everybody okay?" Alex asked.

"Stay low," Hana told them.

Alex scooped up the fallen soldiers' weapons. "Anyone know how to use these?"

Hana took a rifle, checked chamber and clip, and flipped off the safety.

"I've had some training," Clemence said. "Patrice insisted."

Alex gave him the other rifle. Clemence and Hana took spare clips from the fallen guards. Alex turned at Hana's call. She handed him a pistol she found on one of the guards, along with a spare clip. Having no idea what to expect, the group stepped cautiously from the tent.

The valley had become a combat zone. Snipers fired from the surrounding jungle, covering small groups of men rushing toward the camp. Government soldiers returned fire, but seemed less well trained than the attackers.

"Who the hell are these guys?" Hana said.

"I sent a distress signal when the truck was stopped," Clemence said. "I believe you would call them the cavalry." Bullets tore across the earth at their feet.

"Some cavalry," Sunil snapped. They took cover behind a large truck. Alex heard running footsteps and spun around to see Scarface bringing up a rifle. He started to raise his own gun, already knowing he was too late. He stepped in front of Hana as she turned, alerted by his sudden movement. He saw Scarface's rifle line up, expecting the muzzle flash that would be the last thing he'd ever see, when what seemed a hundred bullets tore through Scarface's body. He twitched spasmodically, as if in the throes of some macabre dance, and sank lifeless to the ground.

A black man with a small silver beard and mirrored aviator shades rounded a tractor, trailed by rebel fighters. Alex recognized his face from news reports.

"Patrice," Clemence said.

X

AS THE FIREFIGHT RAGED ON, JACK HUDDLED BESIDE the crane. Pete had taken cover behind a nearby car.

"Call President Botu!" Jack yelled at him. "We need an airstrike!"

Pete banged the radio against the car and held it to his ear. "Nothing's working!" he yelled back. Bullets pinged off car and crane around them. "We have to hide somewhere!"

Jack pointed toward an outcropping of rock that concealed a small cave, perhaps big enough to shelter a few men. He'd stumbled across it earlier, while looking for a place to relieve himself. He checked his watch, which, fortunately, was mechanical. Larry and Becky at Hemmington Oil had insisted on being kept in the loop. He'd been due to check in with another progress report five minutes ago. Hopefully they'd realize something was wrong and call the president themselves, or send in contractors, something. Anything. They had the GPS coordinates; how hard could it be?

AT THAT VERY MOMENT, HEMMINGTON OIL CEO LARRY Price was indeed on the phone with President Botu. "Are you sure about this?" Botu asked, gazing out the palace window at forty acres of exquisite gardens. So much easier on the eyes and nose than the ragged shantytown he'd demolished to make room for it. He twirled a Cuban Bolívar cigar in thick fingers as he listened. When the oilman finished speaking, he told him: "Whatever you want, my man," and hung up. "Like everything else," he said to himself. Scooping a gold-plated radio from his Brazilian rosewood desk, he contacted his most trusted general.

Well, he thought, second most trusted. The first was about to retire, along with that unsightly scar of his.

WHEN THE FIREFIGHT ENDED AND THE CAPTIVE REBEL soldiers were freed, Patrice yelled something at his men, who turned and ran from the camp, pausing only to retrieve weapons from the fallen. Perhaps a dozen men remained at his side.

"Where are they going?" Gustav asked.

"What do you think the president is going to do now?" Patrice said.

"Send more troops?" Sunil guessed.

"That will take too long. We must go. Now."

THIRTY MILES AWAY, A LARGE TRUCK ROLLED TO A STOP beside a rural trail. Hydraulic legs swung down, leveling the vehicle and bracing it for what was to come. In accordance with his general's orders, the launch officer punched the GPS coordinates into the targeting computer and watched as the launch platform elevated and swung into position. The red launch button flashed insistently. The launch officer's finger stabbed down, and the missile leapt skyward on a column of white smoke.

"THE ROCK COMES WITH US," ALEX SAID FIRMLY. "OR no deal."

Patrice seemed to notice the great rock for the first time: a charred-looking mass shot through with slivers of glowing blue. "*This* is Energy X?" he asked.

Alex nodded. Patrice started yelling orders. One of his men jumped into a new Mercedes transport truck and tried unsuccessfully to start it while another man climbed into the crane and fumbled with the controls.

Alex shouted at the man in the truck and pointed to an older vehicle that looked like a relic from World War II. "Use that one!"

Patrice repeated the order in Shona. The driver hopped down, dodging the EX boulder as the amateur crane operator swung it into the side of the Mercedes, knocking it over. The second, older truck started immediately. The driver gestured to the crane soldier to keep the rock where it was and lift it higher. He then drove under it and signaled for the rock to be lowered into the bed. Instead, the metal claw opened and the meteor smashed down onto the truck, bending the frame and stalling out the engine.

Men scrambled to tie the rock down. The driver cranked the engine. It didn't start. He tried again. Still nothing. Cursing and kicking at the floor, he cranked it a third time—and the engine sputtered to life. Patrice ordered his remaining men out of the valley.

"Tell them to take old vehicles," Alex said. "The new ones won't start."

Less than a minute later, they were underway. Alex and Hana rode in the cargo truck, beside the driver. Looking ahead, Alex saw the last of the men who'd fled earlier topping the valley rim.

THE MISSILE FLEW LIKE A BAT OUT OF HELL, FOLLOWING the terrain. A rocky ridge appeared in the distance. The missile's electronic brain told it to rise, because its destiny lay on the other side.

MOVING AS FAST AS THE OLD TRUCKS WOULD CARRY them, Alex and the others neared the lip of the valley. Rebels waiting at the top yelled warnings and pointed to the sky across the valley. The first few vehicles reached the top and disappeared from view.

Alex's truck, weighed down by the meteor, struggled to reach the top, refusing to move. Patrice yelled something from the Jeep behind them, and men poured back over the hill, grabbed onto the old truck, and pushed for all they were worth. Alex jumped down to help. Their effort was just that little bit extra the flagging relic needed, and they started inching forward. Alex looked over his shoulder and saw the missile. It seemed to lose guidance—its electronics taken out by EX—and started to tumble. But he could see it would still land in the valley.

On the valley floor, Jack, Pete, and Phantom—whom they'd found already in the cave—ventured outside, wondering why all was suddenly silent. Phantom was the first to see the missile. He turned and dove back inside the cave, wondering if the overpressure would kill him, thinking it probably would.

Alex's truck stalled again. Patrice's Jeep rammed it from behind, sending it over the crest. Alex saw the tumbling missile hit the crane arm. He had a brief sensation of flying, and then the world filled with noise.

In the valley behind him, the shockwave lifted everything in sight. Jack had a fraction of a second to realize he'd been betrayed, after which he and Pete were thrown into the rocks behind them. Deaf and broken, they could only watch as the Mercedes truck flew toward them, blotting out the sky.

The bowl-shaped valley channeled the force out and up. The fierce wind caught the tail end of Patrice's Jeep, flipping it over. Patrice and his driver fell out; the Jeep kept going, coming to rest in a tree, twenty feet off the ground. Alex's truck was bounced around a bit, but rolled down the other side of the hill and managed to stay on its wheels.

Alex and the other men who'd been beside it were thrown into nearby brush. Hana and the others rushed over to check on him, but aside from a few scrapes and a throbbing ache in his injured shoulder, he seemed to be okay. Patrice walked over, smiling. "That's the first time an airstrike has worked in my favor," he declared. The men around him laughed.

After a moment, they all gathered on the hilltop, looking down on the valley. Everything recognizable had been obliterated. Alex tried to find the crane, but saw no parts he could make sense of.

"Will they think we're dead?" asked Hana.

"Maybe, for a short time," said Patrice.

"We'd best make use of that," Alex advised.

When they tried to restart the truck, the engine made a sound like a jackhammer, then fell silent. "What the hell was that?" Sunil asked.

"It's thrown a rod," Gustav announced. "The engine is now a boat anchor."

"We need to find something to pull it with," Alex said.

Patrice's men gathered what rope they could find in the

vehicles and fashioned crude harnesses, tied to the front bumper. Patrice turned to Alex. "You have some idea where we're going with this?"

"Alex always has a plan," Hana told him, then said hopefully to Alex, "don't you?"

"Of course."

They trekked for almost an hour on a jungle road, Patrice's men pulling the truck in shifts, Alex's group, Patrice, and Clemence walking alongside. Alex consulted a paper map.

"You are sure it will be there?" Patrice asked, observing his quickly tiring men.

"If anyone can get it there, he can. We're still going to need a plane."

"That I can arrange. If I can find a phone your meteor hasn't zapped."

Rounding a curve, they found a paved road skirting the jungle. Parked on the shoulder: an old cargo truck. "And there it is," Alex said. Checking the map again, he walked some fifty yards from the road and scanned the ground around him. He spotted a small pile of rocks, looked beneath it, and plucked the truck keys from their hiding place. "Got it!" he called out, holding the key aloft.

He hurried to rejoin the others. Climbing into the truck, he checked under the seat and found a new satellite phone in a crystal-shielded case. The passenger seat was piled high with cargo straps. He took a deep breath, slid the key into the ignition, and uttered a silent prayer. The engine caught on the first try, and he maneuvered the truck until it was back to back with the first truck. He set the parking brake and hopped down.

Everyone gathered round as he unlocked and opened the tilt-up door at the back. The entire cargo area was lined with great sheets of layered crystal. The door was also covered with crystal. A steel framework inside the crystal cage provided tie-down points, and a second, steel floor had been added above the original floor, resting on giant coiled springs. Winch points allowed the entire crystal cage to slide in—or out—of the truck. The door attached to and moved with the whole thing, forming one wall of the truck-sized box.

"You had Nicholas do all this," Hana said.

Alex nodded. "I didn't know how big the meteor would be. So I told him better too big than too little. He had it modified in South Africa, then bribed some company here to drive it across the border, say it was theirs."

"I don't understand," Sunil said. "How did you know where to park it? You couldn't possibly have known we'd take this road out."

Alex grinned. "That's why there are two others parked beside other exit points."

"How are we gonna get it in there?"

Alex grabbed a lever beside the truck's rear bumper. A hydraulic lift unfolded from beneath the truck. Patrice checked his watch. "A spy satellite will pass over soon. I must have my men out of sight."

"Or they'll know they missed us with the rocket," Sunil said.

"They may already know," Gustav informed them.

"Right," Alex agreed. The others waited for an explanation.

"The same satellite they used to locate the meteor will be used to track it," Gustav said.

"Then why aren't we dead already?" Sunil asked. "They can just send another missile."

"The satellite isn't in range yet," Alex guessed. "Like this spy satellite, it only passes over every few hours."

"This is very bad news," Patrice announced. "This crystal shielding—will it prevent detection?

Alex shook his head. "No. It just keeps the rock from frying electronics."

Patrice muttered something in another language. It sounded like a curse. Then he ordered his men to transfer the rock. As it turned out, they didn't need the hydraulic lift at all; since the new truck's bed was slightly lower than the old truck's, the rebels simply rolled the meteor from one to the other, using ropes to guide the transfer and keep the rock from hitting the walls. They used the cargo straps from the cab to secure the meteor in place.

When it was done, Alex and Patrice shook hands. "I would like you to do me a favor," Patrice told him. "As soon as you are safe, announce our arrangement. Publicly."

"Done. Why?"

"When people hear about this, those who still support President Botu will abandon him. The oil companies may do so as well. If either happens, he is finished and the revolution is won."

"I'm not following."

"The oil companies are the only thing protecting him from military action. South Africa is everything he is not. And so he hates them. In return, they hate him back. Our countries have been on the brink of war for years. Without the oil companies to back him up, my guess is he'll flee the country. Then he will be gone, and we can ally with South Africa."

"You and I speak the same language. You have my full support. Now, about that plane . . ."

AN HOUR LATER, ALEX'S GROUP SUPERVISED AS THE new EX rock was loaded onto a cargo plane by rebels working at the airport. Alex would have preferred to do this on a deserted stretch of road somewhere, but they needed a heavy-duty cargo loader to handle the meteor's weight.

Once done, Alex and the others climbed aboard. The copilot checked to make sure the meteor's shielding box was secure, saw that everyone was properly strapped into the bench seats running down either side of the fuselage, and returned to the cockpit. The pilot rolled the old prop plane down the runway—and then they were in the air.

"Next time you want me to take a fun overseas trip with you," Sunil said to Alex, "do me a favor and don't ask."

"We're making the world a better place," Hana said.

"I agree," Sunil told her. "I just want to be here to see it."

The copilot emerged from the cockpit. Alex could see right away that something was wrong. "We have a problem," he said, and motioned them to follow. He led them to the cockpit door and took his seat beside the pilot. Alex stood in the doorway, the others crowding behind him. The pilot glanced over his shoulder and turned up the radio.

"—will be shot down," said a harsh voice in English. "I repeat: divert your course and land immediately or missiles will be fired. You will not be permitted to leave the country." The warning was repeated in Shona.

"How long to the South African border?" Alex asked.

"Ten minutes," said the pilot.

"How fast are missiles?" Sunil asked.

"A lot faster than we are," said Gustav.

"You have four minutes to alter course," said the radio voice.

"We'll have to turn around," the pilot announced.

"Give me three minutes," Alex urged, dialing the satphone taken from the truck.

"I'll give you two," the pilot told him.

Alex reached Nicholas on his private number. "I need to make a deal with South Africa in the next three minutes or we're all dead," Alex told him. "Who do you know there?" Alex gave him the basics, relayed the plane's position from the pilot, and hung up.

"Time's up," the pilot said, reaching for the radio. "What's that?" the copilot said, pointing. Four black dots raced toward them.

"Too slow for missiles," the pilot announced. They looked frighteningly swift to Alex.

The dots quickly became fighter jets. They roared past, swung into turns and came back, surrounding the plane. The flags painted on the tails were green, yellow, and black. "South African," the pilot said.

"You have one minute to change course or missiles will be fired," the radio announced. Another voice answered with a heavy Afrikaner accent. "Missile commander, be advised: this is Colonel Karel De Bruin of the South African Air Force. We are now escorting your target. If you fire on them, you fire on us."

"Holy shit," Sunil said.

There was a moment of silence before the first voice returned. "Is this a joke?"

"Fire those missiles and find out, pel," said Colonel De Bruin. You'll be at war five minutes later."

Another silence, then: "You're violating our airspace."

"Sue me," said De Bruin.

"You think Botu is crazy enough to shoot?" Sunil asked.

"Definitely," the copilot answered.

They waited. The missile commander was no doubt consulting his superiors—or Botu himself.

"Would we see them coming?" Sunil asked, peering out the window.

"Probably not," Gustav told him. "Nor would we hear them. But the fighters would pick them up on radar."

"Great," Sunil observed. "So if they suddenly split, at least we'll know why."

A charged stillness prevailed. Alex felt Hana squeezing his hand. He'd never known her to be scared of anything. The silence dragged on, until Colonel De Bruin spoke again. "We are now in South African airspace. Welkom!"

The tension fell away, and Alex suddenly felt very tired.

"What did we promise South Africa for that?" Sunil asked.

"I have no idea," Alex replied.

"It's over," Hana said.

"No," Alex told her. "It's begun."

CHAPTER 39
EXPOWER

FIVE YEARS LATER, A QUARTER OF A MILLION PEOPLE gathered at dusk in London's Hyde Park. An announcer recounted the incredible history of the past few years. EXpower had become the largest corporation in history, with more than a trillion dollars in annual revenue. The old energy companies had been wiped off the economic map, the U.S. president had been impeached at home, and Patrice Mahna had been president of Zimbabwe for four and a half years. Occupy the World was now a global force to be reckoned with, and there was considerable evidence that atmospheric CO_2 levels—caused primarily by fossil fuels—had peaked and would soon decline. He finished to loud applause, which seemed tame compared to what came next, when he introduced Alex Watson.

Alex made his way to the microphone and waited for the applause to die down. "The revolution that began five years ago with St. Ives, Zimbabwe, South Africa, and the UK is now complete. North Korea signed an agreement this morning—meaning every nation on earth will now be powered by Energy X."

He waited for the applause to subside, and introduced the people who'd helped make the revolution happen: Sam, Nigel, Sunil, Nicholas, and his wife of four years, Hana—who held their one-year-old daughter in her arms. He also thanked his late friend James.

"Now that everyone's on board," he continued, "paying half of what they used to pay for electric power, we have an announcement to make." He held up a book. "EXpower, in cooperation with Occupy the World, has published its first book. Available free online." The cover appeared on the building-sized screen behind the stage. The book's title was *X/goals*.

"To every EXpowered nation that meets the human rights and environmental goals set out in this book," Alex pledged, "we are offering a 50 percent energy price cut. Every year you meet these goals, you'll pay half the rate you're paying now. EXpower has freed the world of fossil fuel addiction. Now it's time to heal the world." He scanned the huge audience before him. "*WHO'S WITH ME?*"

The crowd went wild with applause. Giant blue letters ignited behind the stage, spelling out EXpower and lighting Hyde Park with the brilliance of the sun.

Alex worked a remote, and the huge image behind him switched to a satellite view of the celebration. The view pulled back until half the Earth was visible. A city lit up in the darkness. Then others, spreading outward at angles. Forming the continent-wide letter: "*X*"

THE END

Thank you for reading. I kindly invite you to share your candid thoughts, reactions, and opinions—positive or negative—on Goodreads, Amazon, or wherever you browse for books. Your time is much appreciated!

ACKNOWLEDGMENTS

All thanks to God, without whom none of this would have been possible.

Mom and Dad, there are no words to truly thank you for what you have done for me.

Ross Browne, you are an inspiration to us all. A Clark Kent with the mildest of manners but donning an intellectual cape to help us minions navigate uncharted waters. Thank you for allowing me to dream big.

John Robert Marlow Sensei, you are the Grandmaster and I am your not so young Padawan. I know, different realms. Thank you for your brutal honesty. Thank you for grounding me in reality.

My sincerest and profound thanks to our esteemed friends at The Editorial Department—thank you Jane Ryder, Liz Felix, Morgana Gallaway, and all the other walk-on-water talented folks who patiently put up with my often-puzzling quirkiness and demands. You all helped nurture this intellectual labor of love.

ABOUT THE AUTHOR

NISFAN NAWAZ is a Sri Lanka-born British American who built a career as a business and information technology professional. He wrote *Energy X*, his first novel, in response to his growing concern about the influence of the world's most powerful corporations and their impact on future generations.

Nawaz lives in North Carolina with his wife and two children. Visit him online at **www.nisfannawaz.com**.